CLEO DANG WOULD RATHER BE DEAD

ALSO BY MAI NGUYEN

Sunshine Nails

CLEO DANG WOULD RATHER BE DEAD

A NOVEL

MAI NGUYEN

ATRIA BOOKS
New York Amsterdam/Antwerp London
Toronto Sydney/Melbourne New Delhi

ATRIA
BOOKS

An Imprint of Simon & Schuster, LLC
1230 Avenue of the Americas
New York, NY 10020

Let's stay in touch! Scan here to get book recommendations, exclusive offers, and more delivered to your inbox.

For Gemma and all the babies who didn't get to stay

I don't believe in getting over it. I believe in
weathering it badly, in nursing the grudge,
and tending pathologically to
the archive of people you have loved.

RAVEN LEILANI, "Death of the Party"

1

I didn't expect the casket to be so small. It looked bigger in the catalog, but I suppose everything looks bigger in pictures. The sight of it rips into me like an arrow and I go back in time, wondering why I hadn't gone with something more bright and colorful to distract from how sadly small it is. There had been so many to choose from. Blue ones covered in clouds and angels. Pink ones with butterflies all over. Green ones with elephants painted on the side. But I didn't pick any of those, didn't want to pick any of them really, which is how I ended up with a twenty-eight-inch casket constructed out of solid Canadian oak in a semigloss finish. Simple, classic, not pretending to be something other than what it is.

Even if I wanted to change it now, I can't. It's too late. You're already inside. And people are entering the reception room. They're forming a line. A line for what I'm unsure. I don't know where Ethan has gone off to. He's been dealing with crippling diarrhea all morning, so he must be in the bathroom, probably cursing the anonymous individual who left that questionable stew on our porch last night with only a hastily scrawled note that read, *Please accept my condolences.*

Oh, he accepted your condolences all right!

I stand awkwardly beside the casket, unsure what to do with my arms, my face, my whole body for that matter, until one of the funeral staff comes up to me and asks if I would like to receive the line.

I freeze. This was not on the itinerary. I had not mentally prepared for activities that were not on the itinerary.

"W-what does that entail exactly?"

"Oftentimes guests want to express their sympathies and offer words of comfort directly to the parents. You don't have to do anything you don't want to. Just tell me what you feel comfortable with and I can make this line go away if that's what you wish."

I feel hot. And irritated. And upset that an immediate decision is required of me. What do I do? Do I say yes, and run us behind schedule? Do I say no, and disappoint everyone I know? Suddenly I feel incredibly drained, like a phone at one percent. The doctor warned me this might happen. That my brain might not be up to snuff after such a seismic loss and that I should not be put in charge of making big decisions, which I thought was an odd thing to say because isn't that what we do when somebody we love dies—make big decisions one after the other, the biggest one of all being whether to keep on living?

"Grief brain" was what the doctor called it as he sent us home with some frightening pamphlets and a shoebox containing a lock of your hair, molds of your hands and feet, and a narrow strip of graph paper indicating your heartbeat. The nurses even gave us the tape that adhered the breathing tube to your face. I think they just wanted to give us as many things as they could in hopes it would distract us from our empty arms.

Ethan is back. His forehead is sweaty and his eyes are bloodshot. I tell him about the line, which looks to have grown to about fifty people, and ask if he's equipped to handle that kind of social pressure. He automatically nods, like a soldier obeying a command, then extends his arms to greet the first person in line. I guess we're doing this.

I've never been more grateful to be married to a textbook extrovert. It had seemed such a curse, having to remember so many friends' names and the stories of how they met and be in constant competition for his attention. It was something I always struggled with, having to accept I wasn't the only one who loved him.

Now I see it's proving quite useful. Ethan gets through the line with speed and proficiency. This comes natural to him. He's always on no matter where we are, no matter who has died, it seems. Ethan does most of the talking, leaving me with the easier task of accepting hugs and nodding my head at the *I'm sorrys* and *I'm here for yous*. I find myself doing a good job, keeping the line moving, not bursting into tears and disrupting the flow. I do my best to not visibly wince at the bright platitudes, all of which fail to downplay the horror of today.

She's in a better place.
You can always have another baby.
At least you got a few days with her.
At least you can get pregnant again.
God needed another angel.
Everything happens for a reason.
I can't imagine.

It's this last sentiment where I find myself gritting my teeth the most. I know that, for most of them, this tragedy defies their understanding of death—that people are supposed to die in the order of age. But surely it's possible to wonder what it might be like, to put yourself in my shoes and consider a world where sometimes, sadly, children die first.

I try really hard not to make a scene or say anything confrontational but when Claire, an underwriter from work, becomes the eleventh person to say the words *I can't imagine*, I explode.

"Well let me help you out with that, *Claaaire*. Just picture your son, Zach, dying right before your very eyes and the one thing you ever loved more than life itself was just suddenly gone and the only thing capable of bringing you a single ounce of joy was your doctor agreeing to prescribe you the strongest sedative in the world so you could sleep a sleep so deep it would feel like you were stone-cold dead."

"Cleo!" Ethan snaps.

Claire looks appalled, as if I've just slapped her across the face. She blinks a couple times before pulling me in for a hug and saying, "There, there."

After we hug the last person in line, I spot Paloma. I haven't seen her since the hospital. She's wearing a black dress that hints at her postpartum pooch. Her hair is pulled into a tight, greasy bun. Her skin is dry and sallow as puffy lids cast shadows under her eyes. Sleepless nights are painted all over her face. The picture of new mom exhaustion.

What I wouldn't give to look like her—delirious and deathly tired—if it meant my baby were still alive.

Here's what you should know about me and Paloma: We are practically a mirror of each other. We live on the same street. We graduated with honors in business. We like our pizza thin-crust, well-done. We drink French 75s exclusively. We drive Kia Souls, surf blue, black roof. Our wedding dresses were signature Theia Couture and, you guessed it, we got married the same year, with the same officiant, at the same venue.

This is all to say that not a single person—not our husbands, friends, or parents—dropped their jaws or batted an eye when we fell pregnant at the same time. It was like a miracle or, at the very least, a message from the divine confirming what we had long suspected: that this inextricable bond between us would never, ever break, even long after we're dead.

Everything had lined up perfectly. Our bellies were growing, the babies were kicking, and our cravings frequently nudged us to Costco for hot dogs and Dairy Queen for Blizzards. And as if we needed more proof of how predestined this all was, we somehow surprised each other with the exact same gift: an orange spotted onesie that said, "YOU BET GIRAFFE I'M CUTE."

Nine months later, when our waters broke only minutes apart, we waddled into our respective Kias—Ethan and I leading, her and Freddie behind. At the hospital, the staff, perhaps seeing how tightly our hands were intertwined, automatically placed us in adjoining rooms. Just as we were meant to walk this earth together, so too would our babies.

There was no cry when you came out. A gurgle maybe, but now I'm not sure. So much was happening. One minute I was pushing you out, the next you were connected to a confounding tangle of hospital wires. The doctor said it was hypoxic-ischemic encephalopathy, a type of birth asphyxia that occurs when the baby doesn't get enough oxygen during delivery. He said the damage to your brain was too severe. That you had to be on a ventilator. That I did nothing wrong. That this was just terrible luck. That he was very, very sorry. And in between all of these statements, he kept peppering in the word *Mum* to address *me*. It was so disorienting. I wanted to tell him to please stop calling me that because out of everything that was coming out of his mouth, *Mum* was breaking my heart the most.

They gave us a private room, dimmed the lights, and let us be alone with you. We ignored the tubes and wires and beeping noises and played family. We gave you a bath. Combed your hair. Changed your diaper. Trimmed your nails. Opened up *Goodnight Moon* and said good night to the socks and clocks. Told you we loved you in Vietnamese and Japanese, our mother tongues. I don't know where we found the fortitude to take selfies, but we did—lots of them—and even laughed as we struggled to get the filter to add dog ears to all three of us. We got some good ones of you beside the wooden disc that we had custom carved with your name: Daisy Dang Hayashi.

Babies were crying all around us. I held you as tight as I could, squeezing you into my chest as if willing you to take shelter inside my heart where it was safest. I rocked you from side to side for hours. The only movement came from your little chest as it filled and unfilled with air from the mechanical ventilator. Your beauty was so startling I couldn't look away. The cloud-like arches of your eyebrows. The tiny curves of your nostrils, like doorways to heaven. I lifted an eyelid. Brown, just like mine. I asked your father to hold open the other eyelid so I could pretend, just for a moment, that you were looking at me with those deep pools of wonder, realizing I was the one whose belly you were inside. That I was your mother.

I closed my eyes and leaned my head back. The silence was dense, the room cold. I didn't know how to pray, so I whispered something like *Please please please oh God please* in hopes the doctors had it all wrong and you'd miraculously belt out your first cry.

Then I heard it. A cry. My heart raced as I looked down, awaiting my granted wish.

But it wasn't you. The cry was coming from the next room.

Paloma's baby was born.

———

I take a seat as Paloma runs around like a veteran stage director on speed. I don't know how she found the time to plan a funeral with a newborn stuck to her breasts all day. When I told her the horrible news, she insisted on taking care of everything. At the time I was so grateful. Now I find myself boiling with a totally irrational, but totally real, resentment towards her because while she may not have slept a wink or bathed in days, she at least had her baby.

"Can I help out with anything?" I ask her.

"Oh gosh, you do not need to do a single thing. The service will begin soon. You just sit tight, sweetie."

I look around the room and am loath to admit how breathtaking it all looks. There are white daisies everywhere, their yellow disks like pops of hope and optimism. The most beautiful display is saved for the casket, where a combination of dainty daisies and wispy greenery delicately cascade across the top.

"Did you see the dumplings?" Paloma asks.

I didn't even notice the plush white dumplings flanking each side of the casket. They were party favors from our baby shower. Because that's what we called you, after all: our little dumpling. I thank Paloma for that poignant touch and tell her everything is perfect, even though everything is terrible.

My mother is sitting next to me. She is like a creature possessed, sobbing so uncontrollably that she somehow falls to the floor from a seated position. Multiple people rush to her aid. They check her pulse, offer her some water and a Werther's Original to get her blood pressure back up, and lift her slowly back to her chair. I ask her if she's okay and that's when she gawks at me. "How are you not falling apart?"

I don't know what to say. I can't explain why I haven't shed a single tear since arriving at the funeral home. At home I can soak pillows into oblivion but here, surrounded by all these people, I can't even muster a drop. I envy my mother for that, the physical release of a good cry.

The service is going to start in five minutes. I go to the bathroom to change my pad, which is on the brink of leaking. Nobody prepares you for all the postpartum bleeding—the sheer volume, the volcanic gushing, the lime-size clots that slide out without warning. I wipe the jiggly mass of blood off the pad and flush it down the toilet.

I remove the cabbage leaves from my breasts. They are warm and wilted, wet with milk from all the hugging. The lactation consultant at the hospital said the sulfur compounds would stop my supply but clearly it's not working because I'm as engorged as a horse in heat. I pop a Tylenol and check my reflection in the full-length mirror, my breasts practically up to my neck. Stupid, sad, pathetic excuse of a body. If it can create a little human from scratch, you'd think it could also detect that the little human has died and immediately signal to the breasts: *Halt! Halt the productions! There is no baby to feed!*

A tall, lanky woman washes her hands beside me. I don't recognize her, but she sees something in me that provokes her to start a conversation.

"It's just so tragic, isn't it? To lose a full-term baby like that? I feel terrible for that woman."

I stare at her, incredulous, wondering whose plus-one she even is. All I can muster is, "Yeah, I can't imagine."

———————

Everybody quiets down as the officiant enters the room and takes out his notebook.

"We open our hearts to you, O God. Let us give thanks to God, who welcomes the stranger . . ."

What the hell is this? I turn around and hiss at Paloma.

She leans in. "He was the only one I could find last minute!"

I grumble and sit there as the clergyman asks for Jesus Christ to welcome my baby into his arms and to bless her abundantly. As a non-Christian, this brings me no comfort whatsoever. For the rest of the service, I worry that my baby has been shepherded into the arms of a bearded, robed man whose credentials I know nothing of. Is he good with babies? Does he have any childcare experience? Does he know about the five S's for soothing a crying baby? It isn't until the clergyman announces that my baby will be in the company of the Virgin Mary and all the other angels and saints in heaven that I begin to feel a little bit better.

After the prayers are done, a handful of people take turns saying a few words. The order and identity of speakers is unbeknownst to me.

Paloma gave no hint as to who would be speaking and what they'd be saying. I wish I had pestered a bit more, because had I known Ethan's uncle was going to sing a "stirring" a capella rendition of *Hamilton*'s "It's Quiet Uptown," the saddest song in musical theater history, I would have submerged that microphone in toilet water. And had I known that my cousin's daughter was going to do a reading of Robert Munsch's *Love You Forever*, the saddest memorial to stillborn babies ever written, I would have doused that book in kerosene and ignited it.

But I had no idea. So I sit through the service, gripping Ethan's hand while still producing zero tears. I look over at him. His face is wet, tears pooling at the edge of his jaw and soaking the collar that he carefully ironed that morning.

At most funerals, people share funny anecdotes or charming quirks or beloved memories of the deceased. But when someone dies before they've truly lived, it complicates the time-honored ritual. Yet, somehow, people still find a way to sum up your short little life. They talk sweetly about how loved and wanted you were, how beautiful you were, how wild and glorious and endless their dreams for you were. Hearing these speeches buoyed me even as they dragged me deeper into a dark abyss.

My mother is the last person to speak. By this point, everybody had more or less said variations of the same thing. That no parent should ever have to outlive their child. That it was fortunate she only ever knew love. That this was a tragic reminder of how we should all hold the ones we love close. What more could my mother say?

"There is so much I don't know about life and death," my mother starts in English before switching to Vietnamese for ease, "but one thing I know for sure is . . . is . . ."

Then, to my utter disbelief, she bursts into tears and collapses to the ground once again.

———

After the service, people say their solemn farewells. A tall white man with a mustache and a protruding belly greets us. He looks to be in his sixties. His mustache is full and thick, shaped like a slug. He wears a checkered waistcoat underneath a very loose-fitting jacket. If he had a British accent, he would be a good candidate for Batman's butler. He introduces himself as Kenneth Timmerman, the director of Monarch Funeral Homes, the person we spoke to on the phone to order the casket. His voice triggers memories of that thick catalog and the dissociative flipping of the pages. He tells us he will inform us when the ashes have been returned from the crematorium, which he estimates to be by the end of the week. We don't know what to say in return but *Thanks*.

"I'm very sorry for your loss," he says. "We hope this service has brought you some semblance of comfort. If there is anything you need at all, please don't hesitate to contact me. It would be a pleasure to hear from you again, whenever that may be."

I want to tell him, *With all due respect, sir, I hope I never have a reason to see you again,* but instead I nod and shake his big, calloused hand, noting the time on his watch and filling with dread that it is only noon, a whole day, a whole life, still ahead of me.

2

The day after the funeral. Some might say it is the hardest day. Harder than the day of the funeral. Even harder than the day you find out your person is dead. Frankly, I don't even know which day is which. Time has collapsed. There are no todays and tomorrows and yesterdays. There is just after.

The moment I wake up, I am greeted by an inescapable, unreachable loneliness. It sits on my chest, jagged edges and all, pressing so hard I don't emerge from the bedroom for days. It smells like death in here, bedsheets festered in a variety of comingling bodily fluids. Blood flowing out of my vagina. Urine leaking out of my bladder. Milk gushing from my nipples. Sweat seeping out of my pores. Tears streaming from my eyes. Snot dribbling out my nose. Bile projecting from my mouth. It won't be long before my anus betrays me, too.

I stare at the ceiling as question after question race through my head.

Did that really happen?
Are you really gone?
Where did you go?
Why are you not here?
Why am I still here?
Who keeps ringing the damn doorbell?

Flowers have been appearing at our doorstep all day. Carnations. Dahlias. Ranunculuses. And they just keep coming. There are already a dozen bouquets scattered around the house in various states of decay. The petals of the orchids have fallen off. Fuzzy mold climbs up the stems of the white roses. The leaves of the peace lily are drooping and wilting to a yellow color, as if it, too, has been weeping for days. It's so hard to keep up. Which ones need water? Which need a trim? Which of them require sunlight? It feels futile keeping anything alive.

"Why are flowers sent to the bereaved?" Ethan asks because he's one of those people who throws random trivia questions at their spouse knowing full well they know nothing.

"I don't know. To terrorize them?"

"They were sent to mask the smell of a decaying body. Prior to the popularity of funeral homes and embalming, the body would simply rest in the house for days. People sent flowers to cover up the stench."

The doorbell rings again. Another flower delivery. Ethan sees my dread and gets the flowers out of my sight.

I suppose I shouldn't be surprised by the warmth and generosity we're receiving, given the fact we live on Willow Avenue. Nestled in the Toronto neighborhood of the Beaches, the street is lined with detached houses that have well-maintained lawns, freshly painted doors, and a glowing neon heart pressed against the window. It's the kind of street where neighbors will put away your garbage bins for you once the trash has been picked up, where children walk over to each others' houses and ask to play with the dog, where misplaced Amazon packages get immediately returned to their rightful owner.

When Ethan and I decided to have children, we knew we only wanted to do it if we could live on Willow Avenue. The daycares and schools all had stellar reviews. The crime rate was nonexistent. The nearby boardwalk was stroller-friendly. But if I were being honest, the real reason I wanted to live on that street was because Paloma and Freddie lived there.

When the house across from them miraculously came up on the market, we put in an offer. We were so desperate we sent the owner a basket of our favorite artisanal jams and scones and included a letter that explained who we were (a married couple in their midthirties), what we did for a living (Ethan an anesthesiologist, I an actuary). We detailed all the hopes and dreams we had of raising our yet-to-exist children in this house. Ethan was going to camp with the kids in the backyard and teach them the difference between Ursa Major and Ursa Minor. I was going to show them how to grow heirloom tomatoes and purple carrots and white bell peppers while blowing their minds with fun facts like how cucumbers are actually fruit. At the bottom of the letter, we attached a silly photo of us eating peanut butter corn dogs at the Ex, in case there was any concern that our very serious jobs connoted a lack of ability to let loose and have fun.

Out of nine offers, the sellers picked us. I like to believe it was because of the wholesome picture we painted in our letter, but given the state of the real estate market, it was most likely due to our high-income jobs and contingent-free, much-over-asking offer.

The day we got the keys, we celebrated with Paloma and Freddie in our new home. All our furniture was still at the old place, so we sat on camping chairs around the fireplace. We ordered pizza that we ate off the floor. We drank champagne, then tequila, then capped off the night with an Amaro apiece.

After they left, I puked everything up and flushed down my esophagus with another Amaro. Ethan and I spread our musty sleeping bags on the living room floor, holding each other tight to generate warmth. That night, after many months of trying, on the century-old, hickory hardwood floors we paid way too much for, you were conceived.

There is not much to do after a death takes place. No need to cook as the fridge is stocked with more food than we could ever eat. No need to rake the leaves or mow the lawn as neighbors kindly take it upon themselves. No need to clean as the in-laws generously gift us with a housekeeper for the month. Ethan's mother hands me a Jizo statue, a tiny bald figurine that the Japanese use to honor lost babies, and tells me she hopes it will speed my healing.

I thank everyone for their generosity. I don't burst their bubble by telling them these gestures keep me bedridden. Because without any clothes to launder, weeds to pull, or eggs to scramble, I have no reason to get up ever again.

My parents are deeply upset by this. They see my bed rotting as a failure of constitution. An indication I'm not trying hard enough to work through the grief in a quick and nondisruptive manner. Proof I'm letting the darkness win.

Ethan is on their side, I know it. He's already gone back to work after exhausting all five of his unpaid bereavement days. Said he preferred to work than sit around at home all day. "But you don't even sit around!" I pointed out, which was true. He had suddenly taken to running at the crack of dawn and close of day and, bewilderingly, in the middle of the night. All this running should be setting off alarm bells, but it's only garnered him praise. Good for him! That's the spirit! If you ask me, running from the sadness seems to be a curse much worse than laying it all bare.

Still, nobody worries about Ethan the way they worry about me. I imagine they all secretly meet behind my back to discuss my despondence and agree upon a plan of action. That can be the only explanation for why, one by one, my parents and friends and awkwardly the housekeeper all desperately try to coax me out of bed.

"C'mon, you have to eat something."

"Seriously, you need to shower."

"Let's go for a little walk around the block, shall we?"

My response is always the same: "I would rather be dead."

Do you know what my mother said? The woman who fell to her knees twice at the funeral?

"Oh, don't be so dramatic!"

Paloma is the first person I see when I wake up. I don't know how long I've been asleep. It could be hours. It could be days. She's picking up clothes and crumpled tissues off the floor. She's giving the nightstands a wipe. She's peeling back the curtains to let in the burning sunlight. She's opening the windows to let out the pungency. And, absurdly, she's removing the bedsheets while I'm still encased in them.

"What the hell are you doing?" I cry.

"You need to get up."

With one mighty yank, she pulls the duvet off me, exposing my pathetic, pantless state, thighs crusty from blood and urine.

"Oh dear god!" Paloma plugs her nose, wafting the air in front of her. "I'm drawing you a bath."

I catch myself in a mirror and see a sad, frizzy, pinched gremlin. Paloma, of course, looks absolutely stunning. Her hair is shiny and voluminous. There's color in her cheeks and a sheen to her skin, as if she's just come from a hot yoga class. She's stylish, too, accessorized in gold jewelry and nary a drawstring or milk stain in sight.

"When did you last eat?" she asks.

I shrug. All the medications I'd been taking—a cocktail of Benadryls, NyQuils, Tylenols, and melatonin—had made it difficult to go to the bathroom. My stomach is hard to the touch. My flatulence is unremitting.

Paloma exhales. I can tell she's frustrated at my lack of desire to improve my state of being. She goes inside the bathroom and a scream erupts from her.

"Good god, Cleo! There's blood everywhere!" Paloma shouts.

I go in to check. There's blood in the toilet, blood dotted all over the white tile, blood dripping down the sides of the cabinet. The garbage is overflowing with soaked pads. The towels are all stained. A brown film coats the porcelain white sink. Toothpaste is splattered all over the mirror and faucet. I really did try to keep it clean, but basic tasks have become Sisyphean.

"Didn't they get you a housekeeper?" Paloma asks.

"I told her to stay out."

The expression on Paloma's face goes from pure disgust to sheer determination. She rolls up her sleeves and says, "Where's the Clorox?"

After the bathroom has been cleaned and the tub has been filled, she strips me of my clothing, assists me in, and—can you believe it?—she just sits there on the toilet staring at me like I'm a fly in her tea. I'm not accustomed to leering eyes while I bathe, but I sense from her furrowed brows that she wants me to take the bar of soap that's on the shelf and rub it all over my body. And so I do, despite my extreme discomfort at being gawked at.

"It's okay to cry, you know? What you're going through . . . it's a lot."

I nod, suddenly feeling pressure to cry on the spot, to show Paloma how bad I'm hurting, but I can't do it. I can't unleash the cries that keep me awake at night, cries so manic with misery and yearning they sound like the howls of an animal struck by a bullet, so instead I offer her a little frown.

Paloma, to my complete horror, gets on her knees and scrubs my back with a loofah. She starts bawling. "I—I just can't believe it," she says. "How did this happen?"

I freeze, unsure if she meant the question to be rhetorical. I hope so because I don't know how to put words to something so inconceivable, something so horrific it escapes narrativization. I know when people ask this question they do it out of curiosity, maybe to put order back into the world. *Surely there is a simple explanation. Surely this could have been prevented. Surely bad things don't just happen.* I think a better question to ask might be, *Why does anything shitty happen ever?*

I change the subject and announce that our mortgage will soon be up for renewal and all the emotion in Paloma's face disappears.

"You can't keep pretending like nothing's happened," she snaps.

I blink and resume what I was saying. "Ethan says we don't have to wait until the maturity date. We can lock in a lower rate at least six months in advance without any penalty. Isn't that such a relief?"

Paloma starts ugly crying again. She yanks some toilet paper off the handle and gives me a few squares, but I don't need them, so she uses it to blow her nose. "I wish . . . I wish things were different," she wails. "Your baby . . . our babies . . . they were supposed to grow up together. Do you know you're the reason I wanted to be a mom? If it weren't for you, I would never have even signed up for this."

I pray she will stop talking, *please.* A sudden urge to drown myself envelops me. I hold my head underwater until my lungs feel like fire and then quickly pop back up. I place my hands over the loose fat on my belly and glide my finger along my linea nigra. Not long ago, I was lush with twice the life. Now I'm carved out, hollow. What is a mother without her child? What is the sun without the moon, the sky without stars, the ocean without water?

I met Paloma on the first day of grade six. The teacher sat us next to each other, presumably because we were both Asian and would naturally get along. We hated that assumption, but the teacher was right. We did get along. We recognized ourselves in each other and formed an unbreakable bond. We shared our school supplies and helped each other with homework and stood up to bullies who said we looked alike when we really did not at all—she was Filipino, I was Vietnamese. It was tough being a preteen, what with all the pimples and racism. So we came up with a secret code to get us through the school year. We had these mini flashlights on our key chains that we'd flick three times in quick succession to let the other know *I love you*. Just that tiny act alone was enough to keep us going. Without Paloma, I don't think I would've made it out of high school alive.

At the two-hour mark of Paloma's impromptu visit, I begin to drop hints for her to leave.

"It's getting pretty late," I start.

"It's eleven in the morning."

"Oh, looks pretty dark out."

"There's not a single cloud in the sky."

I can't tell if she's being obtuse on purpose. She has always tested the boundaries of our friendship. Today, I fear she's willing to stretch it to the point of rupture.

She insists I eat something. A cube of cheese. A slice of apple. A partially melted lozenge uncovered from her pocket. Anything. "Please, for me," she begs. "What if I make you a sandwich?"

As she spreads a layer of fermented chili mayo on the bread—all the way to the crust because she knows that's how I like it—I can't help but feel a hot rage burn inside me. Why is she being so perfectly lovely when it's clear how ungrateful I am? Would it kill her to be a little bit terrible, just to assuage my guilt? I desperately want her to bring up her newborn so that I can lambaste her for rubbing her good fortune in my face. But she doesn't say a single word about her baby. She's too kind and pure to do that. She knows it would be like dangling a garden hose in front of a burning person.

I'd be lying if I said I wasn't a little bit curious. What does her baby look like? What did she name it? Did the baby inherit her cute Filipino nose? And what about the birth? How long was the labor? Did she get the epidural? And oh god please tell me she didn't tear her perineum like she feared?

But I can't ask her any of it. Not yet. Maybe not ever.

"You know I love you, right?" she says. "I hate seeing you like this. I wish I could take away some of the pain you're feeling. You're my best friend. I want you to be happy. I—" She pauses to tend to the tears streaming down her cheeks.

Suddenly there's a drop in my chest, a tightness in my throat. My nostrils flare, and pressure builds behind my eyes. I beg her to please stop crying, to stop saying such nice things, because if I cry now I fear I'll never be able to stop. I know she's only trying to repair the gulf between us, but can't she see the gulf is now oceanic?

"Go ahead and cry," Paloma says. "It's not a sign of weakness, it's the mightiest display of courage there is."

This is perhaps one of the few areas in which Paloma and I differ. For as long as I've known her, she has always been someone oriented towards positivity, someone whose ambitions revolved around some form of self-optimization. She's always talking about the powers of meditation, the buoyancy you feel after a good therapy session, the life-changing magic of journaling. She believes there's a non-pharmaceutical fix for all of life's maladies. I bet she's dying to shake me and scream in my face:

Look on the bright side!

At least you're alive!

Sorrow is a choice!

"You know," she starts, "I'm worried you're letting the sadness take over. I know it's tempting, but you can't let it win. Don't throw away your life because of this. There are so many reasons to live. Daisy wouldn't want you to be sad."

I look up, stabbing her with my stare. "She wouldn't want to be dead, either."

Paloma sighs and drops her head. I bet she's calculating the perfect thing to say next because she believes the only thing standing in the way of my healing is a good old-fashioned aphorism. Instead, she pulls out a business card belonging to somebody named Bonnie Spoon and tells me I should give her a call.

"She runs a grief support group for people experiencing out-of-order deaths. I think it will be good for you to attend, even if it's just one session."

I analyze the card. Bonnie Spoon's official title is Grief Counselor Since 2005 and she has a trademarked slogan: "Become a mourning person."™

Paloma's phone rings. It's Freddie. He doesn't know what to do. The baby is crying nonstop. He has tried everything. Feeding, burping, diaper, five different pacifiers, peekaboo, swaddle after swaddle, bouncy bouncy bouncy, but nothing is working so can she please come home right now? I hear her baby screeching through the phone. Unbeknownst to Paloma, her breasts begin to leak through her shirt. I watch the two wet dots grow larger and larger.

Paloma turns to me, unaware of the state of her chest. "I'm so sorry, sweetie. I have to go."

I hide my smile.

"Please, *please,* eat that sandwich. I'm going to call Ethan later and if he tells me the sandwich is still there, I will rush back here and kill you."

"Whoa whoa, don't tempt me with a good time," I say, raising both palms in the air and chuckling. Paloma doesn't laugh back.

I walk her to the door and wave goodbye. It isn't until I turn the lock that I realize I, too, am leaking.

3

I need to get out of this house. It's been a month and I can't stand the quiet. It's so pronounced I swear I can hear the blood swimming through my vessels. Each swish a reminder of what I've lost and will never get back.

I need a distraction.

I need to work.

I'm not due back in the office for another year because that's how much maternity leave I opted for, back when I didn't know any of this would happen, back when I thought I'd be spending the year bonding with you.

A year is too long. I can't wait any longer.

I put on something civilized, a pleated white shirt and a stretchy pair of black pants that accommodates my expanded waistline, and jump on the Queen streetcar to the Financial District. Once there, it is buzzing with the ambient noise of corporate chitchat and click-clacks and circle-backs. Everyone here is busy. Everyone here has somewhere to be. I march in stride with my phone in my hand and my retractable lanyard at my hip. I blend right in. I am one of them.

Breathing comes easy, as if my airways have widened. Here, I'm not a mother whose baby has died. Here, I'm a senior actuarial analyst for the country's leading provider of life and casualty insurance. I have a nine-year tenure. I'm admired, revered, lauded for being the first Asian woman to hold a senior position at the company. I have deadlines, meetings, and complex problems to solve. Team members rely on me, as do millions of Canadians who choose us for our flexible and affordable insurance coverage. There is no time to rest. No time to dwell or cry or even so much as let out a little whimper. Here, there is no stillness. The ache cannot surface. So long as the screens are on and the notifications keep pushing, the grief recoils.

I take a seat at my desk. No one is in the office yet.

I log in, the password stored in my fingers. I check my email. There are hundreds of unread messages. Most of them are standard company emails. The IT department telling us to please not click on any links that look suspicious. The HR team reminding us to complete the unconscious bias training. The engagement team asking for people to vote on the next company outing.

There are a handful of emails addressed directly to me. The subject lines send a jolt to my limbs:

We miss you
Thinking of you
You are in my thoughts

For a moment, the grief swells to a mass and I can feel my airways thicken, my chest tightening. I quickly delete all these emails.

"Oh my god, you're back!"

I whip around in my chair. There is a young woman in a stylish black jumpsuit standing in my cubicle. Her waist is cinched with a gold belt. Her head a halo of impeccably dark and bouncy curls. There is a bag and coat in her arm. She appears eager to set them down.

"Who are you?" I say.

"I'm Farrah. You must be Cleo. I'm covering your mat leave. I was told you wouldn't be coming back for another . . ."

"Year."

She coughs into her arm. "Right."

There is an uncomfortable silence between us as we stare blankly at each other. A notification chimes from the computer.

"Well, I should be getting back to work," I say before turning my back to her.

I wait to hear her walk away but all I sense is her presence over my shoulder.

"Umm, should I sit somewhere else or . . ."

I am annoyed. I do not see how her predicament is my problem and feel very inconvenienced by her questioning. "I'm sorry. I'm quite busy as you can see. There's a lot of work to catch up on."

"I—I understand. Can I just—"

She hesitantly reaches into the cabinet and grabs a few things. A notebook. A tube of lotion. A picture of the fattest cat I've ever seen. Then she is gone.

I turn back to the blue screen and a sense of peace washes over me. The moment I begin clicking the mouse, I remember how much I relish this ritual: reviewing actuarial tables, pricing coverage for prospective policyholders, quantifying longevity risks, crossing off to-dos like a machine.

Every so often I'll look out the window. Our office is located on the twenty-ninth floor, so the pedestrians look like ants and the cars like Hot Wheels. From this vantage point, it is hard to see the humanity in the people below. They are just bugs. They don't have feelings, dreams, or loved ones waiting for them at home. This way of thinking helps me focus better on work. It reduces the guilt I feel when I'm calculating an individual's life expectancy and price their premiums based on when I think they will die. It's surprisingly easy to forecast a person's mortality, to the accuracy of plus or minus ten percent, of course.

Before I became pregnant, I created a mathematical model to forecast the probability of your death. I know, morbid, but what kind of actuary would I be if I didn't do my due diligence? I researched climate change models and analyzed potential future scenarios of life on Earth. I crunched the numbers to see how likely you'd be to develop some kind of disease. I calculated the odds of you dying by car, plane, and train. The more I looked into it, the more it became quite evident that bringing a child into this world would be incredibly grim. And yet when I thought about how ferociously I would love you, how happy we'd be, it obliterated all the terrifying and startling truths of becoming a parent and I wanted it. I wanted you.

Paloma, on the other hand, did none of these mental gymnastics in her head. The day she realized her period was two weeks late was the day she first thought about babies. She had texted me a picture of a positive pregnancy test and wrote Plot twist lol followed by an emoji of a monkey covering its eyes.

At the time, I thought she was being reckless. Now I wonder if I should've been more like her, more chill. If I didn't want it so bad, if I hadn't tempted the universe, maybe you would still be here today. Maybe this is all my fault.

"Well, well, the rumors are true."

I turn around. It's my boss, Shane Yao. The last thing he said to me before I went on mat leave was *You're gonna love being a mom*, and now here he is, standing awkwardly before me with bewilderment and fear plastered all over his face. I worry I've done something wrong. I worry I might get fired. I worry that when he looks at me all he can think is *dead baby*.

"I didn't realize you were coming back so soon," says Shane. "I assumed you would need more time off. H-how are you?"

He seems flustered. I know he's afraid to bring up the subject, but I do him a favor by putting on my Professional Mask and deliver the kind of curt answer that quells his discomfort.

"I'm doing well, thank you."

His eyes flash with relief. "That's good, very good." He says *good* seven more times and I get concerned that his brain has momentarily short-circuited. "Well, we're happy to have you back."

"I'm glad to be back."

"We missed you around here."

"Thank you."

"Were you able to log back in okay? Any issues?"

"No. Everything is working."

"I see you've met Farrah."

"Yes, I have."

"She's been an absolute champ while you were away."

"I'm happy to hear that."

"There were some very big shoes to fill."

"How nice of you to say."

"And don't stress about the desk situation. We'll find a new spot for Farrah."

"Mm-hmm."

He shuffles his feet uncomfortably. I sense he's run out of things to talk about. Typically, when a mother returns from maternity leave, there are a plenitude of things to ask her such as "How is the little munchkin?" and "Have they started walking yet?" and "Don't they just grow up so fast?" Normal things new mothers get asked all the time. He can't ask me any of those things so instead he resorts to: "Did you hear we upgraded the coffee machine?"

"Oh?"

"It dispenses espressos and tea lattes. Are you much of a latte person?"

"No."

"Well, this thing dispenses hot water, too."

"How ingenious."

"Truly."

Another pause. Shane's eyes are awkwardly darting in multiple directions. I fear he'll burst a vessel. Finally, he finds something else to say to me.

"Anyway, there's a presentation I'd love to get your eyes on. Is it okay if I send that over to you? I don't want to overwhelm you on your first day back."

"Absolutely!" I beam, excited to be discussing matters of work again.

"Great, I'll send that shortly."

He gives my cubicle wall a couple taps and walks away.

I continuously click the refresh button of my inbox, waiting for Shane's email to appear. It's hard to concentrate as the office fills up and gets increasingly noisy. I can hear *good mornings* and *how was your weekend* and *ugh traffic was awful wasn't it?* There's a palpable sense of despair on the floor, as is commonplace on a Monday. Nobody ever seems jovial or rejuvenated despite having two full days off work. It's never enough. But we keep our grievances to ourselves and enter every workweek as if it is.

As I wait for Shane's email to come in, I complete my unconscious bias training. I put on my headphones so I can pay attention to the videos and complete the quiz as best I can.

"In this video, we will discuss the different types of unconscious biases that can be found in a workplace. Grab a pen and paper so you can make note of any biases you think you might display."

I reach into the cabinet to grab a notepad. That's when I overhear someone say my name. I take off my headphones and poke my head up. It's Melody the underwriter and Dolores the analyst, whispering a few cubicles over.

"And she didn't tell anybody? Not even HR?" says Melody.

"No, just showed up out of the blue," replies Dolores.

"Does she seem okay?"

"I think so. If she's back at work she must be fine, right?"

"I feel so bad for her."

"To be honest, she doesn't seem all that sad. Did you see her mom at the funeral? The way she cried? Still haunts me to this day."

"I can't believe Cleo didn't even cry once. I mean, *she's* the mother."

I sit down and sink into my chair. I'm surprised to hear they think I'm cold and icy because I often feel as if I have sadness written all over me.

"I read somewhere that some people can't physically cry. They have some kind of phenotype that prevents it from happening. Like, they could be watching a herd of deer drown in a lake and not shed a single tear."

"Really? That's a bit deranged."

"Who knows? Maybe she could have a medical condition. I have a friend who couldn't cry for a whole year because she had an obstruction in her tear ducts."

"Oh my god, how did she fix it?"

"The doctor told her to watch sad movies every day for a month."

"Seriously?"

"Had to watch *Grave of the Fireflies* over and over again."

"What a nightmare."

They both laugh.

"Maybe she didn't really want the baby. She looked miserable at that baby shower."

"Oh my god, that's right! What do you think she did with all our gifts?"

"Don't even think about asking for it back!"

"I wasn't!" A pause. "But I did contribute a good portion to that Jolly Jumper. When will I get spoiled with free gifts from the company?"

"When you grow a whole human inside you."

"It's so unfair. Do you know how much money I've spent on baby showers and wedding gifts at this office? And what have I gotten in return? Zilch!"

"Hey, I don't make the rules."

"You don't think . . ."

"Don't think what?"

"Never mind."

"Oh, c'mon."

Melody lowers her voice, but I can still make out what she says next. "You don't think she faked it, do you? The pregnancy? She did make out with a lot of highly valuable items."

"No way, that would be absolutely ludicrous."

"I'm just putting it out there. Not to be devil's advocate or anything but it was a closed casket service after all."

"Oh you are sooo bad." Dolores giggles before they both walk away from earshot.

I return my attention to the quiz in front of me but despite my best efforts, I fail.

The grief returns with the intensity of a wildfire. For a moment, I question if I really was pregnant. Maybe I made up the nausea, the cravings, the kicks. Maybe there never was a baby growing inside me. Maybe what was actually expanding in there was the delusion that I was good enough to be a mother.

I put a hand on my belly. I squeeze the fat so hard it hurts. I need to be reminded that you were here. That even if all proof of your existence were gone, my love for you will still cling to the air that feeds the earth.

Suddenly I feel a kick.

Did I imagine that?

I wait to feel another one, but my abdomen is as still as night.

For the rest of the day, I muffle the sorrow with work, work, and more work. When I'm lost in spreadsheets, the grief turns into a harmless speck. Its sharpness is blunted once again. It cannot pierce me. It cannot hurt me.

The overhead lights start to flicker and a custodian interrupts me, telling me they're locking up the building. I look around. It's 8:00 p.m. Everybody has left.

I slip on my coat and head towards the exit.

I pass by Melody's desk. I've never been a violent person, but I also have never met someone as deserving of my fist as Melody. I wonder how much damage I can do to that mousy face of hers, how much blood would spill beneath her skin. I bet it's easy. I bet she'd bruise for months.

There is an unfinished cup of black coffee on her desk. It's cold. An oily film floats on top. A stupid quote is etched on the mug: "I WISH THIS WERE WHISKEY." I pick it up and pour it all over her keyboard and monitor and chair before exiting the building.

4

When I arrive at the office the next morning, coffee is my sole focus. I attempt to use the fancy new contraption Shane was talking about, but I'm unsure which buttons to press and which compartments to fiddle with, so I give up and fill the kettle with water and place a teabag in one of the available mugs in the cabinet. As I wait for the kettle to reach a boil, somebody enters the kitchen before quickly turning around and walking away. A few minutes later, it happens again. People are scared to be around me. It's like I'm a contagious disease. I wish I could scream at the top of my lungs, *It's grief, not herpes!*

Whatever. Small talk drains me anyway.

My phone pings with a message from my mother. It's a picture of a quote. She's been sending them daily since you died. I think it's sweet, even if a little excessive. This one's from Edna St. Vincent Millay:

> Where you used to be, there is a hole in the world, which I find
> myself constantly walking around in the daytime, and falling
> into at night.

Tears pool at my eyes as I text her back a heart emoji.

A woman with pin-straight hair enters the kitchen. I don't recognize her. She makes a coffee on the complicated contraption. I pay attention to the buttons she presses and commit the sequence to memory.

"So that's how you do it," I blurt out.

"It's a bit finicky but you get used to it after a couple times," she says, waiting for the drip to finish.

"Do you work on this floor?" I ask.

"I work downstairs at the creative agency. I'm just here for the coffee machine. Ours is broken at the moment." She puts her finger to her lips and makes a shushing sound. "Don't tell anybody."

I chuckle, grateful to find someone who is not actively avoiding me.

She looks me up and down. "Hey, you just had a baby, right?"

I freeze.

"I remember seeing you in the bathroom one time. Hard not to spot you. You must've been close to the due date at that point. No offense or anything! I thought you were absolutely glowing."

"Oh I'm not sure about that," I force myself to say. "Unless by glowing you mean greasy like a rotisserie chicken, then sure."

She laughs, so I laugh, too, faking it as best I can. I stretch my mouth, flash all my teeth, forcing out sounds that once came easily. It is a strange sensation—like pulling on an old sweater from another life. It never quite fits right.

"Did you have a girl or boy?"

I pause. "It was, um, is . . ." I have a hard time answering, vacillating between present and past tense, so I just say, "Girl."

"Oh, how precious. Can I see a picture?"

A stone sits in my chest, weighing me down. I have to tell her. I have to say the words. But she looks like she's having a good morning, and I don't want to sully it with my sadness. Besides, nobody ever asks to see a picture of you. I take out my phone, eager to have a reason to pull up your photo, and I pick one where there are no tubes, no wires, no signs of hospital in the background. In this photo, you look like you are in a deep, blissful nap. No signs that your heart has stopped beating.

I hesitantly show her the picture. I'm afraid she might notice something is off. I'm afraid she might scream.

"Oh my goodness gracious!" she starts. "Look at those chubby cheeks! I could just gobble them up! How do you come to work every day? I would never be able to leave her side."

The coffee contraption sputters to completion.

"Thank you," I say, watching her collect her mug and bring it to her lips.

"Well, I should be going," she says. "Congratulations! You must be so in love with her."

I smile, holding her gaze. "I am. I really am."

There's a new email waiting for me in my inbox. It's a meeting invite from Shane. Time: 9:00 to 9:30 a.m. Location: His office.

Crap.

The presentation.

I completely forgot to review it yesterday.

I still have half an hour to look it over and come back with remarks. I pull it open and attempt to pore through it as fast as I can. But my brain is uncooperative. It's covered in a veil of fog, unable to dissect the numbers and graphs laid out in front of it, unable to stop reading the same sentence over and over again. Why can't I focus? Then I remember. The hospital pamphlets about grief brain and postpartum brain and how a significant chunk of my gray matter has turned into porridge. That explains why there have been glitches in my cognition, why even simple words don't compute. Once I came across the word *marriage* and read it as *miscarriage*. Same with *corner*, which became *coroner*. And when a commercial for *Deal or No Deal* splashed across my screen I was certain it said *Death or No Death*.

I'm in Shane's office. He gestures for me to sit. Before he can say anything, I get ahead of it. "Look, I'm having a bit of trouble concentrating at the moment, so if I could just have until the end of the day to go over the presentation—"

"Hold on, hold on. That's not why I asked you here."

"Oh?" Relief rinses over me.

"There's something else I'd like to talk to you about. We received some very upsetting news," he says, causing me to shift in my seat. "This morning Melody found her desk in a state of disarray. Somebody had poured a liquid substance all over her equipment. Her computer is rendered unusable now."

"Oh no, that's horrible—"

"Cleo, we know it was you. We have it on camera. You intentionally damaged company property. This is a completely fireable offense. There is absolutely no excuse for this reckless behavior."

I sit there with my head down, shoulders slumped, arms stiff, like a kid being reprimanded for shoplifting candy. It was a harmless joke. Just a little sticky mess. And I know for a fact it costs the company nothing to replace that computer.

"It was an accident," I say weakly.

Shane sighs, furrowing his brows into a disappointed frown. "Cleo, I know you've been going through some tremendous difficulties and I can't imagine what this past month has been like for you. To be honest, I was a little taken aback when you came back to work so soon. I hope you didn't feel any pressure to return early. You have every right to take the maximum amount of leave allotted to you. And should you need an extension, we're more than happy to have that discussion when the time comes."

"What are you saying?"

"I think it's clear you're not ready to be back in the office. You need time to heal. You should stay home and focus on yourself and your family—"

I see where this is going and I don't like it. I don't need to be at home. I need to be here where it's bright and busy and far, far away from that suffocating house that feels like it's filling up with sand.

"But I don't want—"

"Your role at this company is protected so there is no need to worry. Farrah has been doing a great job handling your projects so you can take your mind off work and just focus on taking care of yourself, you know, process everything that's happened. That is all we care about in this moment. Your health." He pauses. "Your physical *and* mental health."

I shake my head. "I'm fine. Really, I am. I've had enough time to process. There's nothing left to think about. Please, I need to work. I need the distraction."

Shane exhales through his nose, his back going completely stiff.

"I think this is for your own good."

"Please don't—"

"You're welcome to finish up whatever you're working on today. But it's clear from the footage I saw that you still have a lot of things to work through and I strongly suggest you take this time off to heal."

Heal.

It's the second time he's used that word. It sounds so quaint and attainable the way he says it, like all I need to do is put on some fuzzy socks and drink some chamomile tea and read poetry next to a sun-baked window. If only it were that easy. If only it weren't an impossible standard.

Shane pushes off his desk and gets up. He extends his arm towards the door, gesturing for me to go. His body language screams, *Get out, get out, get out,* so I walk out of his office. I don't bother saying goodbye to anyone. I know it will only set off a flurry of unsubstantiated rumors, so I silently leave, as quiet as a corpse. As if I'd never been here at all.

5

With the sudden absence of anything to do, my head returns to a fog of unbearable what-ifs.

What if we'd gone to the hospital sooner?
What if it had been a different doctor?
What if there were signs I ignored?
What if I did something to deserve this?

Everything in this house is suddenly a temptation. The knives. The mouthwash. The vodka. The pills. The cord of the hair dryer.

Ethan's at work. What would he do if he were me? He would move. He would put on a pair of sneakers and run. So, I run. Even when it starts raining. Even when it feels like my knees might buckle and my ankles might snap. I run so fast I feel like I might throw up and keep going until I eventually retch into a storm drain.

I walk back home and see a package at Paloma's doorstep. It's getting soaked. The car is gone. The lights are off. Nobody is home. I wonder if she still keeps the spare key inside that fake rock. I look for it in the edges of her garden bed. Not this one. Not that one.

There it is.

I unlock the door and leave the package inside. I should close the door and leave. But her house is warm and inviting and smells like cinnamon and baby powder. I hang out in the foyer, just for a little bit so I can dry up. I walk around the living room where neutral tone furniture is accented with the warm textures of rattan and jute. The monochromatic aesthetic even carries to the wooden baby gym and the beige and tan stuffed animals that dangle from it. Even with a newborn, Paloma's house still has a manufactured elegance to it, like a new doll that has never been taken out of its package.

I'm curious how her ensuite bathroom turned out. The remodel was all she could talk about for weeks. Should she go for glacier white plaster or emerald clay subway tiles? Brass fixtures or matte black? Dual or rainfall shower head? I go upstairs to take a peek. My jaw drops like I'm on HGTV. It looks like something out of a magazine. There's even three plush towels neatly rolled on top of an acacia stool.

I'm sure she won't mind if I take a quick shower. She's let me use her bathroom plenty before during our own renovations. I strip off my wet clothes and step into the walk-in shower. I use her coconut-scented shampoo and lather myself with a peppermint soap that leaves a tingling sensation on my skin. I let the hot water run down my body for several minutes. My breasts are bursting with milk, screaming for the suckling of a baby's mouth. I hand-express all the milk from each of my breasts until they're soft and deflated, knowing full well they'll fill up in two hours, three if I'm lucky.

I dry myself off with their Egyptian cotton towels and slip into a waffle-knit bathrobe hanging off a solid brass hook. Everything is still slightly damp, still carrying the scent of Paloma.

The bathroom counter is cluttered with a mishmash of his and hers items. Razors and trimmers for him. Peri bottles and padsicles for her. I help myself to her skin care, a meticulously curated collection of formulas free from parabens, phthalates, and silicones. Ever since she listened to a podcast about endocrine-disrupting chemicals, she started taking clean living very seriously, going on rants about Horrible Lauryl, the nickname she gives to sodium lauryl sulfate, a common surfactant that is "literally killing us all," and when she does, I furiously nod along to compensate for my deep indifference to the matter.

Guilt slithers up my throat.

Maybe Paloma was right. Maybe if I'd actually paid attention to her, been more mindful about the ingredients I was putting on my body instead of slathering Horrible Lauryl all over me like a pig in sludge, then maybe you would've lived.

I swallow hard, hoping to drown the guilt.

I finish up in the bathroom and mosey around their bedroom. It's the one room I've never seen. Unlike the bathroom and the living room, it's in a state of disarray, the kind of disarray commanded by the delirium of new parenthood. Bedsheets undone. Balled-up diapers on the ground. An empty humidifier with mildew crawling up the sides. The bed is king-size, so when I go to lay on it and stretch out my arms and legs like a starfish, my limbs barely reach the edges. I spot the bassinet in the corner, the mobile of clouds and stars spinning glacially above it. I have the same one. We registered for it together. Only mine is collecting dust and hers is collecting sweet dreams. I walk over to the bassinet. There's tiny baby hairs on the mattress. Thin, wispy, the color of a decades-old penny.

I search the house for pictures of the baby. I want to know what the baby looks like. I want to see if it's possible for my heart to crack once more. Luckily, I don't find any.

I enter the nursery. It smells overwhelmingly of poop. The diaper pail is overflowing. Brown splotches stain the rug. Dresser drawers splayed open. I pull out a onesie. It is white with little clementines all over. There is a faint yellow stain around the collar. I bring it up to my nose. Warm, milky, baby breath. If there's a heaven, I think this is what it smells like.

I open the bottom drawer. Bottles with low-flow nipples. Velcro swaddles made of bamboo. Muslin burp cloths by the dozen. Unopened gripe water. Three different brands of diaper cream. Freezer bags for breast milk. A hooded bath towel with flappy little bunny ears that serve no purpose except to add adorableness.

There is a wooden inscription above the crib. "DON'T YOU EVER GROW UP."

Indelible envy swells through my veins. It isn't fair. This should be mine, too.

I play pretend. I pretend this is all mine. I pretend I'm a new mother, hormones raging with love and bliss and instinct. I'm connecting with my baby. I'm getting into a groove. I'm becoming that thing people say when you have a child. Complete. I pretend Ethan has taken the baby out for a stroller nap so that I could get some sleep but of course I don't sleep because this house is a mess and there are a million and one things to do. There's no time to rest. I empty the diaper pail. Lift the stains from the rug. Fold the onesies and place them neatly back into the drawer. I sanitize the room so there's not a hint of baby poop or throw-up sticking to the air. I plop down on the rocking chair, exhausted but alive and happy and fulfilled. What a life! To be completely unmoored by tragedy. To go one full day without feeling the sting of salty tears crusted to the sides of your face.

I spot the plastic syringe in the crib. Still sticky and dripping of a purple substance. I lick the tip. Grape-flavored acetaminophen. During the prenatal classes, we were advised to have these on hand in case the baby develops a fever. I suddenly feel queasy at the thought that Paloma's child may be terribly sick.

What am I doing?

What is wrong with me?

I shouldn't be here.

As I turn to exit the nursery, I see the plush white dumpling in the closet. They were such a hit at our baby shower that I didn't even get to keep one. I pull it out, staring at its black dots for eyes and pink dots for cheeks and an understated smile that momentarily muffles the sadness screaming from my heart. A strange sensation takes over and I feel compelled to bring the dumpling with me to the rocking chair. I sit down and hold it as if it were a baby. I pull out my breast and press the dumpling's mouth against my nipple. I hum a lullaby, rocking the chair back and forth. I could do this all day, devote myself to unrelenting domesticity. My heartbeat slows. My breath deepens. My thoughts come into focus. It's as if my body has been yearning for this, has been readying itself from the moment those embryonic cells started to multiply.

A ray of light bounces off a yellow spine on the bookshelf. I squint to make out the title. *Mother's First Year: A Daily Journal*. It doesn't surprise me that Paloma keeps a diary. I bet she writes about how motherhood has bestowed so much meaning and purpose to her life, how the love she feels for her baby is all-consuming. There's probably a cloyingly cliché entry in there about how this is the best thing she's ever done and although it is hard she wouldn't change a single thing. I bet every other paragraph is laden with the word *grateful*. Grateful for her health. Grateful for her family. Grateful for the good fortune of having a baby at all.

I resist every temptation to read her diary but what harm could there be in a little peek?

> *Dear diary,*
> *I'm a mom! I can't believe I'm writing these words. I'm an actual*
> *mom! And not just any mom. Mom to the most perfect, precious*
> *little—*

I close the journal. I can't do it. Every word, every exclamation, feels like being skinned alive.

Dumpling moves to the other breast as I continue to rock. There's a golden light shining through the window, and it casts a spotlight on the two of us. I stroke Dumpling's soft white exterior, telling her how loved and wanted and safe she is. How no harm will come to her because I am her mother and that's what mothers do best—protect their babies. I look down at her and think of you. I wonder if you would've grown up to look more like your father or more like me. Would you have your father's meaty cheeks or my hollow ones? Would you laugh if I played peekaboo or blew raspberries on your tummy? Would you inherit my terrible sense of direction and disdain for cilantro? Would you be shy or outgoing? Would you have loved me?

Suddenly a chirping sound goes off from downstairs. I set Dumpling down on the chair and check on the noise. It's coming from the smart thermostat. "It turns on when it detects you're on the way home," Paloma had raved to me when she had it installed.

Shit.

I quickly change back into my clothes, replace the key in the rock, and rush back home. I peer through the slats in my blinds and watch as her car turns into the driveway. Freddie is with her. He's carrying the car seat with one arm, a blanket is draped overtop. They disappear inside their home. After a few minutes, there's movement in the upstairs window of the nursery. Paloma unclasps her bra and nurses her baby in the rocking chair. Dumpling is no longer there. She has been tossed to the ground.

6

Dear diary,
The baby is here! She has a bit of jaundice but otherwise is feeding
well and pooping lots. She's got my eyes and nose and even my
hairy arms. I love her so much. People keep asking if I knew I
could love something this much. Of course I knew. I always knew.

Dear diary,
Is it possible to die from being so tired? She refuses to sleep
anywhere but my arms. She screeches the moment I place her in
the bassinet. What am I doing wrong? Why won't she sleep? Why,
why, why???

Dear diary,
She smiled! Her first smile! I wish I caught it on camera, but it
came out of nowhere. I was wiping down the bathroom mirror and
the squeaks set her off. Oh, my heart nearly exploded with joy!
I didn't want it to stop. I went around the entire house wiping
every single piece of glass I could find. She couldn't get enough of
it. I don't think I've ever been so happy in my entire life.

7

For weeks I stray in and out of consciousness on the sofa, remote in one hand, phone in the other. I watch six seasons of *The Great Canadian Baking Show* while googling things like *What is the life expectancy of Asian women in North America?* The answer, to my disappointment, is astonishingly high at ninety-one years. I think about taking up smoking, wondering how many years that might shave off, but then I remember my chain-smoking grandmother in Vietnam who just turned ninety-five and realize even smoking doesn't guarantee an early death.

One day Ethan decides he's fed up with my listlessness. He insists we engage in activities that once brought us joy. People-watching on the boardwalk. Strolling through Kew Gardens. Cycling down the Leslie Spit. "Your choice. Whatever you want to do!" He says it like I'm picking between prizes. All of these suggestions involve physical effort, I inform him, and need I remind him of the array of alternative activities that also brought us joy: watching movies from the couch, eating snacks on the couch, scrolling our phones while supine on the couch, et cetera.

"Come on! We need to get out of the house. It's not good for us to be cooped up like this."

He tells me about the books he's been reading, including one by a renowned monk who'd lost all three of his children in a helicopter crash off the coast of Oahu and how he woke up one day deciding he no longer wanted to be a passive participant to grief. "He described grief as a kind of tar that lodges itself into our joints and how it's incumbent upon us to constantly move our bodies if we wish to remain unstuck." Ethan goes on to explain to me how *grieving* is a verb and that it's something we do, not something that happens to us, and how the monk committed the rest of his life to one singular motto: "MOTION IS LOTION."

"I really think we should put this into practice," Ethan proclaims.

I look at him, stunned and confused. "You think we should be using lotion?"

"No! The whole *moving our bodies* thing. The more we're still, the more our minds will wander and ruminate on the past. Rumination will rot our brains."

"Could we not just pace around the house?"

"I'm serious, Cleo! Nobody is going to help us but us. We can't keep sitting here feeling sorry for ourselves."

I strongly beg to differ, but I keep my opinions to myself because I know it'll only frustrate him. "Fine."

"Really?"

"Yes," I say without enthusiasm, "but I have one question, though."

"What?"

"Are monks even allowed to have children?"

He pauses. "Well, I guess it's no longer a problem."

We laugh so hard our bellies hurt. Our first laugh! Our first death joke! If there's progress to be made, then surely this would be it. It feels like coming up for air. It feels like hope. A sweet sensation spreads inside me, like thick honey sliding down a sore throat. It's rare and brief but has the effect of making me feel like everything might just be okay.

I change into leggings and a half-zip tunic, and when I come back downstairs, Ethan looks crestfallen.

"What's wrong?" I ask.

"I just got a phone call from the funeral home. The ashes are ready."

———

We're seated across from Kenneth Timmerman. For being a seasoned director, he looks decidedly nervous. There's a sheen of sweat on his forehead. The hairs on his mustache are trembling. One would think he's done this countless times, handing over ashes with the freakish ease of a drive-through worker handing over a burger combo.

He starts profusely apologizing for the delay in delivering the cremated remains to us and reassures us it will never happen again. I want to tell him it's fine since, frankly, who is ever in a rush to collect their beloved's ashes, but my mind wanders to Ethan's tattered army-green jogging shorts, the ones with the hole in the seam of the crotch. I insisted he change into something more appropriate, but he said there was no time since the funeral home was closing soon and he couldn't bear the thought of leaving you alone in a dark closet for another night.

Kenneth stands up and steps outside the room. When he returns, there's a brown box in his hands. It's so small, so plain. Like something to hold inconsequential items lying around the house: pushpins or discarded batteries or elastic bands. He sets it on the table and neatly ties a pink bow around it like it's a present.

Neither one of us immediately reaches for it. My brain can't compute the thing in front of us. Supposedly it is you, but how can that be when you weighed eight pounds and measured twenty-one inches and that thing is just a tiny, insignificant box that people put pushpins in?

"I know this is difficult," says Kenneth. "If you're not ready to bring her home, we can keep her here safely and securely until the time is right."

It's uncomfortably quiet. I wait for Ethan to say something because he's the type of person who always fills dead silences. An eternity passes and still nothing comes out of his mouth.

I speak up. "No, it's fine, we will take her home."

Ethan begins bawling, tears falling onto his pale thighs. Kenneth tells us he'll give us a moment of privacy.

As I comfort Ethan as best I can, I feel a ruinous rage rising. Shouldn't I be the one crying? Shouldn't I be the one who needs consoling? He's supposed to be the composed one, the strong one, the one who reads books with profound insights on how to move through grief. I want to cry, too, but I fear there's not enough room for both our grief, that the room will somehow combust if our emotions were to activate at the same time.

Motion is lotion.

I get up and walk around the room.

There's a corkboard on the wall. I walk up to it and take in every scrap of trivial information, smothering my senses and nerves so I don't have to feel the hurt. There are business cards for florists, caterers, certified celebrants, grief counselors, funeral singers. There are notices about construction happening on the east side of the parking lot, and a routine fire alarm testing scheduled this week that will cause intermittent ringing. There's a job posting for a funeral director's assistant. It comes with a competitive compensation package, a healthy pension plan, and, most importantly, a rewarding career path that allows you to celebrate lives once lived. Requirements: Must be able to lift thirty-five pounds and be comfortable with the transfer of decedents.

I wonder what kind of person would want to be around death all the time. I snap a picture.

"Looks like somebody is interested."

I'm startled by Kenneth's voice. I didn't hear him come in over Ethan's cries, which have now settled into sniffles.

"Excuse me?"

"If you know anybody that would be fit for the job, I'd be happy to take any referrals."

"Not many applications, huh?"

"Actually, we get hundreds a day."

I don't believe him.

"Seriously, we do. People are dying to get in this field." He lets out a deep, throaty chuckle. Something tells me he repeats this joke multiple times a week, but I flatter him with a quick little snicker.

"If I may ask," I start, "and I'm sorry if this comes off offensive in any way, but why would anyone want to work here?"

He coughs into his hand, and I make a mental note to not shake hands later. "Many, many reasons. Some people want to help out others. Some people feel it's a calling. We even had one person work here because they wanted to get over their fear of death."

"Wow."

"It's not a terrible place to work. You should really think about applying."

"Me? Oh no, no, no, no," I say, which is the only correct response to such an absurd suggestion.

"We could really use a stoic presence like you around here."

It flatters me greatly that he can't see the choke hold grief has on me. He doesn't know all the tears that have blinded me and the violent tremors that quake through my body at the mere thought of you.

"I really don't think I'm cut out for the job."

He glimpses over at your ashes, still untouched on the table.

"I think you have more experience than anybody."

I hold back tears. I don't want this man to see that I can break as easily and routinely as an ocean wave. "C-can I ask you something?"

He nods.

"What do you think happens after we die?"

He puts his hands in his pockets, exhaling. "I could tell you what I think happens, but it doesn't really matter what I say, now does it?"

"It does, it does. Of all people you would be most informed."

"Now why do you think that?"

I spread my arms wide. "Because of all this. Because of what you do."

He chuckles. "I certainly have my hunches, I won't lie to you, but I have learned over my many, many years of working here that it's best to keep them to myself. Everybody comes to their own conclusions and who am I to contest their theories just because they don't align with mine?"

"No, please, I want to know."

"Let me tell you what. Come work for me, and I'll tell you what I think."

"What? No. I—I can't."

He sighs. "I understand. It's a grueling job. A lot of people can't handle the schedule. You probably wouldn't want to be pulled away from home at all hours of the day anyway."

My ears perk up. A job that allows me to work myself to the bone so that I can make it through the day without suffocating under the weight of sadness? I'm suddenly intrigued.

"Just think about it," he tells me.

Ethan approaches us with the ashes in his hands. A single teardrop sits on the tip of his cheek, perilously about to fall, and I hug him so tightly the edges of the box leave permanent grooves in my chest.

The drive home is quiet. I'm careful with my turns and slow down well in advance of hitting speed bumps. I don't want Ethan to drop the ashes, even though his grip on the box is tight enough to crush it.

When we get home, Ethan places the box on the table in the entryway. It feels wrong putting it there, like it's just a pack of gum or crumpled receipt. We pick it up and put it on the mantel above the fireplace. Too high, too wrong. We bring it upstairs to our bedroom and set it gently down in the bassinet. Wrong, wrong, all wrong. We're too tired to think of another spot and accept it will never feel right no matter where it goes.

I can't stop staring at it. I take out a tape measure. It's no taller and no wider than four inches. I undo the bow and open it, holding my breath. The ashes are sealed inside a plastic bag, shut tight with a zip tie. There's not much inside. Less than half a cup maybe. Where is the rest of it? Surely there's more. There has to be more. I place it on a scale. Two ounces. I tell Ethan I think they forgot to give us the rest. He shakes his head. He tells me that is everything.

That can't be right. They made an error. They even admitted it themselves. There had been a clerical issue. Perhaps they misplaced some of the ashes and that was the reason for the delay. They've made a mistake. We have to go back.

I should've been there during the cremation, should've followed your casket to the crematorium. It was only an hour away, but I was so beat after the service, there was nothing left of me to give. As we drove east and you went west, I felt like the worst mother in the world. I should have gone. I should have been there. Why didn't I go? Why did I leave you all alone?

"Are you sure this is all of it?" I ask again.

Ethan nods solemnly.

I refuse to believe it.

There has to be more.

There has to be more.

There has to be more.

A sob rises in my throat and gushes out, spilling into seemingly every crevice of my body. Grief cuts through me like a serrated knife. It feels impossible—this stretch of days and weeks ahead I'm supposed to live out. I don't know how I'll do it. There has to be a way out.

I think about emailing Shane. Begging him to let me work again. Pleading my case. I log in to my work email, but the password isn't working. The account has been disabled. Unusable until my return-to-work date, about ten months from now.

I can't wait that long.

I need something to do.

Something that will smother the screams inside me.

I think about Kenneth, how desperate he was for an assistant, how the hours are long and the work taxing. I call the funeral home, and he immediately picks up.

"Do you still need an assistant?" I ask.

8

Kenneth greets me at the door when I arrive and the first thing that comes out of his mouth is, "Oh my, you can't wear that."

I peer down, forgetting what I mindlessly put on this morning. Ripped jeans, Converse sneakers, and a blue hoodie of a cartoon toaster saying, "Time for a bath!" Kenneth tells me not to worry, he has something I can wear for the day. I apologize for not dressing more appropriately. It didn't occur to me that assistants needed to adhere to a dress code policy since, I presumed, I'll just be cooped up in a windowless room inputting data on a dusty old computer and calling bereaved families to remind them their invoice is overdue.

"Oh gosh," replies Kenneth. "You'll be doing plenty more than that." As I follow him towards the back of the funeral home, he waves to a cute, elderly white lady wearing a very work-appropriate gray cardigan. I remember her. She was at your funeral, the one who asked me if I wanted to receive the line. Her name is Maggie, Kenneth tells me. She was his very first hire when he opened the funeral home back in 1982 and is, apparently, a hoot. "Who knows, maybe if it all works out, you could be the next Maggie."

The idea of still being alive at Maggie's age sends tremors down my spine.

Kenneth shows me to my desk. It's directly across from his, in a dark, musky room with one window where light filters through a layer of residue on the outside. The room smells strongly of jasmine, though there are no flowers to be found anywhere. Kenneth tells me about the essential oils they diffuse throughout the place because it's proven to bring about a calming effect among mourners.

Next to my keyboard is a white adhesive name tag. It's just temporary, he assures me. My engraved name tag should be arriving in about a week. He pulls out a black blazer and black pants from an antique mahogany hutch and tells me there's only a size large available. I tell him a large is perfect.

Right above my computer is a poster on the wall listing the dos and don'ts of the funeral home's dress code.

DO opt for dark, conservative colors.
DO NOT wear anything red.
DO wear stockings in black or neutral.
DO NOT wear leggings or tights.
DO wear shoes free of dirt, debris, and scuff marks.
DO NOT wear sandals or open-toed shoes.
DO wear tasteful accessories.
DO NOT reveal your elbows, collarbones, knees, or midriff.

Kenneth hands me a yellow sticky note with a username and password. "These are your login credentials," he says. "Do you know how to operate a Macintosh?"

I haven't heard the word *Macintosh* in forever. I nod.

"What a relief. Because I'll be honest, I haven't the faintest clue how to even train you to use one of these." He leans his head back and lets out a deep laugh. "Now let's get down to business, shall we? You had a chance to read the employment contract I sent over, yeah?"

"Yes, I did."

"And you're okay with our compensation package? I know it's not anything to write home about but I like to think we make up for it by offering you a rather hospitable and fulfilling place to work."

"Mm-hmm." The compensation, as measly as it is, is no concern of mine. I'm not here for the money. I'm here for the promise of not thinking nor feeling.

We take a seat at his desk. Behind him is a framed certificate declaring Monarch Funeral Home Ltd. to be licensed under the Funeral, Burial and Cremation Services Act. Next to it is a stippled painting of a brick bridge leading to a white gazebo. There's a frail man in the gazebo. He's on the ground, hugging his knees. It appears as if he's dying or crying or perhaps both.

So far so good? Ethan texts.

You were right about the hoodie, I text back.

Good to know they have SOME sense.

Ethan didn't think any of this was a good idea. He said returning to a site of trauma seemed very unhealthy, like a criminal returning to the scene of the crime and pitching a tent. Mostly he thought it peculiar that a funeral director would want to hire a newly grieving mother in her delicate time of mourning. I didn't know what to say to this except: "Didn't you say I should be getting back to a routine? Don't you want me to get out of the house?" He didn't have a comeback, that's how desperately he wanted me out of bed.

"Now you're probably wondering why I was so eager to hire you," Kenneth says, leaning back in his chair. "You see, we get a lot of interesting characters that want to work here. People who are morbidly curious about the dead, people who just want a freaky story to tell their friends. One candidate flat-out admitted he was working on a screenplay about the revival of a run-down funeral home and applied for a job here so he could see the inside of a mortuary fridge. Said he wanted to get the description just right. You bet I ended that interview right then and there! Frankly, all the applications we get here are rubbish. And it's my job to weed out these opportunists."

Kenneth pulls out a few strands of mustache hair and places them in a mason jar, which, from what I can tell, houses several more fallen mustache hairs. I look away and pretend what I just witnessed is a totally normal thing.

"This job is about helping people get through the worst time in their life. What I need are people who are warm, kind, empathetic. Who can sit with people's suffering and not look away from it."

He speaks like a robot. His words sound rehearsed, like he's reading from a teleprompter behind me. I turn around to check, but there's nothing there.

"If you don't mind me asking," I say, "what makes you think I have those qualities? You just met me."

Kenneth smiles, spreading the hairs on his mustache. "In all my years of working here, I've seen grief manifest in many different ways. There is one common thread that runs through every single person that's walked through here and have had to say goodbye to their loved one."

"And what's that?"

"Compassion. They all become more compassionate versions of themselves, whether they realize it or not. Everybody thinks grief makes you a monster, but it's my belief that grief makes you more human. It can be, in a way, a sort of gift."

A gift?

A gift?!

How can the torture inside me be a gift? How can there be any positive to any of this? Oh no, I can feel it coming to the surface, the ragesorrowguiltanxietydespair, begging to be released like a long-dormant volcano until finally, tears erupt from my eyes. "I'm sorry," I stutter, embarrassed. Grief makes such a mockery of us, hollowing our eyes, mumbling our speech, marring our faces.

"Don't apologize. If there's any workplace where it's perfectly normal to cry, it's here," he says, handing me a tissue box. "I like to think crying is our final expression of love and one should never suppress that love. And from what I saw at the funeral, what you have with Daisy, it appeared to be a very special, once-in-a-lifetime kind of love."

I can barely take it, his kindness, his earnestness, and now I'm really sobbing. Our exchange takes on an air of familiarity and I immediately warm to him like a child warms to a grandparent. "Now, I give this preamble to every new hire, so bear with me here. It may all come off as rather obvious, but you might be surprised how little people know about this industry." He stops what he's saying to turn on his computer. It is one of those primitive, sad beige machines that still feature a slot for a floppy disk. There are piles of paper all over his desk, along with a calculator and a half-empty plastic water bottle with the label partly peeled off.

"We're open 24 hours a day, 7 days a week, 365 days a year," he jumps right in. "I've had many people come and go because they can't handle the job, so I think it's important that I be completely transparent with you. You will be called at any moment's notice to come in to work. Could be the middle of the night. Could be while you're out at a party. And I'll be frank, you may not see your family and friends as much as you'd like."

I pat my tears away, perking up at this delightful piece of information.

"Now while we're on this subject, are there any days in the upcoming months you absolutely cannot work?" says Kenneth. "I'll mark it in my calendar now so I know not to call on you those days."

I have no plans, no future to speak of. "No."

"Well, if you change your mind, please give me at least one month's notice. We get a lot of new people coming in here expecting to take Thanksgivings, Christmases, and birthdays off. And I do my best to accommodate them, I really do. But holidays, if you can believe it, are the busiest time of year for us and I need all hands on deck. Now here's an interesting piece of trivia I ask all my new hires: Which holiday experiences the most significant spike in mortality?"

This question catches me off guard. I wasn't expecting to be quizzed. I should know this. Why don't I know this? If I answer incorrectly, will I be fired before I even start? I give a panicked guess.

"April Fool's?"

Kenneth belts out a laugh that lasts a bit too long. "In all my years here, nobody has ever guessed that."

"So I'm right?"

"Oh heavens no. I'm sure many heart attacks have been attributed to a good prank, but it's actually New Year's Day. Care to venture a guess why?"

Another unanticipated question. I wish I'd known so I could've come prepared.

"Drunk driving accidents?" I say.

"Wrong again. It's a trick question, actually. Nobody knows why deaths increase on the first of January. They just do."

I lean into the desk, deeply and genuinely fascinated. Kenneth goes quiet as he squints at something on the computer. He tells me he needs to attend to some matter and steps out.

While I wait, I pull out my phone and read up on seasonal and daily patterns of mortality. I commit them to memory, just in case Kenneth springs another trivia question my way.

According to a Statistics Canada report analyzing death patterns between 1974 and 1995, there was a significant spike in deaths on Saturdays, mostly attributed to car accidents and the reckless gallivanting that weekends summon. It also found December and January to be the deadliest months due to higher rates of influenza.

In another study conducted by Harvard Medical School in 2012, researchers were able to pinpoint the time of day people were most likely to die. They found that genetic factors led to a distinct spike in deaths in the morning hours, specifically at 11:00 a.m.

I look at the time. It's 11:31 a.m. and I am still very much frustratingly alive.

———————

Kenneth gives me a tour of the funeral home. There's not a single wall that doesn't have a framed quote nailed to it. They're sickeningly life-affirming and always seem to feature a stock image of a rugged mountain or a peeking sunset. Not unlike the quotes my mother sends me. Today she chose James Baldwin:

> You think your pain and your heartbreak are unprecedented in
> the history of the world, but then you read.

I heart her text and shove my phone in my pocket.

Kenneth takes me to the break room. It's simple yet functional with a microwave, fridge, sink, coffee maker, and a couple of round tables. Kenneth is thorough as a tour guide, every single detail accounted for including where they keep the packets of sugar and creamer and coffee filters. The smell of burnt toast wafts in the air and I locate the culprit, a blackened bagel resting on a plate in front of three smartly dressed individuals. Kenneth quickly runs through their names and the number of years they've worked here: Rebecca, eleven years; Ana, six years;

Rachel, seven months. I wave at them. They all wave back in unison and welcome me with warm smiles. I wonder why they're all working here. I wonder who died and made the pain so unbearable they had to come here to get away from it. I take a guess.

Rebecca, dead mom.

Ana, dead brother.

Rachel, dead best friend.

Kenneth takes me on a tour of the facilities next. There's a lounge tastefully decorated with a tufted velvet sofa and large-scale triptych of the ocean. There's a selection room where sample merchandise is displayed including caskets, urns, plaques, jewelry, and headstones. The coat closet is over here. The guest bathrooms are down that way. We go downstairs to the basement where he shows me the preparation room. It's hard not to notice how cold and sterile the room is compared to upstairs. The lights are brighter, every surface reflective.

"What's that room?"

"Which room?"

I point to the closed door in the back. He tells me that's the closet where they store cremated remains until they're picked up. The walls of my esophagus thicken. "You mean, is that . . . is that where she—" Tears fill my eyes and I can't finish my sentence. Kenneth puts his hand on my shoulder and nods. I dab the tears away and get a hold of myself.

"Can I see inside?"

Kenneth looks straight at me. "Are you sure?"

I nod, even though I'm not sure what I'm hoping to see, just that I want to see it. Kenneth unlocks the door, and a light automatically flicks on, revealing the closet to be just that, a closet. There's nothing to it. Just metal track shelves that go all the way to the ceiling. Plastic bags of ashes in varying sizes sit along the shelves, sealed with a cable tie and metal ID chip. My eyes gravitate towards a plastic white basket at the very top and Kenneth answers my question before I even ask.

"Those are the uncollected," he says. "Still waiting to be claimed."

"How many are there?"

"Three currently, I believe."

"Have they been here long?"

"One has been here longer than ten years."

A gasp escapes me. "B-but why?"

"We do our best to reach family members but after a while, they stop picking up the phone. Or they move out of town and don't tell us how they can be reached. Some people don't know what to do with the ashes, so they never claim them."

"Couldn't you just inter or scatter the remains yourself?"

"We could. We are not required to store these ashes indefinitely. But I can't help but hold out hope one day someone will walk through those doors and tell me they're here to pick up their loved one."

Sadness coats my throat and I want to cry for all the people up there in the basket, waiting to go home—like the last kids to be picked up from school.

Kenneth locks the closet and directs me back up the stairs. There are six reception rooms in total, but he shows me only five. He tells me we don't have to go inside the sixth room, where we held your funeral. I tell him it's okay. Nothing can hurt me more than you being gone, so what's a stupid little room? He opens the door and I take a deep breath. I wait for my pulse to quicken, my head to spin, my legs to collapse from beneath me, but all I feel is confusion.

"Are you sure this is the same room?" I ask.

Kenneth draws his brows together. "Certain."

I don't believe him. "It hasn't been renovated?"

"Heavens no. You think we've got that kind of budget? Ha!"

I walk around the room. It's smaller than I remember. I don't recall the ceilings being vaulted or the carpet being checkered. I certainly don't remember the two flat-screen TVs mounted at the front. And weren't the walls beige, not this aubergine I'm seeing? I feel like I'm losing my mind.

"Are you sure it's not another room?" I ask again.

Kenneth puts his hand on my shoulder and assures me again that this is the same room where we held your service. "My dear. It is nothing to be embarrassed about. Memory loss is a very normal part of grief."

I want to defend myself. This is not memory loss. This is the wrong room.

As we exit, I turn back around and see the tiny casket with the daisies scattered overtop. The white dumplings stare back at me, their beady eyes drilling into my soul, then in one blink, the image is gone.

We return to my desk and Kenneth tells me to play around with the company tools and software on the computer as they can be quite complicated to understand. He leaves me to it and I'm relieved to be alone again. I try to push the memory of your casket from my mind. I pull up the login credentials and type them into the input fields. The operating system hasn't been updated in years and I discover the tools and software Kenneth was referring to is Microsoft Excel and Safari. I launch Safari and search up the terms *grief* and *memory loss*. I click on multiple search results and fill the tab bar.

People who are experiencing heightened emotional stress, trauma, or grief have reported a kind of "fog of the brain," in which they feel reality has been distorted and chunks of time and memory have become completely severed.

In order for a memory to be created, it needs to go through three stages: encoding (the learning of information), consolidation (the process of storing), and recall (the ability to access that information when needed). In moments of shock, memories may not be fully formed to begin with, leading to problems with recollection later on.

The weapon focus effect posits that when a weapon is present, such as a gun or knife, the observer's memory becomes impaired as their attentional resources turn towards the weapon, rendering their inability to perceive the environment around them. The same effect can occur when there is, say, a dead body in the room.

Nausea overtakes me. I want to puke. I shouldn't be here. Ethan was right: This was a terrible mistake. Bile rises fast in my throat. Where's the waste bin? I frantically look for a receptacle but there is none. The hutch. Maybe there's a plastic bag in there, a roll of paper towel, something. I pull on the handle, but it's locked. Kenneth had just opened it earlier to get my uniform, so why is it suddenly locked now? I turn around and see the mason jar. The one with the mustache hairs. I can't hold it in and frantically bring it to my mouth.

For the rest of the day, Kenneth has me reading and signing a variety of paperwork. The mission statement. The employee handbook. The occupational health and safety regulations. The binders are as thick as encyclopedias and if I was thinking straight, I would've gotten up and left. Walked out. Quit right there. Pretend none of this ever happened.

If I do that, that means I'll have to go home. I'll have to stare at the baby bottles in the cabinet and the unfolded stroller in the garage. I'll have to look at that picture of me on the fridge, five months pregnant and radiating with innocence. Then I'll have to go to bed next to that bassinet containing tiny, minuscule, powdery fragments of you. The thought makes my nerves raw, so I stay put and take the gigantic binders from him.

It's not compelling, reading pages that appear to have been photocopied a hundred times, not to mention the language is dense and the paragraph breaks are few. But it's busywork nonetheless, which means the dark thoughts are at bay. Instead of begging the ceiling to collapse on me, I read about the importance of not disclosing any information regarding the appearance of the deceased, the circumstances or causes of their death, or any other relevant information that is not otherwise known to the public. Instead of praying the earth beneath me swallows me whole, I learn about proper hand hygiene and effective strategies for reducing the spread of infectious diseases, about safe lifting guidelines to prevent musculoskeletal injuries, as well as the various types of blood-borne pathogens that may be present in preparation rooms.

I forget all about wanting to die as I engross myself in the proper procedures for handling human remains:

Handlers should use appropriate barrier protection such as latex and nitrile gloves. It is recommended to wear an additional layer of gloves overtop.

Protect your face from coming into contact with bodily fluids by wearing a combination of safety goggles, surgical mask, and plastic face shield.

When moving human remains, careful attention should be paid to appropriate lifting ergonomics. Avoid lifting with your back and instead bend at the legs. Keep the remains close to your center of gravity.

My mind wanders to the hutch. I analyze the combination latch. It's not original to the nineteenth-century cabinetry, which means it was installed after the fact. What could he be hiding in there?

Kenneth walks in, a slice of pepperoni pizza in his hand, looking puzzled as he scans his desk. "You wouldn't happen to know where I put my mason jar by any chance?"

I shake my head, knowing very well his beloved vomit-coated mustache hairs are sitting in the bottom of the kitchen trash.

"Rats, what a dingus I am. Always misplacing everything."

I stare at the bald halo on the back of his head, the sunspots on his hands, the length of his fingernails. I wonder if he's growing them out on purpose so he can collect the nail clippings in a mason jar. I scan his desk for clues into his life. There are no pictures of a spouse or children. No dog or cat paraphernalia. No mug etched with the logo of his favorite sports team. No sandwich wrapped in cellophane with a sweet note that says, *Have a wonderful day, sweetie pie!* I look at his left hand. No ring. He probably has nobody. This job, this funeral home, is probably the only thing he has.

Kenneth licks the tomato sauce from his fingers, including anything that may have lodged itself under his long fingernails, and begins typing on the keyboard. He uses his middle fingers to type. He types so painfully slow, I swear he's going at two words per minute. Once it seems he's picked up his pace, he looks up and lets out a sigh after realizing the computer has been off the whole time.

I watch as he takes large bites out of his pizza. Bizarrely he holds the pointy end and eats the crust first, rendering the tips of his fingers red with tomato sauce. This can only be the work of a devil.

––––––––––

These are the contents of our mailbox:

> A leaflet from our city councillor.
> Flyers from Shoppers Drug Mart.
> Coupons for Pizzaiolo.
> And a card made out to Cleo Dang and Ethan Hayashi.

I open it carefully, bracing myself to read heartfelt words of sorrow from an acquaintance or a distant cousin or an aunt I've never heard of. The irony of death is it brings lots of strangers to life.

But I'm wrong.

It's not a sympathy card.

It's an invitation to a baby shower. Sadie and Fatima are having a baby. Celebrations take place in a month.

My heart tightens around itself. My stomach sinks to what feels like hell. I begin to cry. A cry so loud I'm sure the neighbors can hear. Envy rushes through me like a tsunami until shame pulls me to the surface to choke me out. I wipe my tears away with the back of my sleeve. These are my friends. I should be happy for them. They'd been doing IUI and IVF for years and god knows they deserve this more than anyone. Maybe even more than me.

Ethan comes rushing down to the kitchen. He sees the invitation and from his expression, it seems his stomach sinks to hell, too. He kisses my forehead and wraps me in his arms.

"You don't have to go."

"I have to," I say. "I want to."

"Don't do this to yourself."

"What kind of friend would I be if I didn't go?"

"They'll understand if you can't make it."

"Don't be silly. They were at the funeral. I need to be there for them."

Ethan sighs. "This isn't some kind of transaction."

I know he means well but he doesn't get it. Good friends set aside their difficult feelings and show up for one another no matter what. I've known Sadie and Fatima for almost a decade, watched them get married, cried alongside them with every failed cycle. I've been waiting for this day as much as they have. So yes, I will set aside my grief, put on a smile, and be nothing but happy for them. I don't know from where I'll pull out this version of myself, but I will try. I will figure out a way.

I pull out my phone and type in the URL for the baby registry. I scroll through their selection. A sound machine. A portable playard. Multiple sleep sacks in gender-neutral colors. We have every one of those items upstairs in the nursery. The judicious thing to do would be to give Sadie and Fatima what we already have. They are of no use to us now. But I can't bear the thought of parting with anything that is yours. I click on an expensive bottle sterilizer, enter my credit card information, and hit purchase.

Before slipping under the covers, I look out the window towards Paloma's house. I wonder what's going on inside. I bet she's just given the baby a bath. I bet she's swinging her baby high in the air and smooching those tiny little toes before turning on the sound machine and nursing the baby to sleep. She's probably so tired that she dozes off with the baby in her arms until Freddie gently rouses her awake and, together, they lovingly put the baby down for the night and say in accidental unison, *Night night, darling.*

The pangs of grief return with a fury, angry at me for neglecting it all day, punishing me for having dared to evade it. It ridicules me for thinking I could run away from it, like I'm some kind of god. In bed, I succumb. I have no choice but to feel it all. No screens. No distractions. It's as sharp and excruciating as I left it this morning.

9

I get to the funeral home an hour early the next day. The previous night's cries did not let up, leaving dark circles beneath my eyes and a fiery redness around the rims—stubborn against every remedy the internet recommended: ice cubes, green color correctors, specialty eye-drops that constrict blood vessels. Nothing worked. Such a shame to look like death but still be brutally, excruciatingly alive.

"It's Cleo, right?"

I turn away from the coffee machine to find a young Black woman standing before me with a box of sugar-dappled pastries.

"My name's Rachel. I saw you yesterday when Kenneth was giving you a tour."

That's right, I do recall seeing her in the break room. Rachel, dead best friend. Presumably.

"I remember."

"Random question but do you like beignets?"

"Excuse me?"

"Strawberry rhubarb. They're fresh from a bakery nearby."

"Oh um, no thanks. I should be getting back to my desk." The old me would've said yes, would've devoured that pastry in an instant, lick-ing the jelly shamelessly off my fingers to ensure no part went to waste. Sweets, in all their fluffy delectable glory, were worth being alive for. Now the sight and smell of them make me want to puke.

"Are you sure? You look like someone who enjoys dessert."

I suddenly tense up, self-conscious now. "What does a person who enjoys dessert look like exactly?"

Rachel's eyes go wide with fear. "Wait, wait, hold up! I didn't mean it negatively. I just meant they've got, like, you know, a twinkle in their eye. Less wrinkles on their face. Because they know how to let loose and live life and eat whatever the hell they want."

"Good save."

"I mean it, you really do not have a single wrinkle on your face."

"Neither do you."

"Well I hope not. I'm twenty-three."

Gosh, twenty-three. I think about my younger self and how head over heels I was about being alive. I loved life and life loved me. I knew nothing of loss or grief or unfathomable anguish. That kind of pain was something that happened to other people, not to me. The only thing I ever really had to cry about were curfews and unrequited crushes.

Rachel pushes the box towards me. "Anyway, women are statistically more likely to say yes to desserts than men. So, do you want a beignet or not?"

I push the box away. "No, thank you. I really need to go now."

Rachel seems lovely but I've been actively resisting getting to know the other staff. I'm not here to make friends. Besides, Rachel is twenty-three. Too young to understand what it's like to lose a child. To expel a baby out of your body with more strength and determination than a pro sports team—only to later make the excruciating decision to stop your baby's life support. To walk out of the hospital with an empty car seat and wonder, *What the fuck just happened?*

Before I can slip out, I hear a gruff male voice from the corner of the room. "Geez, Rachel, just call them donuts. She's more likely to say yes if you call them donuts."

"But they're not donuts!" Rachel responds. "They're *beignets*. There's a really big difference."

"They're both fried pieces of dough with jelly inside, are they not?"

"Yes but—"

"My point exactly. One sounds delicious. The other sounds pretentious. It's like those people who think they're fancy when they call mayonnaise *aioli*. It's the exact same thing!"

"It's not the same thing!" Rachel yells and to my surprise, the same words slip out of my mouth.

Rachel looks at me with an appreciative nod and before I can yank myself away, she links her arm with mine, looks defiantly at Donut Dude, and says, "See! Even the new girl agrees with me!" She adds for my sake, "That's Stuart, by the way. He eats egg salad for lunch every day."

"What's wrong with egg salad?"

"Everything!"

Stuart shakes his head and buries himself in a newspaper.

"Seriously, you should try one, Cleo. It's really good. We always sold out before noon when I worked there."

Right as I was about to turn her down again, I pause, intrigued by what she just said.

"You used to work at a bakery?" I ask.

"Mm-hmm, before this job."

"That's quite the career transition, going from donuts to death."

"They're not donuts!"

"Sorry."

Well, that's enough small talk for today. I turn my body towards the door only to hear a follow-up question.

"Where did you work before this?"

Rachel looks at me like I owe her a glimpse into my life since she has just divulged a bit of hers. I would rather not answer. I hate talking about anything from before. It feels like a fable, difficult to articulate, hard to believe. I decide to deflect.

"Doesn't matter. It's nowhere near as exciting as a bakery," I say.

"Yeah I won't lie." Rachel beams. "It was a cool place to work, but believe it or not it had its not so fun parts. For instance, flour would just get everywhere. Like, I mean, everywhere. I'd come home and have to flush my sinuses out every night because there would just be globs of it in there."

A normal person would ask more questions, but I fear doing so would give the impression that I want to get to know her, so I make my way to the door.

"I really should be—"

"I could've stayed at that job forever but then Jenny died and it was hard to be in the kitchen without her. Seeing her apron dangling on the wall, waiting to be worn again. It was too sad, I just couldn't do it anymore."

When somebody mentions a dead person, the polite thing to do is to say you're sorry, thank them for sharing, and perhaps inquire as to what the person was like. That all eludes me; I become desperate to know if my initial instincts were correct.

"Was Jenny your best friend?"

"Best friend? I wouldn't say so exactly but we did spend an excessive amount of time together. I loved opening with her. We would blast Kylie Minogue at four a.m., dancing and singing and punching dough with our fists. We were beyond exhausted and yet wired with sugar and music. I became a morning person because of her. She was the type of person who had infinite energy to give. It was as if she was constantly plugged in to a power source. For two years we were inseparable."

"By all accounts, she sounds like a best friend," I say, wanting very much to confirm my genius.

"I suppose so." Tears pool in Rachel's eyes and I apologize for making her cry.

"Don't be sorry. I'm the one that brought it up."

"Is that why you decided to work here? Because your friend died?"

"I suppose so. I just couldn't walk into that bakery anymore, knowing I'll never see her again. Her fingerprints were still on the fridge door! I saw a job posting here for an attendant and thought, *Why not?* Didn't think much of it. Then Kenneth gave me the job and I just wanted any reason to not go back to that kitchen. It was an adjustment but you know what, it's not all that different, working at a bakery and working here. I was helping brighten people's day with pastries. Here, I'm brightening people's day by helping them honor their loved ones."

"Did Jenny have her funeral here?"

"She didn't have a funeral. She was always against them, said they were too bleak and boring. So we had a dance party in her honor instead."

"A dance party?"

"It was so Jenny. She always wanted to do everything different. Her dream was to open her own bakery and you know what she wanted to call it? Rebel with a Roller." She pauses to collect herself. "Ugh, I'm going to cry again just thinking about everything she won't get to do. Anyway, her parents rented out a banquet hall, hired a DJ, ordered a cake, and told everyone the booze was on them."

"That sounds like a lot of fun."

"It was. It really felt like Jenny was with us. Like it was her birthday and we were all just celebrating what a marvel she was. She would've approved of the whole thing, that's for sure, the music, the food, even the cake. But—" Rachel stops talking. She shuffles her feet, suddenly looking like she wants to change the subject.

"But what?"

"I don't know, it's complicated. It felt right, but also not right at the same time, you know what I mean? Everybody was dressed in fabulously bright attire, laughing, cheering, doing shots. There were signs everywhere that said 'NO CRYING ALLOWED.' They purposely didn't have tissue boxes out because there was no need, it wasn't *that* kind of event. It just felt . . . forced, you know? I went home and cried for three days straight afterwards."

I nod profusely at everything she's saying—the crying that never seems to end, the pretending everything is okay, the faking that's required to be a human being.

"It was a beautiful event, don't get me wrong, but it was weird. Everybody was sad and we all knew it, and yet we were being herded onto the dance floor, twerking and jumping and spelling the letters to Y-M-C-A while shouting *There's no need to be unhappy!* Like what the actual fuck?"

A loud chortle escapes my mouth. I didn't mean for it to come out and apologize for the ill-timed laughter.

"It's fine. It's quite an appropriate reaction to have," Rachel reassures me.

"People are weird about sadness. There's that poster out in the hallway—"

"*Do not cry because they are past! Smile, because they once were!*"

I nod.

"Ugh, I hate that fucking poster! Every time I walk by it, I want to smash it to the ground. It's the *least* helpful thing. Gee thanks, Ludwig, thanks for the advice I'm all better now!"

We laugh in unison and I feel enough of a bond that enables me to ask another possibly inappropriate follow-up question.

"May I ask how she died?"

"She had an asthma attack while clubbing."

"Oh my god."

"Didn't have an inhaler on her. People thought she was performing some kind of break dance the way she hit the floor."

"I'm so sorry."

"It's kind of poetic, if you think about it. She died doing what she loved. Dancing among a raucous group of sexy drunks."

"And her parents still wanted to have a dance party, after all that?"

"I'm telling you, it was the strangest thing I've ever been to."

An unrecognizable sound comes out of her mouth, a sound I'm uncertain of. Could be laughter, could be a whimper. Whatever it was, it's triggered from within her a flood of tears. I hand her a tissue. It's soft, durable, three-ply. The sight and feel of them take me back to your funeral. That chair, that room, the sight of your little casket. I'm crying now, too, so I take a tissue for myself. We cry together without any exchange of words, without encouragement from the other that everything will be okay, without any pressure to hurry it up.

Stuart shuffles his newspaper loudly as if to get our attention. "Geez, guys, can't a guy read about foreign diplomacy in peace?"

We roll our eyes at him and look at each other. "You're a really pretty crier, you know that?" Rachel says after we've dabbed the last of our tears.

A laughter bursts out of me. "I don't think anybody has ever said that to me."

"We should be professional mourners."

"That's a real thing?"

"It is in other parts of the world. There are people who are literally hired to cry at funerals despite never having met the dead person. The more hysterical they are, the more money they get. We could make a killing."

"But why would anybody want that?"

"I mean, wouldn't it be sad if you died and there was just a sea of dry eyes in the room?"

I suppose it would be sad to die and have nobody shed a tear for you. Then again, you'd be dead, so who cares? You wouldn't feel sad because you wouldn't feel anything at all.

"I'm really sorry, by the way, about Daisy," Rachel says, catching me off guard. "It was a somber day for us all when she arrived here. I asked the staff if we could play lullabies for her and we did. We had it playing for her all day."

"Y-you did?" I didn't know how much I needed to hear that, to hear your name, to hear you were taken care of, and every part of me wants to wail to the skies.

"She was beautiful. Like seriously, good job! I don't even know what your husband looks like but thank god she got all your genes."

A whisper of a giggle comes out of me. "Thanks."

"I'm really glad you decided to join us. You're so normal."

I perk up at this compliment since I've been feeling decidedly not normal. "Are there not a lot of normals around here?"

She shoots her eyes at Stuart, who appears oblivious to the dig, before lowering her voice. "Well, anyone who works at a funeral home has to be a little weird."

"Even you?"

"I'm weird in like a cool, edgy kind of way. Some of the folks here are *weird* weird."

I wonder where I fall on this spectrum of weird. "Even Kenneth?"

"Oh my god, he's the weirdest weirdo of them all. Have you ever seen him cry?"

"No."

"Exactly, he *never* cries."

"He must."

"No, I'm telling you, I've been here seven months and I've never seen that man cry once. Does he not realize you're supposed to cry when somebody dies?"

"Maybe this job has hardened him."

"Maybe, but it doesn't explain why we literally know nothing about him. I don't know what he does outside of work. He never mentions his family—that is, if he even has one. It's a running joke around here that he's probably in witness protection or something because he discloses so little about his life. Kenneth Timmerman is probably not even his real name. What a fake-sounding name!"

"What if he's just a private person?"

"C'mon," Rachel continues, "it's one thing to work here, it's another to wake up one day and decide you want to open a funeral home. Who opens a funeral home unless you've got some skeletons in your closet? Like, I'm talking *literal* skeletons."

I think back on my few interactions with Kenneth, the fidgety eyes and the pizza fingers and what the heck was up with the mustache hairs? Maybe Rachel's right. Maybe you have to be really broken to be working at a place like this.

Kenneth isn't at his desk yet. I try the combination lock on the hutch.

1-2-3-4. Wrong.

1-1-1-1. Wrong.

0-1-0-1. Wrong again.

For someone whose computer password is literally *password*, I'm impressed by Kenneth's ability to pick a combination of numbers that isn't easy to guess.

The phone on my desk rings. It's my first phone call as Kenneth's assistant. I haven't prepared my greeting yet and feel flustered when I pick up the receiver. "Good morning, this is Kenneth's desk. How can I help you?"

I regret my words as soon as they come out. Somewhere in there I should have included key information such as Kenneth's surname and the name of the funeral home. My own name might've been helpful, too. I make a note to practice my greeting after this call.

"Cleo, it's Kenneth."

"Oh, I was wondering where you were."

"What are you wearing?"

"Excuse me?"

"The dress code, have you adhered to it?"

I'm wearing the slightly large all-black pantsuit Kenneth provided, in keeping with the policy laid out in the handbook. "Yes."

"Did you drive to work today?"

"Yes."

"Good, good. I need you to meet me at a nursing home in Rexdale. We've got a pickup for a deceased female, ninety-two years of age. I'll text you the address. Please get here as soon as you can."

I look down at the manual on my desk. I still have twenty more pages to read, and I've yet to reach the section that covers the psycho-social hazards of working with bereaved families. I'm not ready for this. I don't know what I'm doing.

"Are—are you sure you don't want to ask somebody else?"

Kenneth doesn't respond. He's talking to someone in the background. Finally he returns to the phone: "Are you on the road yet?"

The body is already in the bag by the time I arrive. Kenneth is speaking with two people who appear to be in their fifties. They have the same high forehead, slumped shoulders, and freckled temples, leading me to believe they are the daughters of the dead woman. Their eyes are puffy; dry patches and broken blood vessels surround their noses. They're holding balled-up tissues in their hands. I instinctively reach into my bag to hand them a travel pack of tissues, but I stop myself. Does the funeral home have protocol on handing clients tissues? Would it be seen as a kind and empathetic gesture, or would it give the impression that I'm uncomfortable with their emotions and would like for them to please dry up their tears?

I keep the tissues where they are and introduce myself. Judging from their body language, they don't look like huggers or handshakers or head nodders. So, I stand at an appropriate distance and offer them my condolences. I want to tell them I know how they feel but this is not my mother and I am not them, so I don't really, do I?

Kenneth directs me to take notes as he asks them a set of questions. The taller of the sisters does the answering.

"What is her name?"

"Meredith Ann Wilkins."

"How do you spell that?"

"W-I-L-K-I-N-S."

"Date of birth?"

"August 5th, 1932."

"Social insurance number?"

"I don't know."

"Weight?"

"I don't know."

The woman bursts into tears and collapses into her sister's arms. My first instinct is to reach over and put a hand on her shoulder, but Kenneth gestures for me to stay put. We stand there in silence and watch these two sisters reel over the loss of their mother. Shouldn't we do something? Shouldn't we say something? Everything feels wrong. I shouldn't be here. I shouldn't be bearing witness to the single worst moment in these people's lives. I feel a knot in my throat and my nostrils start to tingle. Tears collect in my eyes. *Dammit.* Don't cry in front of these people. Don't cry in front of Kenneth. What is it about seeing other people cry that makes you want to cry, too? I look up and pray the tears evaporate quickly.

Once all the information has been collected, Kenneth asks them one more question and prefaces by saying this is a difficult subject but *would you know if you will be choosing a traditional burial or a cremation?* The sisters look at each other and nod, as if they've prepared for this question their entire life, and tell Kenneth they are going with a burial.

They stand side by side as Kenneth and I wheel the body into a white van parked outside. An intrusive thought forms, a picture of myself accidentally tipping the hydraulic trolley over and the sisters watching in horror as their dead mother rolls across the pavement, landing directly in front of their feet. I quickly brush that image away and tighten my grip on the trolley.

After we say goodbye to the sisters, Kenneth tells me to meet back at the funeral home. I drive closely behind the van. There's no signage on the car. From the outside, it looks like any regular van. The kind of van that families of four take on road trips to the beach. The kind that florists use to deliver crates and crates of bouquets to unsuspecting recipients. Its ordinariness makes it unassuming. Which is probably the point. No pedestrians gawking on the street. No curious drivers holding up traffic. I wonder how many dead people I've unknowingly driven past all these years.

Kenneth is driving very carefully. He turns slowly to avoid potholes and presses on the brakes well in advance of the traffic lights. It's clear he's done this many times. I think about Mrs. Wilkins in the back of the van. I wonder if she did everything she wanted to do while she was alive. I wonder if she could hear her daughters tell her they loved her as we closed the back door of the van. I wonder where she is now. Yes, her body is inside the Toyota but where is the essence that makes her *her*? Is she in heaven? Is she in another dimension? Is she *gone gone*? Perhaps she's perched somewhere above, watching her body trudge through traffic. I wonder if wherever she is, you're there, too.

Tears blur my vision. I quickly rub them away and when I focus, I immediately slam on the brakes. My purse smashes into the glove compartment, falling to the ground. I come near inches away from the van. Another intrusive thought enters my mind. What if I crash into the back of the van and crush Mrs. Wilkins's body like a soda can?

When we arrive at the funeral home, Kenneth tells me we need to give Mrs. Wilkins an identification tag and transfer her to the mortuary. I notice he calls her Mrs. Wilkins and not "the body" or "the remains" or "the deceased" or "the decedent," words interchangeably used in the occupational health and safety regulations. I wonder if he does this with every dead person that comes through here. I wonder if he called you Miss Daisy.

Once we enter through the garage, the first thing I notice is a large whiteboard. It has the names of the deceased, the date they arrived at the mortuary, and the date of their visitation and service, if any. There are also notes beside each one.

James Reisberg, dropped off and embalmed, Mount Pleasant Cemetery.

Fisher Pickel, in transit, pacemaker, cremation.

Maria Sabah, transport to Scarborough F.H.

I'm impressed at the efficiency of this whiteboard. The lines are straight. The handwriting is neat. All emotion and personhood are stripped from the process. No room for error. No time for tears. They are no longer people. They are now pieces of cargo that need to be dispatched from one place to the next.

I try not to think about everyone in the cooler but it's hard not to. I think about the people they left behind, how totally destroyed they are. I think about their things. The closet full of clothes, the rack full of shoes, the books they'll never know the ending to, all now in the trash or a Value Village bin waiting to be picked through by thrift seekers. They're probably still getting emails sent in hopes of finding them well. Their hairdressers and massage therapists and baristas are probably unaware, wondering when they'll be in next. It's all so sad and unfair.

Before Mrs. Wilkins goes inside the mortuary fridge, Kenneth pauses and mutters something under his breath before carefully pushing the trolley inside. I don't catch what he said. Should I ask? Is it something I should know for future reference? Do I need to take notes? Is it just me or are Kenneth's eyes becoming glassy?

He instructs me to fill in the mortuary register with Mrs. Wilkins's details. It's fully bound in black leather book cloth, its pages filled with information about people who have passed through this funeral home. I quickly scan the column listing the age at death. Most are over fifty, a smattering in their thirties and forties. One teenager. I keep scanning to see if there are any young children.

Bradley, five years old, pneumonia.

Kaela, thirteen months old, cancer.

Vivek, two months old, SIDS.

Emmett, stillborn.

My heart beats faster, heavier. It feels like my rib cage is getting smaller and smaller, as if it's closing in on my heart and crushing all the arteries. I keep reading. Each entry includes documentation of what items have been placed inside the children's casket. Handknit blanket. Stuffed penguin. Plush bunnies. LEGOs. Gold bracelet. Loveys. Roses. Letters. Tears splash onto the pages, and I quickly dab them away before the ink starts to run.

I'm picturing these mothers, out there, somewhere, attempting to fill the cracks in their souls. I can see them all clearly. Rotting in bed for days. Crying discreetly at their desks. Refusing to eat the food lovingly placed in front of them. Brushing their teeth wondering how in the world they'll get through another day. I've never met these mothers before, but I feel as if I know every single one of them. That's one of the great paradoxes of grief I suppose: It touches each and every one of us, yet it has the effect of filling us with an aching, unignorable loneliness.

I keep flipping the pages. I find a couple more names of children who never made it to kindergarten, never went to prom, never learned how to drive a car. A whole life—there one minute, gone the next.

Then I stop.

Daisy Dang Hayashi.

There it is. Your date of death. Age at death. Place of death. Death, death, death. Sadness ravages my soul. I want to grab a pen and write more along the margins. Because there is more to you than these dates and numbers and time stamps. So much more.

Suddenly Kenneth's shadow looms over me.

"Do you have any questions about the register?" he asks.

"N-no," I stammer, closing the book. "Mrs. Wilkins's information has been entered."

He sees something on my face and softens his eyes. "Why don't you call it a day? You've done more than enough on your second day, don't you think?"

I check the time on my phone. "But it's only two."

"Don't worry about it."

Kenneth walks me towards the exit and before I know it, I'm outside. Full sun on my face. With nothing to go home to but hours of sorrow. I think about Mrs. Wilkins in that dark, confined cooler. How tranquil it must be in there. No pain, no uncertainty, no tears, no surprises, no fighting, no stress, no anxiety, no pretending, no exhaustion, no disappointments, no anguish. I'd give anything to trade places with her.

10

There are two types of people in this world: those who believe life to be long and those who believe it to be short. In this very moment, on this particular weekend, when time seems to tick at a tauntingly agonizing pace, life is most certainly too long. I feel every minute in my bones, my cells, as if I'm being returned to myself. This sends me into a heavy melancholy that doesn't ease up, despite my best efforts at bright siding and finding silver linings, things I've been told would help but don't.

To pass the time, I watch television indiscriminately and to excess. Action movies. Romantic comedies. Silly little sitcoms. I like what TV gives. Hours and hours of narratives so engrossing it's as if the world around me does not exist. The closest thing to anesthetizing the mind. It's comforting to know that everything happening on the screen never really happened. No one ever really died. Plus, I read somewhere that too much TV can lead to a premature death. Every now and then, I excitedly place a hand on my chest to feel for irregular palpitations in hopes all this sedentary activity has induced a pulmonary embolism.

A diaper commercial comes on and each second feels as long as the earth is old. I think of you, your corporeal form. That little strip of peach fuzz above your lips, the milia that dot your cheeks, the cracks in your lips that I gently sealed with Aquaphor after every kiss.

I flick through the channels and stop on *John Wick*. I watch as Keanu Reeves massacres his way through grief with the regality of a Viennese waltz. It's the most sublime thing I've ever seen. I think a killing spree would do me some good. Perhaps we could enshrine into law that every person in mourning shall be granted one free murder. To right the wrongs inflicted on them. To give purpose to the despair. To put the anger somewhere, anywhere.

I check my phone to see what's happening in the world, ignoring all the missed phone calls and texts.

Pro-abortion protests swell across the United States.
A teenage shooter kills thirteen students.
A new virus is spreading fast in Venice.

I click on the last article. "COULD THIS BE THE NEXT COVID?" I get excited at the possibility of another lockdown, of plans canceled, of antisocial behavior as altruism, of government-sanctioned loneliness that would make the entire world as cripplingly sad as I am. What can I say? Misery loves eight billion people's company.

―――――――

In the time I've been recumbent on the couch, Ethan has run, showered, shaved, read an *Atlantic* article, listened to a podcast, called his parents, and whipped up a berry-and-granola-topped Greek yogurt bowl. Now, he hovers a spoonful of that yogurt in front of my mouth. "Eat this. It's rich in protein and antioxidants."

I oblige. He spoon-feeds me like I'm a child and wipes yogurt from my lips, saying *good job!* every time I keep it down. This proves to me what I always knew to be true: that he would've been a good father. The kind of father who sets an alarm for 6:55 a.m. to sign up for guardian swim before spots fill up. A father who spends all day at the library poring over consumer reports about car seats. A father who knows too much about how to relieve gas in a baby. A father who can answer all their nonsensical questions without any hint of frustration.

"What did you do all morning?" he asks.

I can't tell him I've been on this couch all day. When you're in mourning, everybody wants to hear that you've been out. Out of bed. Out of the house. Out with friends. It's a sign you're getting on with life. Returning to a normal state of being. Persevering against the darkness. So I lie and tell him I went to the park and did some light yoga, walked around the block while listening to NPR, talked briefly with the neighbors, and now I'm cozying up on the couch keeping abreast of the news.

Ethan lets out a frighteningly long sigh. Can he tell I'm lying? Maybe the bit about NPR gave it away? He runs his hand through my greasy hair and tells me, "I'm really proud of you for getting on with life."

His eyes crinkle with joy, making the lies feel worth it. "And how has the funeral home been?" he asks.

I know he doesn't approve of this job, but I also know he much prefers me up and about rather than confined to a bed.

"Fine. Somebody brought in donuts."

"Ooh, what flavor?"

"I didn't have any."

"Oh."

The conversation goes nowhere and we fall silent as he feeds me. Now that Ethan has resumed a regular fifty-to-sixty-hour workweek at the hospital, he's often too beat to have prolonged dialogue. Which is fine by me. Less talking means less inquiring. Unfortunately, the silence provokes a question in me and I ask it without any subtlety: "What do you think happens after we die?"

"What?" Ethan's eyes widen with concern. "Why would you ask that?"

"I'm just curious."

He pauses, then says: "Nothing. We decompose and become nothing."

As someone who sedates people for a living and monitors them while their consciousness shuts down to brain-stem death levels, I'm startled by such a boring answer.

"That's it? That's not a very creative guess."

He shrugs. "Well, dying is not very original."

I pester him some more.

"Come on, you work at a hospital. Haven't you encountered patients who've had near-death experiences? That must be quite something. To almost die on the operating table like that? The things they must have seen!"

Ethan looks at me, bewildered. I realize my glee on this subject matter is too obvious. I tone down my delight and pick a blueberry out of the bowl. "What I mean to say is, what a traumatic thing to go through. Wouldn't wish that on a single soul."

We sit in silence until another question gnaws at me. "Is it possible to smuggle out some propofol?"

"For fuck's sake, Cleo! How many times do I have to tell you I'm not administering an anesthetic agent on you?" he yells, burying his head into his hands.

I feel horrible for upsetting him. I didn't mean to. It was a joke, for the most part, and besides, he laughed the previous time I hinted at wishing to be put under for a year. Why isn't it funny now?

"I'm sorry, I won't bring it up again. How is it going at work, anyway?"

"If you don't mind," Ethan says, "I'd rather not talk about work."

"Did something happen?"

He lets out an aggravated exhale. "I had to work the labor ward this week."

"Oh."

It takes me a moment to realize what he is saying. It catches me off guard, the vulnerability in his voice. When he went back to work, it seemed like he had moved on, had tucked away this period as a sad chapter of our lives, never to look back on again. I was astonished at his ability to glide through the stages of grief so quickly and efficiently without disturbing a single living thing, so to see impenetrable clouds of sadness over his eyes right now makes me feel unexpectedly guilty. Of course he is struggling. I should have known. Maybe I didn't want to know. Maybe I took comfort in having him be the strong one. Because if neither of us were strong, how would we ever get through this?

Maggots form two large mounds on my chest. They migrate up towards my face, burrowing themselves into my eyes and ears and nose but not my mouth because my mouth is missing. My mouth. Where is my mouth?

I wake up dry heaving, fingers feeling around my face to make sure everything is there. It was just a dream. I'd fallen asleep on the couch. There's an empty bottle of NyQuil tucked between my legs. The sunlight tells me it's daytime. I sit myself up, terrifically dizzy from being upright, before clutching my chest and screeching in pain. My breasts are throbbing, engorged, as if someone has shoved hot bowling balls inside my chest.

I call Dr. Posey. I tell her the Tylenols and cabbage leaves aren't working. She tells me I can do one of two things: dry up the milk, or donate it to a milk bank. The latter, she warns me, would require me to pump for at least two months or until I produced at least five liters. She tells me this can be incredibly healing for bereaved mothers.

"On the other hand," she adds, "it can be quite depressing."

Donating my milk is the noble thing to do. But the thought of pumping milk into an empty vessel instead of my newborn's mouth every three to four hours sounded like a fate worse than death.

"I want the milk to go away," I tell her.

She writes me a prescription for bromocriptine and tells me it's a dopamine agonist that's very effective at blocking the release of prolactin. It's quite dangerous, she states, warning me of an increased risk of stroke, seizures, psychosis, and even death.

"Not a problem," I tell her. The more fatal the side effects, the better.

"How's your sleep?" she asks.

I didn't want to tell her I bounced between staying awake all night and sleeping upwards of fifteen hours a day, because knowing her, she would say something unhelpful like, "Try to find a balance," and then proceed to not give me the sleeping pills, so I lie and say, "I can't sleep at all."

"That makes sense. Given what you've been through. Try to get out of the house. Go for a walk. Do you go outside much?"

"No."

"You should. Getting out is very important. Have you heard of horizon gazing?"

"No."

"They say when you stare out at the horizon, you're better able to scan the landscape for threats. Once you know there's nothing to be afraid of, this produces a calming effect in the body. Do you have a porch? A deck?"

"Yes."

"I want you to sit out there for one hour a day."

"Is this an evidence-based treatment or—"

"Tongue sunning. Are you familiar with that?"

"No, but—"

"I want you to turn to the sun and stick out your tongue. Set the timer for three minutes. No more, no less. It'll strengthen your organs and give you an instant surge of energy."

I can hear her typing in the background. I imagine she is typing in whatever the medical term is for *shut-in*. Agoraphobia? Social anxiety? Weak-willed?

"Do you have any nightmares?"

I tell her about the maggots. I tell her about the one where I'm pushing you in the stroller and every single person we pass by looks at us in disgust and I don't know why until I pull back the canopy to find you gray and cold as a knife. I tell her these nightmares aren't even the worst ones. "I keep having this recurring dream where my baby smells like green apples."

"What's wrong with that?"

"It's the apples."

"What about it?"

"It's what she smelled like in the casket."

"Oh?"

"Formaldehyde. It's the main ingredient used to preserve dead bodies. It has a very sweet smell."

"Mm-hmm. . . ."

Dr. Posey remains silent as she continues to type some more. Is she writing me up for a psychological analysis? Perhaps some psychiatric medication? Instead she says: "I think you should incorporate some green apples into your diet. Start with a couple times a week. Then work up to once a day."

I'm stunned. She's literally prescribing me an apple a day. What else can I do but act like her advice is not awful? I don't have the energy to dispute her right now. For the past several years I've been meaning to find a new doctor, but there's a shortage in Toronto and I'm lucky to even have a doctor who picks up her phone on a Saturday. So, while her judgment might be questionable and her delivery somewhat unsavory, at the end of the day I always get the drugs I need.

"Now you may not like hearing this, but people who've lost a child are at an increased risk for divorce, mental instability, and family estrangement. Any thoughts of suicide?"

"No," I reply. It wasn't a lie. I have no desire to physically hurt myself. But if a crane were to fall from the sky and come plunging towards me, I'd be in no hurry to get out of the way.

"Talk to your parents lately?"

"They dropped by last weekend."

More click-clacking of the computer.

"Are you sexually active with your husband?"

I remind her that I gave birth two months ago. That I can still feel the perineal stitches poking inside me. That my labia are swollen beyond recognition. That blood clots the size of golf balls are still spitting out of my vagina. That if there is so much as a finger pressed against my engorged breasts, I will lose it.

"Well, as soon as you're able, make time for intimacy. It's good to not be celibate for too long. How's your libido?"

"Is that relevant?"

"You're quite feisty, aren't you?"

I don't know what to say.

"You know what, I'll write you up for flibanserin. This should get you raring to go again. Most marriages don't survive a tragedy like this, so I want to give you whatever leg up I can. No pun intended." She chuckles into the receiver.

Great. Not only have I lost my baby, but I could potentially lose my husband, too? I resent Dr. Posey for making me feel lousy but I can't express any animosity because she has not yet filled my prescriptions and I desperately need these pills.

For the next few minutes, I hear her type some more. Finally, she confirms my prescriptions have been faxed to the pharmacy.

"Now, for your sleep, I normally don't give out more than fourteen tablets at a time, but because of your"—she pauses—"special circumstances, I'm giving you forty. Take no more than one every twenty-four hours, you hear? Any more and you could seriously go into a coma."

I am immediately delighted by this warning and hang up.

One of the best parts of living in the Beaches is how easy it is to get to everything by foot. Craving sour keys? Three minutes away. Need a chiropractic adjustment? Six minutes. Last-minute tooth extraction? Ten minutes tops. The nearest pharmacy is only twelve minutes away and according to everybody I know, walking is supposed to be good for you, so I walk and wait for the benefits to kick in.

They don't.

Two minutes after stepping outside, my chest feels like jagged little rocks are cutting up the interior lining of my lungs. Each breath feels shallow, like I've just run a marathon, and even though I can't see a single person in the distance, I feel like someone might pull a knife on me at any moment.

It's the beginning of summer. The sun and birds are out. Shorts and ice-cream cones abound. There's no threat anywhere. I tell myself I'm okay, I'm okay, I'm okay. I hold it together and keep walking. I go north on Willow until I reach Queen. Traffic barrels past. Cyclists whiz by. Pedestrians push their prams. My chest tightens even more. How is the world still spinning? Shouldn't time have stopped ticking? Shouldn't the newspapers be plastered with headlines that you've died? Shouldn't flags be lowered to half-mast? Shouldn't the entire city have a moment of silence for what I've lost? The fact that everything keeps going as if nothing has happened feels like a betrayal of humanity. It's now clear to me that I live on a whole other planet, one whose rules are governed by the tempestuous whims of my grief.

I keep walking towards the pharmacy and it completely slips my mind that there's a daycare on this route. About six or seven toddlers are playing outside. Some are crying, some are screaming, some are taking turns going down the slide. There's one toddler in particular who catches my eye. She's Asian, her black hair tinged with amber when the light hits it just right. She has brown eyes like teardrops and her cheeks are so fat they jiggle every time she takes a step. I stand just outside the gate and watch her.

Is this what you would have looked like?

She's wearing a matching crewneck and pants with pastel rainbows all over. She's holding a yellow bucket and filling it with all the toys that have been scattered around the playground. A plastic turtle here. A toy car there. Once she has collected all the toys, she dumps it onto the ground, lets out an ear-piercing scream, then starts the process all over again.

I watch for another ten minutes, paying no mind to the terrible, terrible sadness that fills my lungs and clogs my throat. I'm surprised nobody has accosted me or accused me of being a creep. But I know why they don't. Because I'm a woman. And women would never do children any harm because they're conditioned to love and protect them with all of their being.

I catch a glimpse of my face on a reflective surface. Eyes beet red, snot trickling down both nostrils. The little girl looks at me and starts babbling nonsense until finally I make out what she's saying. "Mama cry?"

I get out of there as fast as I can.

The pharmacist tells me to take the bromocriptine once a day with food, at the same time every day. I ask him for how long. He glances down at my large breasts.

"Finish the whole prescription," he instructs. Then he proceeds to warn me that I might start seeing things that aren't there and to not be frightened if I sense someone is watching me.

"You mean like ghosts?" I ask.

"Angels, aliens, leprechauns, landlords, ex-boyfriends, foxes, FBI," he says. "I've heard it all."

I hand him my credit card.

"At least you'll be well rested on the zopiclone. The more sleep you get, the less likely you'll hallucinate," he says before handing me the rest of my drugs.

I crumple up the receipt and shop around. I need eye drops. A pregnant woman who appears to be in her second trimester is standing in my way. She takes one look at me and grins. "How much longer?"

I don't understand her question until she starts rubbing her belly. Oh god. Oh no. She thinks I'm like her, heaving with brand-new life. I look down at my feet, but it's blocked by the bulge that still has not gone away.

There are two options in front of me. I can tell her I'm not pregnant. Or I can tell her I used to be pregnant and leave it at that.

Then there's the third option.

"Four months to go!" I exclaim, caressing my soft, vacant belly and flashing her a fake smile before grabbing the Systane and walking away.

I fill my basket with some air freshener, a box of tissues, and pads. I'm bleeding considerably less than I did before, so I forgo the overnight maxi pads with wings to regular pads with no wings. A fiery ache suddenly blazes from my vulva with such force that I grip onto a shelf. I wince through the pain and proceed as usual. Another thing nobody warns you about is that in the aftermath of birth, your groin feels like it's been punched over and over again by a heavyweight boxer. You're not told that the first time you stand after giving birth feels like descending into lava, yet sitting can hurt all the same. The nurses don't give you anything stronger than an extra-strength ibuprofen, even when you beg and plead and threaten to gouge their eyes out, because the pain is normal they say, it won't last forever, everyone goes through this, you just need to *breeeathe*, remember how you chose this, how you desperately wanted this, and besides it's probably just gas anyway.

I pay for my things and take a different route home to avoid the daycare.

My father lets me into my own house. He pulls me in for a hug, a strange kind of hug that lasts a beat longer and a smidge tighter than what's typical. He asks me how I am, to which I give the kind of response every father wants to hear from his daughter.

"Good. I'm doing good, Ba."

"Yes, well done." He nods enthusiastically, as if I've correctly answered a math equation.

My mother's in the kitchen, filling the fridge with grocery items and precooked meals while my father returns to sweeping the floor with the Vietnamese straw grass broom that Ethan and I almost never use. The soft yellow straws shed with each sweep, effectively producing more dirt as you go. Despite the evidence laid before him on the floor, my father insists it's the correct way to clean. Like handwashing dishes and hand-mopping the floors. The more onerous, the better. You cannot argue with him because he'll always come back with the retort, "This is how our people have always done it." I'm convinced there's something in the immigrant psyche that conditions them to choose the harder choice.

"What is this?" my mother calls out.

I turn my head. A sadness spreads across her face as she realizes she's flipping through the baby book. The one we bought in anticipation of you. Blank pages ready to fill with pictures of your first bath, first smile, first step. Blank lines waiting to be filled with details like what snacks you loved and any nicknames you had, details that mean little on their own but all together make you *you*.

I flip the book shut and take it away from her.

My mother sighs and says, "Do you remember the nickname we gave you when you were a baby?"

How could I forget? The Vietnamese share one fear, the fear that evil spirits wander the earth in perpetuity looking for newborns to snatch up, particularly the beautiful ones. To prevent this calamity, family members refrain from complimenting or coddling the child, and instead they call them ugly or stupid or fatheaded and pray the spirits will overhear these horrendous names and move along.

My parents, however, took it one step further. They called me the vilest thing they could think of: cứt thối, which quite literally translates to Smelly Shit. Some of my earliest memories are of those two words being shouted across the school playground during pickup. "Smelly Shit! It's time to go home, Smelly Shit!"

Out of all the Vietnamese kids, I had the most repulsive nickname. There was Stupid Cow and Big Cockroach and Dirty Rat, so relatively tame and even a little charming compared to Smelly Shit. My parents convinced me that the uglier the nickname, the more loved I was. Still, I begged them to give me a new nickname, but they said it was too late. If we changed it now, the evil spirits would catch on to our trickery and take me away.

Years later, as I became an adult, I started to see the ridiculousness of this folklore, the idea that babies disappear simply because you draw attention to their charm. How foolish. That's why when you were in my womb, I felt confident in calling you my little dumpling. Soft and fluffy, abounding in surprise, and shimmering with steam. A delectable delight adored by everyone.

As I look down at the baby book and stroke the gold foil stamping that reads your name, I wonder if things would have been different had I called you something else, something so horrendous the evil spirits would have let me keep you. I'll never know.

My mother hands me a blank journal. She tells me it's good to write down my thoughts, to let it all out on the page so that it doesn't fester and rot in my mind, making me sick from the inside out. She tells me the practice is called journaling, that it's something people do to keep the demons away, that I could stand to benefit from giving it a go. Coming from a woman who wouldn't let me wear a helmet as a kid because she believed it impeded my brain growth, I'm taken aback by this enlightened suggestion of hers.

She pushes a pen towards me, so I do as she says. I summon my rage to the surface, transferring it onto the page. What comes out is a surprise. It's a list. I even give the list a title. "PEOPLE I WISH HAD DIED INSTEAD OF YOU."

Rapists.
Fascists.
Drunk drivers.
People who drive with loud exhausts.
People who flick their cigarettes into the woods.
People who cold plunge and don't shut up about it.

Wishing death upon others feels good. My mother is right. I feel better already. Why didn't I do this sooner?

I show her my list.

"What is this?" she asks.

"People I think should die."

"Trời ơi! Con điên à?" she screeches. "No good! No good at all! You shouldn't be wishing ill on other people. That will only bring you bad luck." As she takes the journal and pen away from me, I inform her this bad luck she speaks of is already inside the house.

Another thing my mother believes in is the laws of karma. No one can convince her that negative outcomes are not a direct result of our immoral actions and thoughts. When their basement sprung a leak, she blamed herself for not donating to the temple. She began contributing monthly, and claims it's why the house has been incident-free ever since.

I wonder if she attributes your death to something I've done in the past. Perhaps it was the time I scraped a parked vehicle and drove off. Or the time I evaded the three-dollar streetcar fare. Or the time I left a two-star review for that book everyone kept raving about.

Despite her lack of medical degree, my mother considers herself quite the doctor. She takes my wrist to feel my pulse. Steady, but weak, she says. Then she asks me to stick out my tongue. Puffy and swollen, an indicator of digestive imbalance. She tilts my head back and flashes a light into my nostrils. Dry and scaly, prone to nosebleeds.

She instructs me to take off my shirt and lie on my stomach so she can perform cạo gió and "scrape the wind" out of me, some superstitious belief about wind being the source of all sicknesses and negative energies.

I lie face down on the sofa as she oils my back and repeatedly scrapes a silver coin against my body, going over the same spots again and again. I clutch a pillow and clench my jaw. I can feel blood rushing to the areas she's scraping. It's not relaxing in the least. It's agonizing. Excruciating. But that's the point. The onset of pain is supposed to release a mixture of epinephrine, cortisol, and endorphins to help banish the wind. *Out, out, out you go,* my mother hums.

When she's done, I look at myself in the mirror. There are rows upon rows of red welts down my back. If a stranger were to see me, they would think I had been flogged. My mother tells me it will eventually turn purple, then brown, then disappear. Give it two weeks, she tells me.

"Two weeks?" I cry out.

"Don't be so superficial."

I put my shirt back on.

"Now let me do your face," she says, hovering the coin over my forehead.

I swat her hand away. "That is quite all right."

I sit back on the couch and wait for the positive effects of coining to hit me. But there's no noticeable difference. Just overwhelming fatigue.

As I start to drift off, my mother tells me not to sleep just yet. She squeezes my hand three times to wake me.

I sit up straight and ask her, "When does it end?"

"What?"

"The hurt."

"Oh, child, it will dull eventually."

When she says this, I can't help but think about what it would be like to be impaled by a dull knife versus a sharp knife. I suspect being stabbed by either hurts all the same.

Suddenly I feel a strong desire to be a little girl again. I want nothing more than for my mother to swaddle me, to rock me, to read me a story. I want her to tell me that the sorrow coursing through my veins and gushing out the corners of my eyes will stop one day. I want her to tell me that I'm still a mother. I want her to say your name and coat it in that thick, glorious accent of hers. I want her to read me one of her daily quotes, the one about how grief is just love looking for somewhere to go.

But I'm too afraid to ask. It's such an imposition. I can already sense that my sadness is unearthing something in her that she had long ago buried—something she is not equipped to deal with right now. I look at her hands, spotted with age. Her hairline, a thin gray halo. Her miscarriage happened so many years ago, but the devastation remains in the creases of her eyes, the tightness of her jaw, the stiffness of her neck. They say time heals wounds, but time is nothing but a mirage.

I remember it all. The buoyancy in our lives when my mother was pregnant with my little sister. I'd constantly put my ear to her belly, peeking underneath her dress to say hi. I was eager for someone to play with, to swap stories with, to explain with complete authority how to be a person in the world. I pestered my mother a lot, desperate to know when the baby was coming. Then one day, she snapped. Told me the baby wasn't coming anymore.

I hated her. I was certain she took the baby away to punish me, so I lashed out by leaving my toys out everywhere, pushing my food off the table, refusing to brush my teeth. I'd mess up the neat stacks of clothes in my dresser. I'd draw on the walls, aimlessly and haphazardly, to cause the most destruction.

Eventually, she stopped scolding me, stopped putting my toys away and scrubbing the walls. She let the house become a mess. Some days there was no dinner on the table, so my father would drive to the Pizza Hut and bring home a large pepperoni pizza, which she would refuse to eat. I noticed my mother spent a lot of time in her bedroom, not coming out for hours. She stopped driving me to school or going to temple. She instructed us to never pick up the phone because so-and-so was probably calling to snoop, so we'd often have to sit there and endure several minutes of ringing.

It was no longer fun to torment her. It was clear she was already very tormented. So I started to be good. I helped clean the table after dinner and made sure my toys went back in the toy bin and brushed my teeth without fuss. I even kept my crayon scratches on paper.

Not much changed. I'd come home from school and find my mother still in her bed. I thought she'd come down with some kind of malaise, like a viral infection, which seemed to explain why my father had taken to sleeping on the couch, as if to avoid catching whatever had befallen my mother.

More than once, when my father came home from work and found my mother still in bed, the house still a mess, the dinner table barren and the pantry empty, he'd explode:

"I can't do this anymore! You need to get over it! You suck the life out of everything!"

One night when we were sitting in front of the television, I asked my father if he was mad at Má.

"Why would I be mad?"

"Because she took the baby away."

"Oh," he said, "your mother didn't take the baby away."

"She didn't?"

"No."

"Then who did?"

He paused, then said: "Ông Trời."

The old man in the sky. I remember the tale my father told me, about the toad who gathered a troupe of animals to threaten Ông Trời into producing rain. It had been an oppressively long drought; every living creature was on the brink of death. They battled his army and won, leaving Ông Trời with no choice but to submit to the toad's demands. They mutually agreed that if ever they shall require rain, the toad need only croak and Ông Trời would saturate the land with all speed.

I asked my father why Ông Trời took the baby. He let out an exhaustingly long sigh and increased the volume on the TV so that I couldn't ask any further questions.

For years, I fantasized about kicking Ông Trời to the ground and forcing him to tell me where he was keeping the baby. I dreamed of rescuing the baby and delighting my mother and father with a reunion. I dreamed we were one happy family again. I'm not sure when I realized this was never going to happen.

———————

My mother gets up and goes to the kitchen. She makes me a soup of pork spareribs, potatoes, and carrots. I watch her pour salt on the meat and brush the grit off the bones. She parboils it in salted water not once, but twice, scooping the impurities as they rise to the surface. She pours everything into a bowl, topping it with black pepper, and tells me this will renew my strength, replenish my mental fortitude, and thicken my uterine lining so that I may bear more children. I say nothing and sip the broth.

My mother watches me eat. She smiles every time I bring the spoon to my mouth and practically propels into the air with glee when I finish the bowl and ask for another helping.

Relief splashes across my parents' faces when they head home, satisfied by how much food I've eaten. They don't need to know that I throw everything up into the toilet later that night, or that I take a medically inadvisable amount of medication so that I can sleep into oblivion. I keep that to myself, being the good daughter I am.

11

There's a knock on the door, a slow succession of taps that can only belong to Paloma.

"Surprise!" she shouts.

"What are you doing here?" I say, keeping the door slightly ajar.

"I miss you! What are you doing? Wanna go for a walk?"

Not another goddamned walk. Why does everyone insist on walking? This impromptu visit is a shock. I've purposely ignored all her calls and text messages. A normal person would've taken the hint and left me alone. That's not how Paloma operates. The more you push her away, the more she shoots her way back in like a coiled spring.

I peek my head out, scanning the porch or walkway for a stroller. "It's just you?"

"Yes! So, what do you say? Can I steal you away for a walk? It's such a gorgeous day out."

I look down the street. The lake is sparkling and the sky is spotless. Neighbors and pedestrians have forgone their sweaters to soak up this unseasonably hot June day. Days like this used to fill me with pure bliss. Now, it only accentuates the inexplicable sorrow I feel inside.

Paloma sees my hesitation but ignores it and grabs my hand. "Come on, put on some shoes and let's go!" Like a dog on a leash, I follow her commands and toddle alongside her despite hating every minute of it. The sun is bright and the air is balmy and the edges of my heart are raw.

We sit on the last free bench on the boardwalk. Paloma asks if I want an ice cream from Beaches N' Cream. I shake my head. The thought of eating anything right now makes me queasy. Luckily, she doesn't push it any further.

"The real reason I wanted to see you is because I wanted to talk to you about something," she says.

Paranoia runs down my back. Does she know I was in her house? What gave it away? Did I leave the rock in the wrong spot? Was something amiss in the nursery? When I put the journal back, had I left it a few inches away from its original location?

"About Sadie and Fatima's baby shower—you know you're not obligated to go, right?"

I sigh with relief. Then realize this, too, is a topic I'd rather not broach.

"I want to be there."

Paloma gives me a look like she wants to shake me upside down until all the crap falls out.

"Really," I insist. There's a pause, and in this pause I realize I do mean it. There are moments, if ever fleeting, when I want to be around people. And this is one of those rare moments. I miss my friends. I feel out of touch with them. Since the funeral, our interactions have dwindled to text messages filled with heart and hug emojis that say everything and nothing all at once. I worry I've become something of an outcast. Nobody knows what to say to me anymore. I think they're scared to bring up my loss, scared it'll make me cry and send me spiraling. What I want to tell them is: It makes me happy to hear your name. To speak of you as if you're still here. And besides, I'm already spiraling anyway.

"Well, if you want, we can go together," Paloma says. "If it becomes too much, just give me a safe word and we'll be out of there pronto."

"A safe word?"

"Yeah, just pick any word and I'll get you out of there."

"You mean like *margarita*?"

"Sure."

"But what if I actually want a margarita?"

"The point is to pick a word outside of your regular vocabulary. Something you wouldn't use on an ordinary basis. That way I know you're using the safe word."

I think long and hard about this. A word comes to mind. It came from an article I read about the four stages of human decomposition. The first stage is livor mortis when the blood vessels collapse and a dark purple discoloration appears on the skin. Second is algor mortis when the body cools down significantly after it no longer produces heat. Third is rigor mortis when the buildup of lactate and phosphate causes the muscles to stiffen. The last stage, which occurs about two weeks after death, involves the destruction of soft tissues by microbes that feed upon the proteins and carbohydrates of the body. It's the name of this last stage that I propose to Paloma.

"I beg your pardon?" Paloma responds with a flustered look.

"Putrefaction," I say. "I want *putrefaction* to be the safe word."

Paloma lets out a tired sigh. I bet she's wishing we had stuck with *margarita*.

"Whatever makes you most comfortable."

She shifts uncomfortably in her seat. So much of friendship is about picking up on cues when there's something not being said, and I can tell Paloma is holding something back.

"What? What were you about to say?"

"Nothing."

"You were going to say something."

"I wasn't."

"Paloma, come on. You've never shied away from telling me anything. Remember the hemorrhoids you wouldn't stop going on and on about? What could you possibly be afraid to say to me now?"

She purses her lips. "I was curious if you've called that grief counselor I recommended."

"Oh," I say, forgetting all about that. "No I haven't."

"Do you plan to?"

"Eventually," I lie.

Twice I'd been tempted to pick up the phone. Once, when a series of phantom kicks jolted me out of bed. Then again, when I woke up clutching my throat after a horrible dream in which I was choking on a green apple. Both instances wrecked me to my core, made my mind go to the darkest place imaginable, and still I couldn't get myself to call the counselor. I didn't want to talk. I didn't want to tell the story of how I lost you again and again and again. I lived it. There was no need to *relive* it.

Paloma looks out at the lake, as if she's sick of looking at me.

"I don't mean to be such a nag but I really think you should talk to someone," she says.

"I'm sure she's great at what she does, but it's not for me."

"How will you know unless you try it?"

"I'm fine. You don't have to worry about me all the time."

"Of course I worry! You haven't been replying to any of my texts."

I clutch her shoulders, forcing her to look at me. "I'm fine! Seriously! You're my best friend. You'd be the first person I tell if something were wrong."

She smiles when I say this and I know I've hit the right note. "Do you really mean it?"

I bury my head in the crook of her arm so that I don't have to answer.

As she holds my head, stroking her fingers through my hair, I stare out at Lake Ontario and wonder how many people have drowned in it. How many bodies it has swallowed up. How many still remain in the depths of its murky waters.

Paloma violently flinches and clutches her left breast. I sit up, asking if she's okay.

"I think I might have a bleb."

"W-what's a bleb?" I ask.

"It's from a clogged milk duct. We've been having some latching issues and my breasts are filling up faster than the baby can drink. I've tried every kind of nipple shield out there and nothing works. I don't know what to do. I'm at my wit's end."

A horrible sting rises in my throat and my heart spasms in my chest as I'm reminded Paloma is a mom. A mom with a living baby. I wonder if she realizes this is the first time she's acknowledged the existence of her child. I swallow the sting down. I concentrate on the lake and count the number of geese floating on the surface. Four, five, six. I stop blinking and let the breeze dry out my eyes.

"Does it hurt a lot?" I force myself to ask.

"Let's just say I'm pretty sure the baby has swallowed more blood than milk at this point."

She massages her breast over her shirt and moans in pain. A group of people flash us a disturbed look.

"Maybe you should take a pause from the feedings. Give your breasts a break," I say.

"That's the worst thing you can do."

"Oh." I sink into my seat.

She absentmindedly continues, "The only way to remove a clog is to keep emptying my breasts. Stopping altogether would just make everything worse."

"I had no idea."

I gaze out at the lake again, sullen with the realization that I know nothing about the mechanics of mothering. What else do I not know? What other experiences have I been deprived of? How much deeper could our bond have been had things played out the way they were supposed to? I have nothing else to contribute to this conversation. I have no sage words of advice, no helpful anecdote to relay. The conversation is now stilted, awkward, and it dawns on me how different our lives have become.

"I've got an appointment with a lactation consultant tomorrow," says Paloma. "She's been booked up for weeks. I practically had to harass the receptionist to squeeze me in."

A horrible thought forms in my mind, which involves a pillow, my face, and the constriction of oxygen, but I immediately shake off the thought.

"I think if I leave an hour early, I can avoid rush hour," she continues. "It'll also give me time to find parking. I don't know how anybody drives downtown. It's impossible to find parking there."

I nod and nod, my ear sharply tuned to the triviality of her problems.

"Did I tell you we got rear-ended last week? Thankfully the baby wasn't in the car. We were at a four-way stop and this idiot was glued to his phone! Let me tell you, you do *not* want to get into an accident. The insurance process alone makes the collision feel like a nap!"

I drop my jaw and stretch my mouth open, feigning horror at this news despite the fact that it all feels rather quotidian to me. A fender-bender? Seriously? That's your biggest problem?

"It's the worst!" Paloma goes on. "And I'm barely getting any sleep on top of that. Luckily we'll be staying at Freddie's parents' tonight so I can get a few extra hours of uninterrupted sleep. I can't wait. Isn't it sad that I'm excited to get four hours of sleep? Four! The average woman needs seven to nine! All this lack of sleep can't be good for me. You know, sometimes I fantasize about doing absolutely nothing but staring at the wall and eating crackers."

I shift uncomfortably on the bench. This was bound to happen— her divulging the minutiae of motherhood with me. We'd gone so long pretending her baby didn't exist that I wonder what changed. A small part of me wants her to keep whining, to keep digging herself a deeper hole, so that I could deliver the ultimate rebuttal: No matter how hard taking care of a newborn is, grieving the loss of one is a million times harder. And she'd have to concede my point and accept my wounds are bigger and bloodier than hers, therefore I'd win.

Paloma stops mid-sentence and turns to me. "How are you doing? Sorry, I know that was a lot. Are you okay that I'm talking about this stuff?"

I meet her gaze, strap on my Optimism Mask, and tell her, "Of course!"

As we get up to walk, the lake calls to me even louder than before, promising me refuge from this hellish land.

———

When Paloma and I were eleven, we operated a daycare. Not a real daycare, of course. A pretend one. We turned our dolls into a cast of toddlers and our bedrooms into learning centers. We were precocious in that sense, always exhibiting an entrepreneurial spirit even during play. We got a kick out of barking orders and disciplining bad behavior and sending dolls to The Chair.

We gave personalities and idiosyncrasies to all the children. Baby Alive was a booger picker. Polly Pocket peed herself daily. Sally Secrets gave everyone lice. Stinky Pingu spat on Purple Bear and got suspended for one week.

One day Stinky Pingu went missing. I searched for him everywhere but he was nowhere to be found. Paloma and I declared him dead and broke the news to the rest of the children. We took them all outside to the backyard, laid them down in a semicircle, and instructed them to look up at the sky. We explained that Stinky Pingu was up there now, playing with another group of children in the clouds. Polly Pocket asked if we could join them up there. I told her no. You have to wait your turn. When it's time, you'll be invited to come up. "Don't worry," I said. "Everyone will get a chance to play."

Later, it came to light that my mother had thrown Stinky Pingu in the trash because he reeked of, in her words, "a drunkard's butt crack." I didn't tell Paloma. I didn't want to crush her heart the way mine was when I learned Stinky Pingu was not merrily frolicking in the clouds but, in fact, lying in a landfill somewhere. To this day, she still doesn't know.

I watch Paloma and Freddie drive off to the in-laws' for the night and make my way over. I remove my shoes at their front door. It's the polite thing to do, to not track all matters of dirt, debris, and infectious diseases into a person's house. Especially when one of the residents is an infant with an undeveloped immune system.

Dumpling is in my arms again. I fetch her from the corner of the nursery where she still has not been picked up after being haphazardly tossed to the floor. I let the sweet, wonderful weight of her slow my thundering pulse, and I read her a book about a boy who befriends a little rabbit.

It is important to make storytime a part of your baby's daily routine. Print books are preferred over e-books, as screen time is not recommended for children under two years old.

My brain is full of information like this, gleaned from the countless parenting books I devoured during the third trimester haze.

Your baby should not be immersed in water until their umbilical cord falls off.

Sunscreen is not recommended for newborns under six months old.

The most common choking hazards for children under four are hot dogs, whole grapes, and hard candies.

All this wisdom floats aimlessly in my head, waiting for the day it will become useful.

Paloma's diary sits on the nightstand. A pen rests on top, its cap perilously dangling on the edge of the table as if she was in too much of a hurry to put the cap back on, as if the baby had been fussing, crying out to her, forcing her to write fast and get all her thoughts out before mom brain kicked in and she forgot what she was going to write. I open to the last page.

> *Dear diary,*
> *This feeling is indescribable. It's unlike any experience I've ever*
> *had in my life. It's like my heart has jumped out of my body and is*
> *now resting in that crib, snoring the cutest little snore. I get it now.*
> *I get why people say they would die for their child because I would,*
> *I absolutely would.*

My heart sinks as rage bubbles inside me. I desperately want to take that pen and write in the margins: Oh really? You would die for your child? Well who fucking wouldn't when the alternative is having to go on living without them here?

Breathe.

I close my eyes and let the anger flush out of my system before putting down the pen and placing everything back exactly where I found them. I grab another book off the shelf and read it to Dumpling. It is a short book, about a baby chick who can't find its mother but in the end, they're reunited and happy again. Of course they are. I close the book and cry into Dumpling's plush white body.

Everything hurts so much I wonder if it's possible for my guts to wrench and my heart to twist any further. Let's see. I pull out my phone and scroll Instagram. It's a minefield of hurt as the algorithm pushes bump photos, birth announcements, and family photo ops in relentless succession.

Each post feels like a paper cut to my lips. Their happiness magnifies my sorrow. Their blessings laugh at my misfortune.

And yet I can't stop scrolling, a bloodletting gone wrong.

Bayleigh, a former university classmate, has five-month-old twins named Ethel and Nella. She dresses them up in matching outfits and headbands with very large bows. She likes to write out her posts in the POV of her babies: We have just learned how to roll from tummy to back but we are still trying to figure out this whole tandem breastfeeding thing. We know Mama is getting frustrated but we promise we'll get the hang of it soon.

Next up: Felicia, an actuary I used to work with. She's currently on maternity leave. She has a baby boy named Reign. Her grid contains back-to-back photos of her son lying next to a plush cream bunny. Next to his head is a number indicating how many months he has been alive. He is the light of her life. Her prayers in the flesh. Every post ends with the hashtag #boymom.

Next up: Ada. I do not know who Ada is but she appears to be quite popular with over a hundred thousand followers. The app has recommended her to me based on my interests, so I take a gander. Ada has pinned a black-and-white ultrasound picture to her profile. She's twenty-four weeks pregnant and is beyond excited to be welcoming a fall baby to her family. There are hundreds of congratulatory comments below.

Omg omg omg! Congrats girrrl!!!
Woohoo, I'm gonna be an auntie!
ADA, this is the sweetest news!!!!

The flood of responses makes me want to add my own. I hope everything works out for you, I type and follow it with three praying hands emoji.

To my surprise, Ada replies immediately: Why wouldn't it???

I begin to type up a response regarding the statistics of perinatal loss. How one in four pregnancies end in a miscarriage and one in 175 are stillborn. How the fetal mortality rate currently stands at 4.7 per 1,000 live births. Not to mention how mothers are dying at alarming rates, especially Black mothers, who are three times more likely to have fatal complications than white mothers, and Indigenous mothers, who are two times more likely. Ada appears to be of mixed race, so I hope this information is helpful to her. Before I can hit send, the app informs me that I have reached the maximum character limit and everything I have typed up somehow disappears.

Next up: Sienna, an old friend who has moved to the suburbs. She is a #momoftwoundertwo. She has a Halloween family. They like to dress up in themed costumes and make silly poses for the camera. Last year, the parents were soy sauce and the children sushi. The year before, chefs and lobsters. What will they be this year? Bacon and eggs? Spaghetti and meatballs?

I notice Paloma has liked every single one of her posts.

I click on her profile.

I haven't checked it in a while. There are new posts I haven't seen yet. Including the birth announcement of her child. Born on April 29 at 9:09 a.m. Approximately three hours after you were born. It's the first picture I've seen of her baby. Thick eyebrows, brown complexion, two dimples on the chin, and hair blacker than the night. An irrefutable duplicate of Paloma.

I fight back tears but they drip down my face anyway, following the curves of my jaw and neck and chest until they're absorbed by my cotton bra.

I turn to my own profile.

There is no birth announcement. No baby pictures to fawn over. Just photos of a person I don't recognize. She smiles a lot. She hangs out with friends and takes pictures of trees. She reads poetry and uses exclamation marks in her captions. She is happy to be alive, indicated by several posts where she uses the words *blessed* and *lucky*. She doesn't know what's coming. She has no idea her world is about to tip off its axis. I wish I could reach into these photos and warn her.

The last photo was posted four months ago. She is standing in front of a pastel balloon arch with a sign that says "Our Lil' Dumpling Is On The Way." Her hands are placed around her belly to accentuate her bump. Her hair is thick and shiny. Her skin is glowing. Her eyes are glistening. The caption reads: What an absolutely beautiful day being showered and spoiled by loved ones. Our baby girl is already so loved beyond measure. We can't wait to meet you, little dumpling!

I turn off the phone.

After wiping the wet off my face, a strong instinct to do something, anything, kicks in. I place Dumpling down in the crib for a nap. On her back, of course. *Babies must always be placed on their back in an empty crib free of loose blankets or soft objects.* I see a pile of laundry that needs to be folded so I tackle that first. I use the Marie Kondo method that I painstakingly practiced during my nesting phase. How did it go now? Right. Lay onesie down flat. Fold in left side, then right side, then the bottom a third of the way, then fold, fold, fold. File into a drawer in an upright position. I do the same for the pants, the sleepers, the itty-bitty socks. I repeat this until the laundry basket is empty. I am so focused on ensuring my folds are crisp that I don't even shed a tear when I come across the onesie Paloma and I bought together, the one that says, YOU BET GIRAFFE I'M CUTE.

I scrub away a yellow milk stain on the rocking chair. I refill the caddy with fresh diapers and wipes. I empty the diaper pail. It weighs a ton and smells sour and tangy, but I don't mind. A baby that produces lots of wet diapers is a healthy baby, an alive baby. I would take this smell over the smell of nothing.

I keep going, cleaning every inch of the nursery. I want the room to be so sanitized, it's as if there was never a baby in here, as if the baby never came home from the hospital. Like you.

I disinfect the toys, teethers, and pacifiers. Anything that can get in the baby's mouth. *Regular sanitizing will reduce the risk of the baby contracting illnesses and infections.* I grab a mixing bowl from downstairs and concoct a solution I find online. It is a one-to-one ratio of hot water and white distilled vinegar, along with a few drops of mild dish soap. Soak in solution for thirty to sixty minutes. Rinse thoroughly. Let air dry on a clean rag or rack.

I bookmark this recipe for future reference. It's from a blogger who proudly calls herself a Crunchy Mom, whatever that means. A cursory online search describes a Crunchy Mom as someone who likes unmedicated births, cloth diapers, and anything organic. On the list of things they do not like are Big Macs, Fisher Price, and Paw Patrol.

This got me interested—the idea that motherhood came with its own set of rigid taxonomy. I'm curious to know what type of mother I would've been. I take a quiz online. I answer the questions to the best of my ability. At the end, it generates a result: You Are a Scrunchy Mom! I read the description.

A Scrunchy Mom toes the line between a Crunchy Mom and a Silky Mom. You possess the hippiedom of Crunchy Mom while dabbling in the IDGAF attitude of Silky Mom. You want your kid to eat the healthiest foods but do not stress if they have a Dunkaroo or two. You vaccinate your children but prefer homeopathic remedies to beat colds. You are not opposed to letting them watch TV for hours, but you'll make sure they touch grass every now and then. You let your kids play with low-stimulating wooden toys as well as loud electronics with flashing bright lights. You would grow chickens in your backyard if you could, but for now you will settle for buying frozen chicken nuggets in bulk.

My throat tingles with despair and I cry into a rag. I should feel relieved to discover that I would've been such a laid-back mom but the truth is I don't actually care what kind of mom I would be—I just want to be a mom.

I continue to wipe down the kitchen, removing all manner of fingerprints and grease and residue off the surfaces. I freeze when I get to the fridge. The baby shower invitation is pinned to the door.

It's in two weeks.

Everyone will be there.

The Crunchy Moms. The Silky Moms. The Scrunchy Moms.

They will all gather in packs and bond over their shared experiences of parenting. They will compete over who has had the least amount of sleep and commiserate over diaper rashes that just won't go away. They will share their dramatic birth stories, and mouths will gape when they get into the gory details before breathing a sigh of relief that everything turned out fine. They will take turns holding each other's babies and congratulate each other for making such cute creatures, basking in those compliments as if it was hard earned, as if they had personally hand-picked the combination of genes their child had inherited.

And then there will be me.

The Sad Mom.

Who stupidly said she would attend.

It's too late to back out now.

12

Dear diary,

I'm an awful mother. I took the baby to the doctor and she lost nine ounces. Nine! The doctor was terribly upset at me, asking a lot of questions that I didn't know the answers to. How many wet diapers does she have a day? How many ounces does she have per feeding? How much sleep does she get? I don't know, I don't know, I said. I was so embarrassed I stormed out of the office. The doctor ran after me and said I forgot the baby.

Dear diary,

I'm writing this as she sleeps in my arm. I can't stop staring at her. She's so peaceful, so serene. Part of me wants to wake her so I can hear her coo at me. But I know once her eyes open, the work will start all over again so I will remain as still as possible, for as long as it takes, because I never want this moment to end.

Dear diary,

Every day there is a new worry. I worry she is too cold, too hot, too hungry, too full, too stimulated, not stimulated enough. I worry I worry too much. I worry my milk will go sour from all the worrying I'm doing. I don't know how to turn it off. What if there is no off button?

13

When it comes to death, our hearts work faster than our brains. The heart crumples the instant we learn someone we love has died. The brain, meanwhile, needs a little more time to process. The brain could watch Uncle Tim's lifeless body get lowered into the dark, damp earth and still implore, *Wonder what Uncle Tim's up to this weekend?*

Neuroscientists discovered this by placing a lab rat inside a black box. They put a little blue tower inside too, and every time the rat investigated the blue tower, object-trace cells would fire from its brain. When scientists took the little blue tower away, the same object-trace cells continued to flood the brain. The rat kept looking for that little blue tower, even though it was no longer there.

I think about this experiment as I greet mourners during today's service. These poor people, with their solemn faces and black attire, searching frantically for their little blue tower.

I am friendly and welcoming to each person who arrives. I am diligent not to smile too excessively, as Kenneth has instructed us all to do. We don't want to appear inappropriate, nor do we want to come off as cold. It's a delicate balance, a skill one must tune in front of a mirror. One wrong turn of the mouth or a slight crinkle of the eyes and you could obliterate somebody's day.

It's going to be a full house. Two reception rooms have merged into one to accommodate up to three hundred people. They're all here to pay their respects to Clyde, a husband and father of four, who dropped dead of cardiac arrest while out for a morning run.

In the break room, I overhear Rachel and Rebecca talking.

"It's probably the saddest thing I've ever heard," Rachel says.

"Sadder than the young father who died a few months ago?" Rebecca asks.

"Well yes, I mean, he had one child. This man has four!"

Here at the funeral home, we are trained to view all loss as equally tragic. There's no hierarchy. No 0 to 10 scale of human suffering. No grief Olympics. Repeated multiple times in the employee manual is this sentence: *The worst kind of loss is always your own.*

Secretly, we do it anyway.

We compare hardships the way we compare our homes, finances, bodies. We assign points based on the age of the deceased, the nature of the death, how sudden—or not—it was, who they left behind, and the closeness of those relationships. We add and subtract and multiply these points to arrive at a number that quantifies the devastation. This way we know exactly how much sorrow someone should feel and consequently how much compassion they deserve.

It is a terrible game.

Everybody who plays it is a loser.

———————

The service starts in ten minutes. Every seat is taken. Latecomers stand behind the last row of chairs; some sit cross-legged on the floor. Noses are blown. Children shushed.

It's a beautiful day. Not a cloud in the sky and the breeze is as gentle as a sigh—the kind of weather that feels like a slap in the face when you're burying someone you love. For this reason, we do our best to lower as many blinds as we can for the service. No need to remind them the world is moving on without a care.

Clyde is in the visitation room, resting in his casket. His hair is combed to the side and his facial hair has been neatly trimmed. He is wearing a black suit and a red corduroy bow tie. There is a wedding ring on his finger, engraved with "C&K."

I scan the room looking for his wife, Kaitlyn. It's not hard to spot her. Just look for that pained expression of disbelief. The eyes that appear to be elsewhere. The closed lips that seal up the screams. I know that look well. It stares back at me in the mirror every single day.

To all the mourners, I give out a small pamphlet that contains the schedule of readings along with a few pictures of Clyde selected by the family. A picture of him and his wife on a mountain peak, with their arms outstretched in celebration. A picture of him and his four kids at Canada's Wonderland. A picture of him as a toddler in a canoe.

"Excuse me, miss?" A woman taps on my arm. "Can you tell me if it is an open casket or closed casket?"

"It is open, ma'am. Do you know how to get to the visitation room?"

Before I show her the way, she waves her palm in the air.

"No, no. That won't be necessary. I prefer not to see him in that state, you know? I don't want that to be my last memory of him."

"That is understandable, ma'am." What I really want to say is how perfect and peaceful and put-together Clyde is, how there is nothing to be afraid of, how she might regret not seeing him one last time. Neuroimaging studies have shown that viewing the body can help tremendously with the grieving process. When the brain sees the body, it provides visual confirmation that the dead are dead. Neural networks change how they fire based on this new reality, paving the way for healing to begin.

I wish I could tell her this, but employees are not permitted to say such things. According to the manual, employees shall not impose their beliefs onto the families. Even if their beliefs are scientifically accurate. Even if it is for their own good. At Monarch, we must allow people to grieve in whatever manner they choose.

The most delightful thing about being dead is how nice everyone is to you. All your negative personality traits are forgotten. Any lingering grudge becomes irrelevant. Those insufferable things you do—like ignoring texts for weeks or correcting people's grammar or tipping too little—is forgiven.

I stand in the back of the room and observe as, one by one, people go up to the podium and say incredibly generous things about Clyde. They share funny anecdotes—like the time he thought he was petting a dog, only to realize it was a coyote. That was Clyde for you: always believing the good in everything and everyone. He was also a passionate carpenter who loved carving masterpieces out of nothing. But above all, his most important role was that of husband and father. He was a good family man who would do anything for his wife and kids.

Clyde's childhood priest, Father Paul, walks up the steps and faces the mourners. He leans down so the microphone reaches his mouth.

"Forty years ago, a young couple came to my church and asked me if I could do the honor of baptizing their son, Clyde. This little boy had cheeks like apples and eyes like blackberries. Even as an infant, he was hard not to love. It has been an absolute joy seeing him grow into a caring, intelligent, and might I add genetically gifted man."

The crowd laughs. A much-needed reprieve falls upon the room.

"Now I know you are all reeling over such a senseless loss. It is hard not to get angry when someone dies well before they are supposed to. We think, was this God's plan? How can God do this to someone who has done everything right? But I implore you not to see it this way. Our relationship to God should not be transactional. We do not do good by each other with the expectation that God will reciprocate us with a long life. We do good because we are good. Clyde was the best of us. It is clear by how many of you have showed up here today. Our Heavenly Father will see to it that Clyde is at peace. More peace than any of us can ever imagine. A kind of peace that all of us will one day experience in our own time. So, if you are still wondering if this is God's plan, the answer is God always has a plan. And we must trust in our Lord Jesus Christ."

They all mumble their amens, cross their heads, lips, and hearts, and pray to the heavens that Father Paul is correct, that Clyde is now at peace, that he is in the careful hands of God, because any theory other than this simply cannot be stomached right now.

"Now the question I get asked a lot is, 'Father, how long does the grief last?' I wish I had an answer. I wish I could say six months, one year, five years. There is an expectation that grief comes with an expiration date, that it eventually releases its grip on us so that we can finally breathe and feel like ourselves again. Unfortunately that's just not the way it works. Now you may not like hearing this, but it is my view that grief never expires. When people ask me how long grief lasts, this is what I ask in return. 'How long will the love for your person last?' They tell me forever, and then I tell them, 'Well, that is how long the grief will last, too.'" He takes a long pause to let the words sink in. "I know, I know. It's a hard thing to hear. Now you can see why I'm not the most popular priest."

The crowd breaks out in fits of laughter. They all rejoice in this brief moment of levity, clinging to it like a life raft because they know it won't last.

The final speaker to step up to the podium is Eli, the eldest child, who looks to be about eleven or twelve years old. He reads from a sheet of paper that looks to have been crumpled and recrumpled over and over—as if nothing he wrote was good enough. His grandparents stand by his side as he whimpers through his speech, their mournful eyes downcast the entire time. The crowd is holding it together surprisingly well until the boy struggles through his final line—"I love you, Daddy, you will always be my best friend"—and the room is once again wrecked with grief. A cacophony of cries and sniffles fill the entire room. It is so loud I see a pair of birds flap away through the window.

After the service, we direct everyone to head to the dining hall where our caterers have set up a delicious, comforting buffet featuring the foods Clyde loved to eat: Buffalo chicken wings, buttermilk waffles with whipped cream, roast beef sandwiches, and creamy three-cheese macaroni. These offerings are not nutritious or well-rounded by any means, but here at Monarch Funeral Homes we don't judge.

According to the core values of the funeral home, we believe food to be essential to any funeral reception as it provides comfort and nourishment during difficult times. Eating together is a memorable way to honor our loved ones, and it is highly encouraged for visitors to partake in a meal following the service.

Looking at all this food lends a metallic tang on my tongue. How can they even think about eating? How can they be so ravenous? I fear I will never experience it again, the feeling of wanting food and enjoying it so much that my body keeps it down. It's as if my stomach is burnt out. Tired of mechanically breaking down food for a body that clearly doesn't appreciate it.

I spot Kaitlyn at a table with friends. Everybody is eating but she hasn't touched her plate. Her friends keep adding more things to it. They hover loaded spoons in front of her mouth and tell her how tasty the food is, but her lips don't move. Her eyes are blank, fixed on a mound of creamy macaroni growing colder by the second.

No one is observed as intensely as the widow at a funeral. Even though it looks like everyone is chatting and chewing and minding their own business, I catch their eyes flicking towards Kaitlyn, their gaze filled with sympathy and anticipation as they await her first bite. *Come on, come on, eat something.* But nothing enters her mouth.

It's hard not to look at her. She wears her grief like a bright red lipstick, like she wants it to be seen by everyone near and far. The shade clashes with her complexion and has a formula that chaps her lips, bleeds at the edges, and leaves stains so stubborn no amount of oil could ever remove. And that is just how she likes it.

I study her face and body language. She looks like she may never laugh again. She looks like she's wondering how she got here, how she went from planning what to make for dinner to planning her husband's funeral. Then something in her face switches. Her eyes look contemplative, maybe a little guilty, like she's thinking something she shouldn't. I think she wishes she weren't here. I think she wishes she were dead.

Her youngest son plops down on her lap, and she snaps out of it. She scowls at her child, as if he's just roused her from a dazzling dream. She looks around the table and realizes she can't tell any of these people what she's thinking. She can never tell anybody.

———

When the last of the guests depart, Rachel tells me to head to the break room. The staff like to congregate after a big service like that. It takes a toll observing such intense displays of grief, even if they are strangers, even if it's your job. Even Kenneth, who has become so accustomed to death, is looking a little worse for wear after putting Clyde to rest.

Kenneth suggests we all play a game. A game to get to know each other better. "But there's a twist," he says. "Instead of sharing one interesting fact about ourselves, why don't we all share one really boring fact?"

Everybody perks up. This is a much less intimidating game than its counterpart. The pressure is low, our averageness not on trial. Stuart goes first.

"I like cereal, specifically Raisin Bran."

Oohs and *aahs* erupt from the room as we all laugh at our mutual absurdity.

Rachel goes next. "I recently switched to an electric toothbrush."

About time!

Ana stands up. "I put a splash of lemon in my water every morning."

Good for you!

"I can't sleep without a night-light," Maggie says.

Aww!

"I separate my socks into two bins. Indoor socks and outdoor socks," Rebecca says.

Clever! I'm stealing that trick!

More trivial and horrifying revelations come forth one after the other—from a love of tea to a recent purchase of a garlic press to an evangelical obsession with a bidet. It's all so silly and yet so natural, so easy, like our bodies have been bending us towards frivolity. The sorrow we all felt from Clyde's funeral was not gone, just set aside, making room for joy and laughter and giddiness.

I realize it's my turn. I don't know what to say. Every part of my life feels engulfed in flames. Nothing is stable or ordinary or dull. Eyes drill into me, waiting for a response, so I spit out the first thing that comes to mind: "I don't like flowers."

"Whaaat?"

"Who doesn't like flowers?"

"Even dahlias? Peonies?"

It appears I've broken the rules of the game because my statement seems to fascinate everyone. I'm suddenly an interesting person. People turn their chairs towards me, wanting to know more.

"I don't know," I say. "They require a lot of work for something that will just wither away. They're a waste of money. The thorns hurt like hell. And not to mention they're terrible for the environment. They produce so much waste, something like a hundred thousand tons of single-use plastic."

They all gawk at me as if I've just told them I hate puppies. I change the subject by pointing at Kenneth, reminding them all that he still has yet to share his boring fact. They forget about my transgression and turn to him, eagerly awaiting his revelation. From what I've been able to glean so far, Kenneth is something of an enigma. Nobody knows what he does outside of work. We only know he owns a dozen waist-coats, drives a silver 2006 Toyota Prius, and keeps a book of crosswords at his desk, though it is unclear if he actually does the crosswords. We also know he opened Monarch Funeral Homes in 1982. What compelled him, we don't know, but a quick internet search informs me the mortality rate in Ontario had spiked significantly in the early eighties. Maybe he was trying to capitalize on the surge, to go where the market was and guarantee he'd never have to suffer the ill effects of a recession again. I asked some of the staff if they've ever just, you know, asked him. They said he always says the same thing. That he just wanted to help people. Nothing more to it.

Kenneth clears his throat and all ears are at attention. Finally we'll have one more factoid to add to our boss's short, sad biography. Maybe he watches *Wheel of Fortune* every night. Maybe he organizes his book-shelf alphabetically by author. Maybe he has a wife and kids and lives in a quiet cul-de-sac where everyone keeps a whimsical goose on their front porch.

"I love my job," is all he says.

I return to my desk and draft an invoice for Clyde's family. I follow a template to ensure nothing is missed: embalming and preparation, staff services, van transfers, facilities, burial, documentation, catering, mortuary products. As the total creeps up and up, reaching five digits easily, I feel disgusted. I want to replace all these numbers with zeroes. Just this one time. I think about poor Eli, growing up without a father, and I think about Kaitlyn, raising those four kids alone, and it just doesn't seem fair to make them pay for a tragedy they never asked for. They're going to be so hurt when I send this to them. They're going to question every hug and sympathetic gesture we extended them because when money is involved, all that kindness feels conditional.

On the other hand, I get it. This is a business. We have to be able to cover the costs of operating so we can continue to provide compassionate care to future families. This was all laid out in the handbook and still, I wish it wasn't like this. I keep Clyde's invoice in the drafts folder for now. Too soon to send it.

My eyes dart to the hutch. I still haven't forgotten about it. There's an impenetrability to it that makes me uncomfortable, like the sight of an unattended bag at the airport. Whatever lies inside can only be nefarious.

I'm convinced I can crack the combination. I ask Google what the most common four-digit codes are. There are ten thousand possible combinations with a high likelihood of being an even number, a significant year, or a couplet like 2424 or 6969.

I look up at Kenneth, who's squinting at something on his computer. Since we're in the routine of learning the most mundane details of each other's lives, I ask him a series of questions. When is his birth year? What is his favorite number? What was the address of his childhood home? He answers each one without hesitation or suspicion, peppy at the idea that I'm showing so much interest in his life. I write down his responses, hoping one of these combinations will work.

I can't do anything right now, though. Not with Kenneth right there. I keep waiting for him to dash off to an appointment or an off-site meeting, but he hasn't moved since we returned from the break room.

I bide my time by typing in questions like, *What happens after we die?* The search engine populates a series of results. I put on my headphones and watch a grainy YouTube video of Steve Jobs giving a commencement speech at Stanford University. He's telling the graduates about his brush with death after being diagnosed with a very rare form of pancreatic cancer. He tells them death is the single greatest invention of all time because nobody can run away from it, because its very existence is the reason life has any meaning at all.

I move on to another search result.

A computer scientist has invented a chatbot that plays back the voices of dead people. The voices are startlingly accurate. Should you miss someone, all you'd have to do is pay a monthly subscription fee and you can converse with them all you want. I read the fine print. Only adult voices can be replicated. There are legalities involved with replicating the voices of the young.

Next.

The *Journals of Gerontology* asked people over the age of sixty-five what they thought about the afterlife. The researcher selected participants who had recently lost a spouse and asked them if they believe they will reunite with their loved one when they die. Sixty-eight percent said yes. The ones who said no, or were uncertain, were more likely to report anger, intrusive thoughts, and depressive symptoms. The researcher concluded that believing in an afterlife and reunification after death can psychologically protect bereaved individuals from the pain of loss.

I scroll through the rest of the study but discover that it doesn't reveal whether the afterlife does, in fact, exist. I close the window.

I wish there was a way to know where we go after we die. If only there was a trial period, or visiting hours, or even a small porthole window where we could have a little glimpse. How is it possible that scientists—who have figured out how to clone celebrity pets and send aluminum junk into outer space and reincarnate the once-extinct woolly mammoth—still have no idea what happens after we die? I would give absolutely anything for this answer. My house, my car, my sanity, my entire savings. But of course, there's only one way to find out.

Maybe I should just do it, take a risk. Anything is better than this, right? But wait, what if I die and the suffering persists wherever I end up? What if I die and you're still not in my arms?

Tingles travel up and down my spine and a darkness penetrates every inch of me. Dammit, I need proof! I need data, numbers, evidence,

models, testimonies, calculations, spreadsheets. There has to be answers out there.

I scroll and scroll until I find something instructive.

A new study published by the *Resuscitation Journal*. In this study, researchers visited twenty-five hospitals in the United States, the United
Kingdom, and Bulgaria where they monitored patients who were experiencing cardiac arrest. While doctors performed CPR, researchers
attached devices to the patients' heads and tracked their oxygen and
electrical activity. In some patients they detected notable spikes in brain
activity, leading the team to believe consciousness can occur when an
individual is technically dead. When asked about their near-death experience, some patients recalled seeing faceless figures, a vast field of
grayness, men with hooded white robes, demons and monsters. One patient saw their dead grandmother who told them, "You need to go back."

"All right, that's enough for today," Kenneth says, jolting me from my
screen. He stands and starts packing up his bag.

It's five o'clock already? I haven't had a chance to try the lock.

"I'm almost done here," I tell him. "Go ahead, I'll head out shortly
after."

Kenneth takes my sweater from the rack and hands it to me. "Come
on now. I won't have you working late after a day like today."

"I don't mind, really. I'll be finished in half an hour tops."

Kenneth slings his messenger bag across his chest. "I was just being
nice, dear. I need you out so I can lock up this room."

I'm not sure if my vision is playing tricks but I swear Kenneth's eyes
quickly dart to the hutch before landing back on me.

"Well in that case, I'm happy to close up if you like. Is there a check-
list or set of procedures you would like me to follow—"

"I know what you're doing," he interrupts. I freeze, bracing myself
for what he's about to say. "I know it's very hard to sit with the grief. It's
tempting to plunge yourself into work and while I agree it does take
some of the sting away, you cannot avoid it forever. Even the sun needs
to set after a long day."

I should feel relieved Kenneth hasn't caught on to me but all I feel
is indignant at being known so intimately. Am I really that transparent?

I accept my sweater from him, grab my bag, and walk out the door. The sun has indeed set, leaving a hint of pink across the entire horizon. I wave goodbye to Kenneth and walk to my car. The wind whips across my face, swinging my hair sharply to one side. I get in the car quickly, glad to have escaped the blustery weather, but now I'm alone. Just me and the rage and the sorrow and the hopelessness that I keep trying to push down.

14

Whenever I go to bed, I pray to wake up in the future. In films, when the main character loses someone they love, the plot fast-forwards several years to when they are less mopey. They are chipper and clean and, most importantly, not in bed. It makes for a better viewing experience because there's nothing more insufferable than watching someone cry all day. Viewers want a redemptive narrative arc. They want to see a plucky protagonist who takes on the world with gusto. They want to see big teethy smiles and hear belly-aching laughter. They want their happy ending, preferably in the form of a wedding or birth or reunion or dream finally realized. Anything to confirm our protagonist has outrun despair and learned how to live with joy again.

A repulsive smell keeps me from falling asleep. I follow the stench, and it leads me to the nursery.

Nobody has gone inside since you died. Ethan and I often found our bodies migrating towards the room like there was a magnetic pull. We lingered outside the door, hovering our hands over the knob, convincing ourselves none of this ever happened and you had been napping in the crib all along.

The smell is sour, almost sulphuric. A dead mouse?

I open the door and see a future that never was. Boxes of unused diapers. Baby clothes with tags still on. Board books with uncracked spines. Bibs that have never seen spit-up. Stuffed animals that have never been clutched. A crib that has never been gnawed on by tiny little teeth. Everything remains devastatingly untouched—a glaring anachronism, belonging to a time when things were still good.

I collapse to the floor and cry until my skin burns from the salt. Ethan rushes in and attempts to soothe me, but he's distracted by the smell.

"God, what is that?" he cries out.

The stench of rotting flesh is more palpable than ever. It's coming from behind the rocking chair. We pull the chair back and plug our noses.

The orchid.

I'd forgotten all about it. I put it here after reading an article about how plants should be placed in nurseries to remove volatile airborne chemicals and alleviate babies from coughs and headaches. The author made it seem like it was something I *had* to do, something of utmost importance to the health of the baby, and that neglecting to do so would make me an unfit parent. So, I went out and bought a plant, not in fear of your health but in fear of not doing everything I could to give you the best life possible.

Miraculously the orchid is still alive. The flowers have opened to reveal a deep purple hue. The pendant leaves are green and glossy. For such a pretty little thing, it smells downright atrocious.

"I'll get a plastic bag and throw it out," Ethan says, still plugging his nose.

"Throw it out?"

"Well yeah, it smells like death!"

Ethan momentarily unplugs his nose and gags.

I don't mind the odor now that I know what it is. Does it smell like a dozen deer carcasses rotting in the blazing sun? Yes. Is it the most beautiful plant I had ever seen? Absolutely.

"I want to keep it," I tell him.

"Are you kidding? There's obviously something very wrong with it."

"I think it's perfect."

The stench went away after three days. Now it smelled like, well, a flower.

"That's more like it," Ethan says.

I do not say a thing. I prefer the way it smelled before.

———

Ethan and I decide it's time to go through the nursery. Some things are easier to let go of than others. Things about to expire, like infant formula, diaper cream, and medication are tossed without emotion. But things that were once warm against your skin all stay. The comb we used to scrape the birth off you. The pink mittens that protected your hands from the cold hospital air. The pillow used to prop your head up. The opened packet of Aquaphor we used to hydrate your lips. The zippered pajamas the NICU nurses had to cut the feet off of so they could attach the pulse oximeter to your big toe. We inhale each one of these items in hopes of summoning your essence. We carefully place them inside a box, praying the scent of you will still be there the next time we open the lid.

We cry in each other's arms, producing long, guttural sounds that have never come out of us before. An expulsion of everything that has ever hurt us. Our grief, when combined, feels too big, too violent for your sweet little nursery.

We distract ourselves from missing you by sorting through the rest of the room. I open an unmarked bag of clothes. My maternity clothes. Overalls and dresses and pants that stretched as you grew. These clothes repulse me. I decide they're all cursed and add them to the donation pile.

"Really? You don't think you'll need these again?" Ethan asks.

"Yes, I'm sure."

Because he's so abundant in hope, he frowns when I say this. I can see it in his eyes, the desperation, the want for a baby. Like a choking person wanting air.

"Don't you want to try again?" he says.

I flinch. *Try again.* As if you were a botched experiment, an obstacle in the way of a greater destiny.

"I don't know," I respond.

"I'm not saying right now, but maybe one day?"

I let out an "Mm-hmm," but it bears no meaning. I just want this conversation to end. It is the most painful thing, talking about a future without you in it. The more he tries to convince me to keep the clothes, the angrier I get. I want to scream in his face, *Don't you realize we could have dodged all this pain by not getting pregnant in the first place? By not tempting the specter of forever?* But I can't say it. If I tell him how

I really feel, that I never want to be scorned by hope again, I fear he will leave me.

We agree to talk about it later and continue adding more things to the pile. Socks that seem impossibly too small. Onesies with a million buttons. Baby Nikes that were already useless to begin with. I post them on a Buy Nothing group on Facebook, uploading pictures and writing the saddest sentence in the world: BABY ITEMS, BRAND-NEW, NEVER USED.

Within minutes, I receive multiple messages:

I'm interested! Can I pick up today?
I'll take it! I have a baby on the way!
Love these! Your location please?

I freeze. A maternal protectiveness washes over me, and I am suddenly unwilling to part with your things. The thought of another baby wearing your clothes, playing with your toys, drooling on your bib makes my throat close up. Why should some other baby get to enjoy them when you couldn't?

"It's just stuff," Ethan tells me.

I shoot him an annoyed look. "It's never just stuff."

That night in bed, I lose myself in my phone. I play crossword after crossword, pausing when the word *bereavement* comes up in one of the puzzles. Curious, I look up the meaning of that word. It's derived from the Old English verb *reafian*, which means to pillage or plunder— like how soldiers might reafian villagers of all their possessions during wartime—so to experience bereavement is to have something violently stolen from you.

I tear up at the sweet clarity of being seen.

That got me wondering what other validating words were out there. I look up the word for a parent who has lost a child, hoping there might be an equivalent to *orphan* or *widow* but my search comes up empty. It's almost as if the neologists of the English language mutually decided it was too sad a word to coin and moved along. I look up other languages and find *vilomah,* Sanskrit for "against a natural order." I come across even more words. *Thakla* in Arabic. *Shakulim* in Hebrew. *Shidu* in Chinese. *Verwaiste mutter* in German. All of which translate more or less to bereaved parent.

I text my father and ask him if there's a Vietnamese word for me. He texts back within seconds.

No ... No word will ever be good enough.

15

The morning of the baby shower, I conceal my gift in wrapping paper and add a satin yellow bow on top. I'm not sure why I go to all this trouble because Sadie and Fatima are the ones who have requested this specific brand of bottle sterilizer, so it should be no surprise when I give it to them.

I never quite understood why the conception of a child necessitated financial contributions from other people. The shopping list, or registry if you want to be formal about it, almost always includes practical things like nail clippers, washcloths, and rectal thermometers, which always struck me as bizarre because most of these things are under ten dollars and could the parents not simply pick them up the next time they visited a Walmart?

But then I got pregnant.

And filled my registry with things I could easily afford myself.

And got a surge of dopamine each time my phone pinged with a notification that somebody had purchased something off my list.

I understood the ritual now.

I peek out the window and look at Paloma's house. She has offered to drive us to the baby shower. She called this morning to say she won't be bringing her baby because she wants one goddamn afternoon to herself and griped that this better not be one of those ridiculous baby showers that only serves mocktails. I sensed she wanted me to ask why she was so agitated but I didn't for fear she would start complaining about how hard being a mother is. I didn't want to hear it and besides, I was relieved her baby would not be coming.

"Wow, you look beautiful," I gasp when she opens the door. Paloma is wearing a pistachio-colored linen dress that frames her breasts in a sexy yet elegant manner. She smells brightly of bergamot. I, on the other hand, am cloaked in an oversize black crewneck and a pair of ripped jeans that highlights my hairy scrotum knees. Paloma orders me inside and hands me an indigo dress to wear. The sleeves are ridiculously puffy, resembling inflatable armbands found at the kiddie pool, but I keep my mouth shut and thank her.

On the car ride there, I quell my nerves by playing a game of pretend in my head. In this game, I am at the baby shower with a baby strapped to my hip. I am chatting up the other women about wake windows and developmental milestones and the best hacks for calming a teething baby. I am effortless. I am fun. I am one of them.

"You seem nervous." Paloma breaks up my daydream, pointing out the purple claw marks I had drawn on my arms.

I wouldn't be so nervous if I knew who would be in attendance. Do the people coming know what happened? Do they know not to ask me if I have any kids? I wonder if Sadie and Fatima had sent out a memo to all the guests in advance of this party, something along the lines of:

> One of our dear friends, Cleo Dang, has suffered the terrible, terrible loss of her baby girl. We kindly ask you to bear that in mind, for it is a sensitive subject as you can rightfully understand. Anyway, don't forget to RSVP if you haven't already done so!

If such a memo had been sent out, I wouldn't know whether to be horrified or grateful. There is something inherently humiliating about being the subject of someone's concern. The constant check-ins. The forced gentleness. Like I am a toddler on the brink of a meltdown. I can picture it now, the sidelong glances, the tensed-up bodies, the paralyzing fear that they'll say or do the wrong thing.

Paloma tells me multiple times that I don't have to go, that she could turn this car around right this second and take me home. I tell her not to be silly. I am fine. Really, really, I am. Besides, I have a gift.

I am in a dress. I have gigantic floaties on my arms for Christ's sake. It would be preposterous to back out now.

"I'm really proud of you," Paloma says in response. "It's good you're getting out."

I pull down the sun visor mirror and apply a light layer of pink lip gloss. I practice smiling. Not too wide. Not too narrow. A little teeth. Not too much. I want it to be believable, how ecstatic I am for the couple, how delighted I am to be in the presence of all the moms and babies and bumps. I compile a cheat sheet in my head of appropriate things I can say at the baby shower:

This food is delicious!
How old is your little one?
We got really lucky with this weather, eh?

When Paloma turns onto their street, I take in a deep breath and put on the Happy Mask. It is one of many masks I have procured as of late. When I wear one of these, it helps me blend in with my environment so that I don't stand out. To the observer I appear completely fine, jovial even, like I am one of them. Nobody can see what is going on underneath. Nobody can see the sadness that strangles me.

———————

The festivities are taking place in the backyard. There are beautiful decorations everywhere. The smell of frosting hits me instantly with its sickeningly sweet notes of vanilla. All the food look like works of art. Towers of intricately piped cupcakes. Toast topped with mashed avocado and bacon. Paper bags prefilled with popcorn. Sandwiches cut up in neat little squares. Cups preloaded with zesty chickpea salad. Multiple bottles of Prosecco sitting on ice, already uncorked and ready for consumption. This is where Paloma has dashed off to, leaving me alone and at the mercy of anybody.

There are lots of people here already. Women sip champagne under the shade while toddlers chase each other around the tree. Dogs go sniffing for food that has fallen to the ground while babies practice tummy time on the grass. I try not to look at the babies and focus my attention on the dogs. I lure a corgi over with some popcorn. He likes my offering and stays close to me. Good boy.

As I rub his belly, I overhear a conversation among a group of mothers. They're all in agreement of how wonderful it is to have children, how it has injected a sense of purpose into their lives, how their hearts have expanded by a billion. Then they lower their voices and get wistful about their pre-kid days: how they miss the sex, the sleep, the sanity, the spotlessness, the silence, the scrolling and shitting in peace. Oh god, remember when you didn't have to suck the shit back up because somebody was banging on the door screaming MOMMY MOMMY? Once the confessions have been expelled like a much-needed exorcism, they return to their original volume and reaffirm how much they love their children and would never, ever change a thing and how maybe, just maybe, they'll go ahead and have another one.

There's a relaxed certainty in which they talk about having more babies, like it's a done deal. Like it's as easy as ordering another round of bread for the table.

Someone drops a plate of cubed cheese and the corgi abandons me. I'm alone again. That traitor.

"Cleo, con ơi!"

My mother is here. Why is my mother here?

"Are you surprised to see Mummy?"

"What are you doing here?"

"What do you mean what am I doing here? Sadie's mom and I go to the same aqua fit class. You're the one who introduced us!"

Right, that was me.

"You look very pretty. Is this new?" She touches my arm floaties.

"It's Paloma's."

"Paloma! She's here? How's she doing?"

"Fine," I say. "We drove here together actual—"

"Why haven't you replied to my texts?"

I stop chewing my popcorn, taken aback by her tone. "I've been meaning to," I lie.

She scrunches her eyebrows, then with a soft voice says, "I've been lighting incense for her every night."

"You have?" This is the first time I'm hearing of this. Joss sticks are typically lit for gods, ancestors, and the deceased, to pray for their peace. The thought of your photo, perched high up on an altar before a statue of the Bodhisattva and photos of your great-grandparents, gives me a kind of comfort I didn't know I needed.

"I laid out some fruit this morning," she says. "And a small cup of milk. I think Daisy would like that very much."

Tears fall down her face, creating streaks through her foundation. She dabs at them to avoid smearing her makeup. Watching her cry triggers an avalanche of tears behind my eyes, too, but no, no, not today. I tighten the straps on my Happy Mask, sealing up all that's underneath. I will not cry. Not here. Not during such a happy occasion. Must not disrupt the atmosphere of this gorgeously sunny Sunday with my tears. Unless they are happy tears, of course. Happy tears are allowed.

Now that my mother has come up to me, so do other people. I'm like a traffic accident nobody wants to approach until someone does it first.

Darcie, Julianna, and Flora all come over and say hello. We talk about time, how it goes by so fast and it seemed like yesterday we all graduated from university. We talk about Julianna's cute ice-cream earrings and how nobody wears statement earrings anymore. We talk about the catered food, how delicious and beautifully presented it all is. We laugh when one of the dogs humps Darcie's leg. It's a great time. Everyone is in a good mood. The Happy Mask is working.

An ear-piercing screech forces our attention towards a hysterically giddy toddler who's holding what appears to be a chunk of feces. We watch in horror as the mother uses her bare hands to free the feces from his grip. Flora looks back at us, her eyes black holes of disgust, before exclaiming how wildly happy she is to be child-free. I stare at her with longing, so free, so unencumbered, and I bring my hand to my vacant belly, wishing I had not wanted this, either.

Sadie's sister calls on all of us to gather around and play a game. It's a trivia! About babies! And there are prizes! Despite my best efforts at not participating, I can't stand by as everyone continues to shout the wrong answers. How do they not know that babies are born with three hundred bones? That they can simultaneously breathe and swallow during the first three months of life? That the first color they see is red? I find myself whipping my hand in the air and spitting out the answers over and over again.

There are some questions that throw me for a loop, though. For instance, I didn't know a baby's DNA can transfer to the mother's bloodstream, that the fetal cells embed themselves in her organs and tissues, remaining there for decades.

"So when people say your baby is a part of you, it's not just hyperbole. It is quite literal," the sister tells the whole group.

Is it really true? That you're still in me? I wipe away the tears before anybody can see and focus on answering the remaining questions.

Points are counted and the results are irrefutable. I win. The prize is a snake plant. I walk up and claim my reward, reading the card that comes with the plant. Its Latin name is *dracaena trifasciata*. It's native to tropical and subtropical regions of Asia and Africa. It should be watered every two weeks and the soil should be dry before watering. It likes direct sunlight but will tolerate indirect light, too. It's most famous for being incredibly difficult to kill.

I look at the plant and name it after my favorite vengeful hero. Keanu Leaves.

He looks hardy and resilient.

I fear I will find a way to kill him somehow.

Just when I think I might make it through the baby shower, someone brings up the big terrible thing, followed by another person and another person. When you're grieving, people are curious to know how you're doing. They soften their eyes and hug you just a little longer and tighter than usual. When you tell them you're hanging in there—or some proverbial expression like that—they commend you for being so strong.

Internally, they're picturing themselves in your shoes and you can see it on their face, the fear. You are their worst nightmare. The possibility is too much for them to bear, so they change the subject. You don't mind. You play along because, like them, you would rather pretend the big terrible thing never happened.

One woman marvels at the fact that I'm even at this party. She asks if I've returned to work and when I tell her I have, her eyes glimmer with amazement. She looks at me like I've just pulled off the greatest magic trick of all time and, with a genuine expression on her face, asks, "How do you do it?"

I want to ask what she means by "it." But I keep mum, not wanting to prolong this interaction, and let her question hang awkwardly between us.

She shakes her head. "I think I would die if anything happened to my children." She sheds a tear. Tears for me or for her hypothetically dead children? "I just don't think I could do it."

She dabs her eyes and blows her nose. I know she's trying to empathize but all my brain hears is: *You must not love your child as much as I love mine since you are here, alive, attending this fabulous party in that pompously hideous dress.*

A tray of shrimp cocktail emerges from the kitchen, and I use that as a reason to excuse myself.

There's a dog at my feet with a bright orange vest that says "ANXIOUS, DO NOT PET." I wish I had a vest like that. My vest would say "BABY DIED, DO NOT APPROACH." It would've come in handy at the cupcake tower when somebody asked if I was eating for two. Or when a toddler pointed at my postpartum pooch and shouted for everyone to hear, "Are you going to poop out the baby?" Or when Fatima's great-aunt wondered why I hadn't had any kids yet and insisted I "chop-chop" before all my eggs shrivel up like hers.

A vest would be useful in situations like these. Maybe I can start an Etsy shop. Maybe I can offer a variety of colors and fonts. Maybe there are hundreds of mothers out there waiting desperately for somebody to invent this vest.

———

When I finally get a moment alone with Sadie and Fatima, the first thing they say to me is: "It's really good to see you."

I smile back and say the things I rehearsed in the car.

Congratulations!
You must be so excited.
Better get some rest while you still can.

We talk about their birth plan and how they've already prepared a playlist for when Sadie goes into labor. Mostly orchestral music from their favorite fantasy games. Sadie goes on to explain how she would prefer to give birth without the epidural and how she read an article about music being an effective method of pain relief. I tell her that's such a smart idea and refrain from exposing the truth of how terribly painful it is to give birth without anesthesia.

They thank me for the bottle sterilizer and tell me my presence means so much to them. "Of course, I wouldn't miss it for the world." I'm surprised at how well the conversation is going. My words flow out like a stream. I remember to smile as they talk, and laugh when they make a joke. It helps that they're old friends—friends who have desperately wanted a child and have undergone failed embryo transfers over the years. They know what it's like to dream of a future of cuddles and kisses, only to later have it dismantled. I feel a kinship to them. And because of this, their happiness doesn't hurt me the way other people's happiness does.

Until the baby kicks.

"Oh my god, she's kicking so much!" Sadie says, pressing both hands to her belly. "Hurry, feel this, Fatima!"

I watch as they brush their hands across Sadie's belly, awing each time they feel movement. Look at them, holding their entire future in their hands. So sweet.

"I'm just so happy for you guys," I say. Except my voice cracks on the last word.

Shit.

My throat feels tight.

My eyes fill with tears.

My face scrunches up.

The Happy Mask is slipping off.

No, no, no.

Sadie starts to tear up, too, and I tell her, please please please don't cry, I'm fine, really I am. But my voice goes squeaky when I talk and all that does is make Sadie cry some more. Now mascara is running down her professionally made-up face and Fatima is consoling her while I apologize profusely for making her cry at her own baby shower. I hand her some napkins, but Fatima tells me to give her some space.

"The doctor says she needs to avoid stress right now," Fatima tells me.

I take a few steps back.

People are now coming up to Sadie and asking what happened, whether she is okay, if there is anything she needs. Then one by one, they all look at me like I'm a monster. Who makes a pregnant woman cry?

My chest tightens. My throat tickles. My skin goes damp with sweat.

I am a monster.

I am all of their worst nightmares.

All the commotion sets off a sleeping infant, who shrieks so loudly it upsets all the other babies, and now all the day-drunk mothers are moaning that their kids have been abruptly awakened.

Suddenly I'm back in the hospital.

I'm pushing and pushing and pushing. I'm pushing so hard I think my eyeballs might burst and my teeth might break. The doctor tells me to keep going, that I'm doing so good, so I keep pushing and think of nothing else but getting you out, and when you finally emerge, my body collapses with relief. The doctor puts you on my chest and I'm amazed at how breathtaking you are. We await your first cry, but it doesn't come. You seem to be struggling, like you're choking on something. The doctor takes you away from me and I keep waiting to hear you cry but you never do. All I hear is the doctor telling the nurses to go get something right away, now! His voice is hurried, and I notice his hands are trembling.

Somebody yanks my arm and I'm back at the baby shower. No doctors. No nurses. Just moms bouncing their babies and begging their toddlers to put their shoes on while Sadie is sitting in the shade being fanned and handed an ice-cold drink. Paloma ushers me away from the frenzy.

"Putrefaction," she says.

"W-what?"

"Come on, I think it's time to go."

In the car, I lower the window all the way down to get some air. I think about putting my head through the window and raising the glass towards my neck. What if something happens to Sadie's baby and it's all my fault?

"You did nothing wrong," Paloma says unprompted.

"I ruined their baby shower."

"You didn't ruin anything. It was a lovely event. Those pregnancy hormones make people so emotional. You know that."

I say nothing for the remainder of the ride. I shouldn't have come here. The Buddhists believe if you attend a wedding shortly after attending a funeral, you will soil the newlyweds with your bad juju. Maybe the same applies to baby showers. Maybe I have soiled their matrescence.

The snake plant is in my lap; I didn't realize Paloma had carried it out. I run my finger along the edges of its thick, swordlike leaves. Not sharp enough to draw blood.

I stare at the long-haul trucks on the highway and picture one of those giant tires coming loose and barreling towards us at a hundred kilometers an hour. I would die on impact, but Paloma's life would be spared. People would be sad. They would mourn for a while. Then they would move on. Everybody always moves on.

"What's going on inside that head of yours?" Paloma says when we leave the highway.

"Nothing."

Except everything.

"You will have what they have one day," she says. "Don't give up hope."

A ball of grief forms in my throat and I swallow it whole.

I don't want just any child.

I want you.

16

There's a drug to treat grief: acetaminophen. Yes, the active ingredient in Tylenol. The everyman's drug. Used to treat migraines, sore muscles, toothaches, menstrual cramps, colds, and fevers. It's part of a class of medication known as analgesics, which are designed specifically to relieve physical pain. New evidence has emerged suggesting these painkillers can also blunt emotional pain, as well as suppress any negative thoughts of death. Since physical pain and social pain share the same neurochemical pathways, the drug treats both types of pain as if they are one and the same.

When I bring up this neat little fact to Kenneth and suggest we leave out glass bowls of Tylenol throughout the facilities for our guests, he looks at me like I've lost my head. I whip my head back and laugh a loud and obnoxious laugh so that he thinks it was just a joke. He laughs in return, tells me *good one*, and we are silent once again, our eyes returning to our computers.

It's a slow day at the funeral home. There's a list of things I could be doing. Cleaning the hearse. Hounding doctors for death certificates. Filing burial permits with the city. None of it sounds appealing to me. I'm so bored I blurt out an intrusive question to Kenneth. "Do you ever cry?"

He looks up, answering me like it was a normal thing to ask. "It's been a while but yes, I have shed a tear or two."

"Do you remember why you cried?" I know my questions are invasive but I'm curious to see if he takes the bait.

"I tend not to focus on the negatives. I'd rather focus on the reasons why I don't cry, like this weather for instance. What a gorgeous day we're having, eh?" He beams as he stares out at the tranquil blue sky, a sight that elicits no emotion from me. How does someone get to be so happy? He's probably someone who wakes up every day feeling grateful to be alive, who sings as he waits for the coffee to brew, who stops to pay respect to a million-year-old tree. It all feels unnatural to me, this zest for life.

I return to my emails, skimming the promotions folder to see if there are any sales that catch my eye. The old me was a diligent spender, never going over budget, never purchasing extraneous things. The new me buys everything without friction. A new pair of running shoes made of high-density foam. A three-wick candle that smells of smoked rum. A percussive massage device that relieves sore muscles. A fluffy shag rug to go beside the bed so that my feet are shrouded in softness the moment I wake up. With every click of that Buy Now button, a spark ignites within me and the sadness dissipates, the void in my heart gone. I feel in control. What I want I get. What I see is mine. I chase that feeling over and over again, paying no mind to the monthly statements that warn me of my depleting credit limit.

I scroll through today's promotions. The higher the discount, the faster my heart beats.

35% Off EVERYTHING
50% Off ALL Bathing Suits
FINAL HOURS: Save 60% Storewide

My eyes stop on a particular subject line: *How are you enjoying your new car seat?*

I click on the email.

Hi Cleo,
We hope you and your little bundle of joy are enjoying the
BumbleBee Infant Car Seat. By now you've probably taken baby
out to explore the world, so we wanted to send a quick reminder to
never leave your baby unattended in the car seat, even when they are
buckled in.

We would love to hear from you, so please consider leaving a star rating in the link provided below.

Thank you for riding with us!

I search frantically for the tiny blue unsubscribe link and click it.

I haven't seen the car seat since that day we got home from the hospital. It's tucked away in a closet somewhere. I still remember the neighbor's reaction when we got home. She knew we were expecting, even dropped off a warm peach cobbler during the last weeks of my pregnancy, and waited eagerly for the baby's arrival. When we pulled into the driveway, she ran over to greet us, screaming, "Oh my god, the baby's here! Let me see that darling little angel!" After peeking inside the car seat and seeing there was no baby, her entire face turned gray with dread. We did not have to say a word. She knew.

The display room is in the back of the funeral home. This is where we showcase a selection of our finest merchandise including caskets, urns, liners, and burial clothing. Not everyone comes back here. Most of the families purchase directly off the catalog over the phone. But a handful prefer to come in person to see and feel the merchandise for themselves. It's a big decision after all, choosing your loved one's eternal resting bed. You don't want to get it wrong. No refunds or exchanges.

A fully lined, half-couch casket sits in the middle of the room. It's our bestselling item. Made of solid pecan wood cut from the deciduous trees of southeastern United States, its rich brown color and natural dark grain—and competitive price, might I add—is the number-one pick among countless families.

I take a damp cloth and clean the dust on the casket. One wipe reveals a thick layer of gray fuzz, suggesting this casket has not been washed in a while. I go to town, scrubbing every crevice until it's shining. Once the exterior has been cleaned, I take out the mattress and bedding set and fluff them out. The steps to making a casket bed are not much different than making a regular bed. I stretch the fitted sheet over the thin mattress. Carefully lay down the cover sheet. Position the pillow at the head of the casket. Finally, I smooth out any wrinkles in the crepe material.

The casket calls to me. *Come and rest your head.*

I look at it. I could use a rest.

I hoist myself up and slump down onto the bed. I close the lid and picture my funeral.

Everyone says they want their funeral to be a celebration of life, one where all their friends and family dress in bright colors and party in their honor and regale each other with funny anecdotes. Like what Rachel's friend had.

I don't want that.

I want everyone to wear black. I want my casket to be open. I want everyone to peer down at my dead body. I want every single cheek to be wet with tears. I want sad songs blasting from the speakers. I want clouds colliding and thunder clapping. I want speeches that tug at the heart and twist it beyond recognition. Most of all, I want everyone to know I died because of you. That my love for you reached the depths of the ocean and the heights of the earth and split the world in two. I want them to incinerate my body, reducing it to its most basic fragments, and then I want them to mix my remains with yours like we're flour and sugar so that we may never be separated again.

"If you follow me this way, I can show you our collection of caskets."

Shit. It's Kenneth. He's coming this way.

I push the lid open and jump out of the casket. I flatten my hair and straighten the creases in my pants.

When Kenneth shows up with a customer, I quickly fix up the bedding.

"Ah, Cleo, perfect! If you don't mind, could you please show Mr. Garrison around?"

I nod. "Glad to."

"Great, you're in good hands, Mr. Garrison. Cleo knows our collection inside and out."

———

Kenneth tells me he has to leave early for an appointment and that he'll see me in the morning. Perfect. I'll have the entire office to myself. When he's gone, I immediately fiddle with the combination lock again.

I try his birth year. 1-9-5-3. Nope.

His birth month and birth date. 0-2-1-6. Nope.

Maybe 1-6-0-2? Nope.

His birth date, repeated. 1-6-1-6. Nope.

His childhood address. 2-9-0-6. Dammit.

The more failed attempts, the more I'm convinced Kenneth is hiding something. Who makes their combination so difficult to guess unless they're hiding something so sinful, so depraved it would ruin their entire life?

Suddenly there's a knock on the door. It's Ana the mortician. She asks if I have a free moment and if I wouldn't mind helping her prepare a body. At first I hesitate, but Ana appears desperate, telling me it will only take half an hour and I will be back at my desk before I know it.

Even though she spends most of her days in a bright, cold, windowless room, Ana is astonishingly pretty. Auburn pixie cut, rosy cheeks against clear brown skin, long lashes coated with mascara. I find the makeup endearing because in her line of work, it is entirely optional.

She instructs me to put on personal protective equipment and as I do, she tells me the deceased woman's name is Leona, sixty-two years old. "Heart cancer, if you can believe it."

Ana tells me that primary cardiac tumors are very rare, affecting 1.38 in 100,000 people each year. That's because the heart is made up of specialized muscle cells that rarely divide, making cancer extremely abnormal. Even if there was a tumor, it's usually benign, nothing a little surgery can't fix, so to die from a malignant tumor means you would have to get really, really, really unlucky.

I feel so bad for Leona. I wonder if she ever fell to her knees asking, *Why me? Why me?* I know I have.

Ana takes me to Leona's body. The first thing I notice is the skin on her hands, the color and warmth that peeks through her freckled knuckles. Ana has done a good job painting the pink back into her skin. From her forehead to her fingertips, it's as if she is blushing with life.

She has no hair, most likely as a result of chemotherapy, but her family has provided a wig. California blond locks with layers, highlights, and thick side-swept bangs. Ana tells me this wig is made of virgin hair from Mongolia, the highest quality on the market. How it must have run them thousands of dollars.

"Holy shit!" I blurt out.

"You won't believe how much people spend on funerals."

"I guess it's worth it to the family. It's the last gift they'll ever be able to give."

"Actually, Leona bought this herself."

"She did?"

"That's what her kids said. When the doctor told her things weren't looking good, she went online and ordered the prettiest, most expensive wig she could find because she said there was no way in hell she was getting buried as a baldy!"

A loud cackle escapes my mouth, a sound so foreign and startling it makes me feel momentarily alive. Ana gently brushes the wig, smoothing out all the tangles and knots. She asks me to hold the wig as she carefully lifts Leona's head. She instructs me to slip the wig on and I do so, slowly and delicately, like I'm crowning a member of royalty. We readjust her wig so it sits where her natural hairline would have been. We sweep the hair across her shoulders, framing her face in a way that doesn't hide any of her features. Once we get it to where we like it, I take a step back. The hair brings out her eyebrows and cheekbones. And though her eyes and lips are sealed, you can tell she lit up every room she entered. Leona, the belle of the ball, the life of the party.

For her clothing, the family chose a sequinned, skin-toned dress with fluttery sleeves. It's the dress she wore to her son's wedding. I know because the family has included a photo of her for reference. In the photo she's resting her head on her son's chest, beaming from ear to ear. Upon closer inspection, her eyes look slightly puffy, as if she had been crying, as if she had been wondering how her cherubic little boy got to be so big and grown. She's practically clutching at him, like she knew there wouldn't be much time left.

The dress is hung up on a rack. It's stunning. From every angle it glimmers like fireflies at night. Ana has cut the back so it's easier to put on. We make sure the dress is symmetrical across her chest, tighten the fabric around her shoulders, and tuck in the sides with pins. Once it's perfect, we both agree she looks like a movie star. Like a Farrah Fawcett or a Goldie Hawn.

We finish with accessories. Diamond stud earrings, platinum tennis bracelet, and a rosary draped around her left hand, as requested by the family. I notice a tattoo on the inside of her arm. It's a lemon tree branch wrapped around her forearm with a name delicately inscribed underneath: Hannah. I wonder who Hannah could be. A sister, a friend, a lover, a daughter?

"Her best friend," Ana answers before I even utter a word. "They've known each other since they were just kids. She'll be giving a eulogy at the service. Such a sweet woman."

I think about Paloma being dead and what I would say at her funeral, but the thought goes no further than that because my gut instantly fills with dread. I can't imagine losing another person I love.

"Did you know you can preserve tattoos after death?" Ana says.

"Like in photographs?" I ask.

"No, like in the flesh."

"You mean—"

"Yep. Once the skin gets extracted, it undergoes a special preservation process and then gets put into a nice frame and shipped to the family."

"Oh."

I want to wince but remember to keep my expression neutral. My mind whips back to a paragraph in the employee manual.

Here at Monarch Funeral Homes, we believe grief looks different on everyone, which is why employees should strive to withhold judgment on how clients choose to mourn. Grief is an individual and idiosyncratic experience. It is diverse from culture to culture, person to person. There is no right way to grieve, no timeline for healing. As employees, we must practice compassion, patience, and openness with every single person who walks through those doors.

I can't lie and say I haven't passed judgment on other people for the way they grieve. Years ago, Ethan openly wept at the news that Regis Philbin had died of a heart attack. I balked and reminded him that he had never even met the guy. As soon as I said this, Ethan lifted his head out of his hands and looked at me like I was Satan. "What does that matter? I grew up watching him. *Who Wants to Be a Millionaire* was a staple of my childhood." He continued to cry, which made little sense to me. I wanted to cheer him up. So I pointed out that Regis Philbin was eighty-eight years old. A long life by any measure. He had a wonderful career, was adored by millions, left behind a legacy that will live on for generations. I hoped saying all this would knock some sense into him and demonstrate that the level of sadness he was experiencing had not been earned.

It didn't work. He didn't talk to me for days.

It's all coming back to me now, the horrible things I said to people in their worst moments and thinking I was helpful.

What I said to Paloma when her childhood dog had died. "You can always get another one."

What I said to my father when his ninety-eight-year-old mother was dying. "At least you don't have to worry about her anymore."

What I thought to myself when I watched a TikTok of someone filming themselves crying over the death of a friend. "Craving attention much?"

I think about the royal family—how the world lambasted them for not flying the flag at half-staff or releasing a statement in the immediate aftermath of Princess Diana's death.

"SHOW US YOU CARE," the headlines pleaded.

"HAS THE HOUSE OF WINDSOR A HEART?" wondered the British press.

The public begged and begged for the family to put their grief on display, for them to grieve in the manner that was deemed most appropriate. We picked apart their reaction and judged them for grieving too little and not enough.

I wonder what people think of me, what they say when I'm not around. Would they think it strange that I sleep beside my baby's ashes tucked inside her bassinet? Or that I run my baby's pictures through an AI generator to see what she might have looked like when she's five, ten, twenty? Or that I sneak inside my best friend's house and read bedtime stories to her infant's plush dumpling? I never want to find out.

Once Ana puts on the final touches of makeup, Leona looks perfect. Her service is not until the morning, so we gently close her casket for the night. Ana thanks me for helping and tells me I'm free to go. I try to go but my legs freeze up and I'm left lingering awkwardly in front of her. There's a question I've been meaning to ask, a question I'm certain she's been waiting for.

As if she's read my mind, Ana pulls me in for a really long hug.

"I see the resemblance," says Ana.

"You do?"

"Kenneth told me you're the mother of that sweet little pea. Now that I'm standing in front of you, it's so evident: Daisy is the spitting image of you."

I try to hold back tears. "Really?"

"She was absolutely beautiful."

"Y-you remember her?"

"I think about her every day."

Tears well up in Ana's eyes, which surprises me. For someone who is around death on a very intimate basis, I didn't expect her to be so emotional. I thought the key to succeeding in this profession was to put up walls, commit yourself to apathy, and remind yourself that death is as normal as life itself.

"As you know, we don't see babies very often and when we do, we take care of them with deep reverence. I can assure you your baby was cared for like she was one of our own children. Daisy left a huge mark on me. On all of us here. We told her she was loved every day."

My eyes sting with tears. I don't know what to say back. Until now it was a complete unknown, those unaccounted days from when we left you at the hospital to the morning of your funeral. Where had you gone? Who was looking after you? Were you warm and safe and snug?

"It was the honor of my life to dress her, and I just want to thank you for putting your trust in us," Ana continues. "Did you pick her outfit? If so, I'd say you have a promising career as a baby stylist."

An unexpected chuckle comes out of me. I'm grateful for her switch in tone. The levity briefly slows the buildup of sorrow in my throat, giving me a chance to breathe.

I tell her I can't take full credit. It was all Ethan. Two days after the doctors pronounced you dead, we were desperate to get away from the thick tendrils of sadness clinging to every single surface of our house, so we went to the mall. We hoped being around all the noise and people and music would anchor us to the living world. We bought new salt and pepper shakers, new forks and spoons, new throw blankets made from one hundred percent natural Alpaca fiber. We walked over to Crate & Barrel and bought the most expensive couch on display. The store clerk said the fabric was kid-friendly and we simply nodded as we swiped our credit card.

When we left that store, that's when Ethan spotted the daisy-print mustard romper in a window display. He pointed to it and said, "That's the one." We walked inside, found the dress on the rack, and pulled out the smallest size we could find. We brought it up to the counter where the cashier applauded our selection.

"This is *soo* cute. Did you just have a baby?"

Ethan and I awkwardly shuffled our feet and sheepishly nodded. We didn't have the strength to put to words our reality, so we faked it just to survive the interaction. The lady beamed. "Congratulations! I guess you aren't sleeping much these days, huh?"

I mustered a smile to match the cashier's excitable energy. Even Ethan played along. "Do the bags under my eyes give it away?" he said, following up with the fakest laugh I'd ever heard from him. A laugh so unrecognizable I thought he was having a stroke. When we walked out of that store, we both felt sick to our stomachs.

The thing about faking happiness is that your body can always tell.

"That must've been very hard for you," says Ana. "Thank you for sharing that."

"Everything feels upside down. It's like I'm in someone else's story and I just keep waiting to switch back." I'm surprised to find myself opening up. Since working here, I thought I'd be limiting exchanges to quick head nods and cursory statements about the weather. I had no interest in fostering real relationships because that meant putting your-self out there, sharing your stories, and I couldn't bear talking about your death over and over again.

Ana is different. She draws words out of me with ease. She shows an endless capacity to be with my sadness. With her, I don't need to wear any of my masks.

"Do you want to say more about that?" she asks.

"I don't know how to describe it. I just felt like I was out of my body. Like I was watching myself walk aimlessly around that mall going from one store to the next. It didn't even feel like it was me down there. I don't know if that makes sense. God, I don't even know what I'm say-ing. It all sounds so cliché."

"It's cliché for a reason," Ana says. "It's very normal to feel that way. That is just your brain's way of protecting you when you're feeling over-whelmed. Our bodies are very intelligent in that way."

I pause, a new thought occurring to me. "Can I ask you a question?"

"Sure."

"What happens after we die?"

Ana scratches her head as if she's never thought about it before. Surely she has a theory or two about the afterlife.

"As an agnostic person, I don't believe in a heaven or hell. The only thing I know for certain is that when you die, you are never, ever com-ing back to life."

I slump my shoulders, disappointed that her answer is not more groundbreaking.

"But," she continues, "I think we come to life in people's minds. The memories of us that once remained dormant in other people are roused so that we can live again. That's why we live, right? To safekeep stories of the dead."

Ana walks me back to my desk and asks if she can fetch me a glass of water. I shake my head, telling her I'm fine. I thank her for letting me be a part of Leona's dressing. She tells me I was a tremendous help and gives me another long hug.

When Ana leaves, I close the door. I lower the blinds. And I pull up a video of you on my phone. You are sleeping. Your cheeks are rosy. Your hair is feathery. A tube runs through your mouth. Leads are placed on your chest and stomach. There are little animals on them. A duck. A frog. A bear. An elephant. The animals move up and down as you breathe. I turn up the volume to hear your breathing, but all I can hear is the beeping of the machine. I play the video over and over again, hoping in one of the replays your eyes will flutter open.

I squeeze my eyes shut, remembering the first time I changed your diaper. How proud I felt for doing it on my own, for navigating the various tubes and wires that connected you to the life support machines, only to be told by the nurse that I had put the diaper on backwards. I know, for certain, if I had more practice, I would have gotten better.

Suddenly I'm hit with a flashback.

The respiratory therapists are removing the tubes from your face, stopping the flow of oxygen keeping you artificially alive. My fists are tight. My knuckles white. I want to tell them to stop, even though Ethan and I agreed it was time. As we watch them weave the wires through the openings in your onesie, a sound suddenly trickles out of your mouth. A soft, pitchy, drawn-out sigh. She's alive! She's okay! She's making baby noises! I tell them. But the respiratory therapists shake their heads, explaining the sound is a result of excessive respiratory secretions.

The flashback ends as quickly as it begins and I'm back at my desk, the video of you playing on a loop from my phone. My neck and back crumple from the weight of remembering. All that's left to do is to sob—body-racking cries—in the desperate hope that you might hear them, wherever you are.

17

My calendar informs me I have a postpartum checkup with Dr. Posey. I don't want to go. When I call in the morning to cancel, the receptionist threatens to charge my credit card $200.

"Are you serious?" I blurt out. "That's absurd!"

She responds in a rather sassy tone, "It's quite a bargain compared to the costs you would incur should you let a postpartum infection go untreated for weeks. Worse if you are unfortunate enough to develop a life-threatening abscess in your pelvic wall, but I'm sure you're fine. You'd know it if you had it. The smell coming from your genitals could wake up a hibernating bear. Could evacuate an entire population. Could tip the economy into a recession—"

"Fine, I'll keep the appointment."

I opt not to drive. I don't trust myself to not veer into oncoming traffic. So I walk. I'm on the sidewalk waiting for the red light to change. There's a baby beside me. About four or five months old. As you should have been. It's strapped inside a carrier. It's got long lashes, fat ankles, and ears that stick out. A sock perilously hangs off one foot, about to fall to the ground any moment now. The mother doesn't notice, so I reach out and pull the sock up.

The mother swiftly turns her baby away from me. "What the hell are you doing?"

Her reaction startles me. "I was just—the sock was—"

"Get the hell away from us!"

The light turns green and the mother marches across the road in a huff. She looks back and screams, "You can't go around touching other people's babies!"

People are staring at me now. They are holding their children tighter.

They are crossing the road to avoid me. One person is recording me on their phone.

I put on my hood and walk faster than I've ever walked.

My heart turns into a brick, its rough edges grinding against my thoracic wall. The air feels like molasses—too viscous to enter my lungs. It's hard to breathe. Why are my clothes so tight? Why is everything so loud? Why are you not here?

I look at the time on my phone.

I'm going to be late. If I'm late, they'll charge me $200. I keep on moving. The rest of the way, I remain silent, crushed, glum. I don't dare make eye contact with another baby. I fear I will do something wrong again. Like I'm hardwired to hurt them. Maybe that's the kind of person I am—the kind who shouldn't be a mother.

I'm five minutes late, but Dr. Posey is fifteen minutes later. The sassy receptionist asks me to put on a mask, sanitize my hands, and wait in the waiting room.

There are two other people waiting: an elderly man with a terrible coughing fit and a large-chested woman who has heavily doused herself in bad perfume. I do some quick math in my head and choose a seat that's as far as possible from both individuals.

CP24 is playing on the television. I read one devastating headline after another.

The deadline to cut global emissions in half came and went.

An apartment fire sends eight people to the hospital.

A commuter was stabbed in an unprovoked attack while riding the bus, the fifth assault on public transit this month. The chair of the Toronto Transit Commission appears on the screen, assuring the public there is no need to be alarmed. "Hundreds of millions of riders get to where they're going safely and it cannot be said enough, the TTC is one of the safest transit systems in the world. I repeat, one of the *safest* transit systems in the world."

He goes on to list several statistics. How the rate of offenses against riders is historically low at 2.15 incidents per one million boardings.

How the types of offenses have become less aggressive in nature. How the presence of special constables has triple-folded since the year before. Translation: Chill out, you worrywarts!

I think about that poor person who got stabbed. They were just minding their business, trying to go places as we all do, and now they're probably lying in a hospital bed right now, watching TV to distract from the pain of having been impaled by a knife, until they see this headline splashed across the screen: "RIDING TRANSIT IS SAFER THAN EVER."

When you've been on the wrong side of statistics like I have, like Leona has, numbers mean shit. You no longer trust the data. You stop putting faith in it. All the facts and figures could tell you your biggest fear is an improbability but you'll still feel as if doom is around the corner.

"Cleo?"

Dr. Posey is wearing a purple polka-dotted turtleneck tucked inside pink polka-dotted pants. She is sporting some kind of patent leather loafer in a bright orange color. There's red lipstick smeared across her pale, wrinkly chin. She looks like a clown. And she smells of mothballs.

I proceed to take a seat, but she stops me and hugs me tightly. I do not expect this, so my arms dangle uncomfortably on the sides of my body. I hear her sniffling. Then I feel a cold sensation spread across my shoulder. Is her nose dripping on my shirt?

She pulls away and gathers herself.

"Is everything okay?" I murmur.

"Honey, *I* should be the one asking *you* that!"

I'm taken aback but this unusual display of empathy on her part. As I wait for her to ask me how I'm doing, she turns towards her computer and starts hitting the keys with unmethodical intensity. She asks me to verify my name, address, birthday, and the number of children I have.

I freeze.

"Oops," she says. "My bad, I was just going off the sheet. Full name please?"

I answer, even though I know she knows who I am.

"Now tell me, I've always been meaning to ask you, is Dang really your last name? It's not a stage name of some sort?"

"No. I don't need a stage name. I work in insurance. Or used to, rather."

"Right," she responds, peering at me over her thick-rimmed glasses. "And your birthday?"

After I tell her, she pulls up a calculator on the screen. She types in the current year, then subtracts it by my birth year.

"Thirty-five, eh? Are you aware pregnancies past this age pose significant dangers to the mother and child?"

I nod. She has given me this lecture on three different occasions.

"Nothing you can really do about it now. Though I do know of some tinctures that will improve the effectiveness of your uterus. Works wonders. You'll have the uterus of a nineteen-year-old again. Terrible bloating, however."

Dr. Posey vigorously clicks her mouse and pulls up some records.

"I know we spoke on the phone recently, but it looks like the last time I saw you in person was . . ."

I remember. I was thirty-six weeks pregnant. Swollen, agitated, and wild with happiness. It was spring. Tulips were in bloom. Temperatures had hit the double digits and you still had a heartbeat.

Now it's fall. All the flowers are dead, and I may as well be, too.

The sorrow in my body screams through flesh and bones, exiting through my eyes. My crying is not silent nor still. It's the kind that commands touch, closeness, acknowledgment. But Dr. Posey does not offer any of those. Instead she asks me to strip down and lie on the bed. I put my legs on the stirrups and stare up at a very bright white light. She tells me to scoot down further so she can get a better look. Is there something down there that requires extra scrutiny? Have the sutures busted wide open? Are they brimming with infectious pus?

"Good news. Your incisions are healing perfectly," says Dr. Posey. "It's like you never even had the baby."

I stare at her, incredulous. "What did you just say?"

She doesn't pick up on my indignant tone and tells me to sit up. "If you wish, you may proceed with bearing more children to replace the one you lost. You may be what we call advanced maternal age but don't let that stop you. We've got people in their forties popping out kids like it's champagne."

Dr. Posey straps the blood pressure monitor on me and looks at the gauge for what feels like an awfully long time. I'm hung up on something she said. *Replace.* The cuff tightens uncomfortably around my arm. I wish it was around my neck.

After mumbling something to herself, she goes back to her computer and types with vigorous energy again.

"Any lightheadedness or dizzy spells when you stand?" she asks, still looking at the screen.

Yes. "Nope."

"And how is your appetite lately?"

Nonexistent. "Fine."

"Wonderful," she responds, finally turning around to look at me. "Now I'm going to touch your breasts. Just a warning: My hands are a little cold."

A few weeks ago, I would have shuddered at the thought of my breasts being touched, but thanks to the bromocriptine, the engorgement has diminished significantly and I'm back to having the small milkless breasts of my dreams.

With two cold fingers, she presses firmly around my nipples in a circular motion. The sensation triggers something in me and a paroxysm of grief takes over again. I'm startled by my reaction, but Dr. Posey doesn't seem disturbed whatsoever. She proceeds with the exam and assures me it is very normal to cry when being caressed.

"Physical touch can activate our orbitofrontal cortex," she says, her fingers traveling up towards my armpit. "That's the part of the brain that stimulates our emotions. Don't be surprised if you suddenly burst out into laughter. Do you like to laugh?"

"Um, I guess," I say between sniffles.

I can't tell if Dr. Posey is making conversation or asking as a concern for my health. Her question has a studied quality to it, like it was ripped from a routine patient questionnaire alongside *Where is the pain located?* and *Do you have a family history of this?*

"Well, you seem to be doing much better than when we last spoke," she says as I put my clothes back on. I'm not sure what on my face gives her that impression—the gush of tears or the absolute look of dejection. "But of course, I know some people can appear stronger than they actually are. So tell me the truth, how are you really?"

"Good," I lie, wanting this to be over.

Dr. Posey shoots me a baffled look. Her bedside manners may be awful, but she is an excellent detector of bullshit.

"All right fine," I say and proceed to tell her that the sadness is too unbearable, that my body cannot withstand the pain any longer, that unless she can write me a prescription for the strongest anesthetic available on the market then I might as well die.

She frowns into the computer screen. "Are you telling me you want to hurt yourself?"

"No, that's not what I mean at all."

"Then how would you die?"

I shrug. "I don't know, but every inch of me hurts so much I swear I'll die of a broken heart."

Dr. Posey laughs and laughs, each expulsion making me feel smaller. "My dear, at your age it's quite rare to die from takotsubo cardiomyopathy."

"What?"

"It's the formal name for broken heart syndrome. A weakening of your heart's left ventricle. It can be caused by acute emotional stress, such as the death of a loved one. You would know it if you had it. Have you felt any pain in your chest, arm, or shoulders? Any shortness of breath, loss of consciousness, nausea, or vomiting?"

"Yes, yes, all of that."

She strokes her chin. "Hmm. Well, like I said, you're young. It's nothing to worry about. I'll write you up for propranolol. Powerful stuff. It should dampen those strong emotions you're feeling. I give it to all my sad patients. Take this and you should make a full recovery in a matter of weeks."

"This will get rid of my grief?"

"Of course! There's nothing modern medicine can't cure." She prints off the prescription and hands it to me.

"Do you have any friends?" Dr. Posey asks.

"Yes."

"Really? You don't strike me as a sociable person. Name one friend."

"Paloma."

She cocks an eyebrow. "Why did you say it like that?"

"Like what?"

"Like she's the shit on the bottom of your shoe."

"No, I didn't."

"Yes, you did. There was so much disdain in your voice. Has she done something to you?"

I scratch an itch on my hand. "No."

"You know, it's very common for people to disappoint us in our worst moments. They either say the wrong thing or say nothing at all. They tell you they're going on a short work trip and the next thing you know they're half-naked on a beach in Bali with a woman they promised was just a colleague."

I am stunned into silence.

"Take it from me," she continues, "if there's someone in your life that's sucking your energy, cut them out now. They're a cancer. They'll just spread and spread and spread."

I ponder her words. Paloma wasn't a cancer, though. By all accounts she's been an incredible friend who constantly checks in on me, makes me sandwiches, cleans my home, folds my clothes, waters my plants, replaces my Brita filter. She even abstains from talking about her baby to the point where I wonder if she even has one.

If anybody is the cancer, it's me. I'm the one spreading to places I'm not wanted. Her house. Her bed. Her nursery. I'm the one who should be cut out forever.

"Can I ask you a question?" I say.

She nods.

"What happens when we die?"

She rubs the space between her eyes and looks at the time on her watch. "I can't go into all the details, but essentially your vital organs would stop working. Your heart stops beating. Your brain stops—"

"No, no," I interrupt. "I mean, what happens *after* we die?"

Dr. Posey sinks into her chair as if she's been waiting to be asked this question her whole life. "Well, the medical community has no official statement on this matter, but if you must know, I'm convinced we all become electromagnetic energy. You see these lights, this computer, this device?" She holds up her phone. "All powered by the dead. Haven't you ever wondered why we see a bright white light just before we die?"

I don't blink nor speak, processing what I've just heard. The lights momentarily flicker and Dr. Posey points up. "See? They're listening," she says. I don't know whether to roll my eyes or cast them to the ceiling. I look up at a single bulb that's rapidly blinking like it's trying to send a message. What if she's right? What if you're here in this room trying to tell me something? I want to ask Dr. Posey more questions— What are they trying to say? How do we communicate with them?— but there's a loud knock on the door.

"That's my next patient. Time to skedaddle."

I hand my prescription to a young man. He's new. He has the wide eyes and shaky awkwardness of a recent pharmacy graduate, which pleases me greatly because I'm confident I can convince him to give me twice the dosage Dr. Posey has prescribed.

"Can I see your ID please?" he says.

I roll my eyes. The downside of young pharmacists, however, is that they can be quite the Goody Two-shoes. I hand over my card.

"I'm sorry. The name on the prescription doesn't match the name on the ID."

"What?"

I look at the prescription. My name is spelled wrong. It says Chloe Dong. Fucking Posey.

"The doctor clearly made a mistake," I say.

"I can't fill the prescription as is," he insists. "You'll need to come back with the correct papers, ma'am."

"Are you fucking serious?"

His lip is trembling. He looks petrified. There's a completely stocked row of beta-blockers right behind him. I soften my eyes, untuck my hair from my ears, and pull out a hundred-dollar bill. "See behind you? Any one of those will do."

"Umm . . ." He looks back at another pharmacist, but she's occupied on a call. I tap the counter to get his attention back on me.

"You look suspicious. Don't look suspicious."

"I'm sorry. I—I can't—"

"Listen, my doctor is booked up for weeks. I need my prescription now."

He fiddles with his glasses and shrugs his shoulders. He looks like a good boy, the kind who cries at videos of dogs getting adopted. I try to exploit his empathy.

"Look, I'm very worried. I don't know what I might do if I don't get these today. I've been having these very vivid, very dark thoughts, you know what I mean, and I don't know what I'll do if I don't get what I need."

"I'm sorry you're feeling that way, ma'am. But I can't. I'll get in trouble."

"Listen here." I lower my voice, my patience waning. "If I showed up here with a knife lodged in my throat, blood spurting all over the place, would you turn me away because I didn't have the proper identification?"

"No, of course—"

"Don't you think I'd be given prompt medical care? Surgery, X-rays, antibiotics, pain relief, intravenous fluids, the whole shebang?"

"Why yes—"

"Whatever it took, I'd be given all the pharmaceutical and medical assistance I needed, you see, or else I would die."

"I don't see how this is the same."

"Are you an idiot? It's exactly the same!" I shout.

"Excuse me, can I help here?"

An older woman emerges from the back with the precision of a manager. She has deep eleven lines between her eyes and looks like she has zero tolerance for nonsense.

"I—I was just asking this young man where I could find bandages," I tell her.

"Aisle five."

"Thank you."

I shoot the young pharmacist a look of disgust before taking back my hundred-dollar bill and using it to buy a basket full of NyQuil.

18

The sound of the garbage truck jolts me out of my nightmare. I clutch my chest to make sure it's still there, that it hasn't been hollowed out by faceless monsters. I'm in one piece, but the nightmare leaves me drenched in sweat, angry red scratches up and down my arms. This has been par for the course lately, these nightmare-fueled nights. It's different every time. One night I'm being strangled by snakes. The next I'm in a car steadily tumbling down a cliff. In every single one, I always wake up before I die.

I pull back the curtain and peer out the window. The truck is gone, the sun high in the sky. Ethan is working the weekend shift, which means I'm alone, nobody to soothe me from my disturbed awakening. Every morning I have relied on the sight of Ethan's face to tether me to reality, to assure me within seconds of waking that I'm home and safe. When he's not there, I feel like I'm still in my nightmares, plummeting to the bottom of a pit lined with spikes.

Paloma's car is gone, too. Her home looks empty. This is my chance to see Dumpling.

Within minutes I'm rocking her in the chair, singing lullabies, and reading her a book about a princess that outsmarts a dragon. Then I press her against my chest and reassure her there are no such things as bad dreams as long as I'm here.

There's a cold, sticky sensation in my underwear. I check myself in the bathroom and see bright red blood on the gusset. It has seeped onto my shorts and inner thighs like a massacre. I know immediately what it is. My first postpartum period.

I want to throw up. Dr. Posey had warned me this would happen.

"Mothers who aren't breastfeeding menstruate sooner than mothers who do. It's a sign your body is ready to move on."

I ball up the underwear and throw it in the trash. There's no use scrubbing out the stain. Blood has a way of sticking around long after it's been washed out.

I step inside their shower and get the water as hot as I can bear. The smell of copper intensifies with the steam. I watch the stream of red water flow down the drain and wait for it to turn clear. I step out, still wet and dripping, and find a stack of pads in the cabinet. I sift through Paloma's underwear drawer and pull out a pair of cotton blue Hanes. She has so many, I'm sure she won't notice. I stick the pad on her underwear as fast as I can, but my swiftness is futile. Drops of blood trail behind me on the porcelain floors.

———

I rock Dumpling back and forth and hum the tune to "You Are My Sunshine." The lullaby and the motion and the NyQuil make me so drowsy that I fall asleep, just for a second, and when I wake Dumpling has fallen to the floor. I quickly pick her up and squeeze her against my chest, telling her over and over how sorry I am, how it will never happen again, how Mama was just very tired.

I need to stay awake. I pull out my phone and consume a gluttonous amount of content. Videos of startled cats falling off things. Videos of pranks between lovers gone wrong. Videos of people applying makeup while talking about a date from hell.

A video comes up of a mother whose child recently died of hypoxic-ischemic encephalopathy, the same diagnosis as you, and I stop scrolling. I watch the video too many times to count, committing the mother's story to memory, crying and nodding at every word she says. I didn't know there were others like me, others whose lives have been upended by a medical condition they can't even pronounce or spell.

Until now, I had been too scared to learn about your condition, too afraid I'll come across an article titled "SIX EASY WAYS TO PREVENT HIE AND KEEP YOUR BABY ALIVE" and then hate myself for not knowing any of this sooner. But now, after seeing one mother talk so openly about it, I type the acronym into the search bar and learn everything I possibly can.

I learn it has an incidence rate of approximately 1.5 out of 1,000 live births. It's caused when there's reduced oxygen or blood flow to the brain. It can happen whether the baby is ill or perfectly healthy. It can occur at any time before, during, or after birth. It's one of the most common causes of death among newborns. It is mostly unpreventable.

I click on another result and discover this condition has inspired the creation of multiple charity foundations, annual half marathons, and T-shirts that say "FUCK HIE." There's even a whole month dedicated to fundraising and awareness spreading.

I click on a peer-reviewed study about a groundbreaking new treatment that will decrease the mortality rates of HIE and the first use-cases of this treatment has been shown to be very promising. It is still very early, however.

I read about the mechanisms of birth-giving. I learn that with every contraction, the uterus compresses the umbilical cord and momentarily restricts the flow of oxygenated blood to the baby. According to a Stanford engineering professor, the very act of being born represents 430 micromorts, where each micromort represents a one-in-a-million chance of death, making it akin to undergoing major surgery or BASE jumping off a skyscraper. In fact, it is safer to use heroin than it is to be born or to give birth.

Next, I stumble across a forum full of parents whose babies have died. I'm astounded by all the ways they could die. There was HIE, yes, but there was also chromosomal abnormalities and preeclampsia and intrauterine growth restriction and bacterial infections and placental abruption and premature rupture and umbilical cord prolapse and SIDS and congenital heart defects and if it's none of these things, then it's something else. There is always something. And these are just the deaths with a known cause. Most of the parents in this forum don't know why their baby died.

Why hadn't I known any of this data in advance? Why hadn't I done the proper research instead of obsessing over what brand of crib mattress to buy and what hypoallergenic wipe to use? Why had no-body warned me?

I create a new profile and pose a question for all the parents in the forum. *Does it ever get better?* That's all. I don't extrapolate or provide any identifying details. I wait a couple of minutes and pretty swiftly, a few answers pour in from anonymous users.

One of my twins died in utero. I had to carry her to term and gave birth to both my children, all while knowing I could only keep one. The pain will always stay with you. It's like a scar that never goes away. But with time, it will fade and soften and you eventually get used to having the scar there all the time.

My darling boy is supposed to turn five tomorrow and I'm an absolute wreck! I wish I could say it gets better. Some days it feels like I'm doing fine and then other days I feel like I've been bludgeoned to near death. It's like the worst roller coaster ride you've ever been on and there's no stop button.

Fourteen years and counting over here. I'm not sure about better but you do get stronger. I like to think of grief as a solid boulder strapped to your back. The weight always stays the same. But if you constantly exercise the muscle, it won't feel as heavy to carry around.

People say grief shrinks over time. Personally the grief has only expanded for me. Every day, every moment they aren't here is a new loss to add to the pile. Pretty sure by the time I'm dead, the autopsy report will find nothing inside but grief for my child.

I want to reach into my phone and pull these people out so I can sit with them and have a chat, ask them more questions. How do you stop blaming yourself? Do the what-ifs ever end? What do you do with all that rage? Where do you put it? How do you get over the unfairness? Did your marriage survive? Your friendships? Would you do it all over again, knowing what you know now? From where did you find a morsel of desire to live? Can you tell me how you did it, how you got better, please, please can you help me?

I refresh the page. There are even more responses now. I can't believe how many people are answering my query. People I don't know. People who don't know me. The only thing we share is an unspeakable kind of pain. I don't deserve their stories, yet they are laying it all bare for everyone to see. Each response is considerate and thoughtful, as if they're talking to a little sister who knows nothing of what it means to live in this world.

> After our Henry died, I lost my job, my house got foreclosed, and my wife and I separated for a few years. It was awful. I'm not sure how I got through that but somehow I'm still here, sitting on a park bench eating lunch and basking in the sounds of sweet birds. So I'd say right now, things are all right.

> Do you know that feeling when you leave your house and feel like you've forgotten something? I feel like that 24/7 and it's been a decade. I will never not feel like I am missing a part of my body.

> It did for me, but I also paid thousands of dollars for therapy if you've got that kinda money kicking around.

> There are good days and bad days but the most important thing to remember is that whatever day you have will end. Nothing is permanent. Sorry for the cliché.

> There's a great quote by Julian Barnes that goes like this: "You do come out of it, that's true. After a year, after five. But you don't come out of it like a train coming out of a tunnel, bursting through the Downs into sunshine and that swift, rattling descent to the Channel; you come out of it as a gull comes out of an oil-slick. You are tarred and feathered for life."

I'm no longer the same person I was, but weirdly I prefer who I am now. I don't care anymore about how others perceive me or if I'm succeeding in life, whatever that means. That stuff doesn't matter anymore. All that matters is that I'm surviving.

I don't know if *better* is the right word, just different. It's like everything comes into focus and I see the world through a more sharpened lens. I notice the pinkness of the flowers, the softness of my dog, the sweetness of a pear, the relief of a good song. I truly never paid attention to things like that before my baby died and it's made me appreciate every day I get to live.

Before I can read the rest, my phone goes black. The battery has died and my charger is at home. I should head out anyway. I gently place Dumpling back on the shelf and do our usual bedtime routine. Three kisses, two squeezes, and *Night night, I love you forever and always*.

19

Dear diary,
Why is it that everyone seems to have an opinion when you
become a mother? This morning a woman at the grocery store told
me babies shouldn't be wearing socks, that they inhibit their toe
gripping ability. Wtf! I told her I will do with my baby as I please.
She called me stupid and walked away. But now I can't stop
doubting myself. What if she's right? What if that's why the baby
has not started crawling yet? What if I've been doing irreparable
damage? Just to be safe, I threw out all her socks.

Dear diary,
Did you know babies say dada before they say mama? What
fucking patriarchal bullshit is that? I was loading the laundry
when it came out of her. Just sitting on the tip of her tongue.
Daa-daa. Like, excuse me girl I'm the one who made you! Kidding
aside, it was very adorable.

Dear diary,
I gave the baby peanut butter for the first time and within a few
hours she developed an angry rash on her neck. I ran straight to the
emergency and they told me it wasn't an allergy rash. It was a drool
rash and that I should keep her neck folds as dry as possible.
I've never been more embarrassed in my whole life.

20

Paloma has asked me to lunch. A Mexican restaurant she's been dying to try. What could I say? She knew I didn't participate in social engagements on weekends, or really ever for that matter, but I reluctantly agreed as long as she paid.

I'm the first to arrive and there's a long line. The sidewalk is covered in yellow leaves and the winds are haphazardly scooping them up into the air. I claim my spot in line, the skin on my cheeks prickly from the leaves hitting my face. I overhear someone say it's at least a forty-five-minute wait. Living in this city sometimes feels like a prison sentence despite how much diversity and delicious food there is. I wonder if grieving would come easier had I lived somewhere else, some place quieter and with fewer people, some place where it's sunny and warm all the time so that my body is constantly coursing with endorphins and serotonin. I read that the country with the happiest people in the world is Finland due to the robust public services and adjacency to the sea. But I think it's no coincidence that it also happens to be the place where the sun never sets from May to August.

Paloma texts me that she's running late. I tell her there's no rush. The line is barely moving. There is a couple in front of me arguing. I pretend to give them privacy by putting on my headphones, but I don't queue anything up. The woman is texting somebody on her phone while the man is telling her they need to bail on their plans. "The baby-sitter has to leave at two o'clock, Jules! There's no way we're going to make it home in time. Just tell them we'll reschedule."

Jules responds, "Look, they just let those people in. We'll have plenty of time."

The man rolls his eyes and kicks a pile of leaves. I wish he would stop fidgeting. I accidentally make eye contact with him, which seems to double his anxiety because now he realizes his outburst was on full display. He turns his back to me. I want to tap his shoulder and tell him to get a fucking grip, that he's worrying himself over nothing and how he's lucky to have children to go home to but their two friends join the line and he's suddenly as happy as a clam.

Just when I reach the front of the line, Paloma arrives. She's forty minutes late. I can't help but feel I've been used as a line sitter. "I'm so sorry," she says, pulling me in for a tight hug. "A streetcar broke down and there was this huge backup. I swear walking would've been faster."

Paloma is wearing knee-high leather boots and a chunky knit sweater dress, which is much more elegant than the establishment calls for. Meanwhile my Merrell hiking shoes leave an embarrassing trail of months-old dirt inside the restaurant.

Before we sit down, I catch a glimpse of Paloma's legs. They are slender with well-defined muscles that can only be obtained through weight-bearing squats. I wonder if she exercises in between wake windows. I wonder if she lifts the baby into the air until her quads burn and they both collapse into a fit of giggles.

I remember reading somewhere that breastfeeding burns five hundred calories a day. I picture her slimming down as her baby grows fatter by the day, rolls traveling up its arms, milk spilling down its mouth, hands twiddling her nipples for more. I wonder if it's possible to get the life sucked out of you by a baby.

"Good day, what are we feeling today?" the waiter asks, pen at the ready.

I select the least caloric thing on the menu, a shrimp ceviche.

Paloma orders three kinds of tacos with a side of chips and guacamole. "And oh what the heck, I'll get the grilled octopus, too."

"Any drinks?" the waiter asks.

"Two French 75s please," I say.

"Actually"—Paloma lifts up a palm—"could I get a Limonada?" She beams at me and hands the waiter our menus.

That's weird. Paloma always has a drink with lunch. I know it's not because she's breastfeeding because she had Prosecco at the baby shower. Something comes over me. A pang of despair, a twinge of envy. My mind races with reasons for Paloma's sudden sobriety. The only time she does not drink is—

No.

It can't be.

Is she pregnant again, only six months after giving birth?

I want to pull out my phone and look up the probability of conception within the first year of birth but her eyes are glued to me.

I am overreacting.

Paloma wouldn't do this to me. She would never double down on her bliss in the face of my anguish.

Then I remember. In her first trimester, she always craved lemonade.

I want to throw up. It's hot in here. A pit forms in my stomach and my heart quickens as I lay a hand on my stomach, gathering a fistful of flesh. I sink my fingers deep into the subcutaneous fat, wishing there was a baby of my own in there.

I take a deep inhale and exhale.

Maybe I'm wrong. Maybe she just wanted a lemonade.

Throughout the course of lunch, I look for more signs that she could be pregnant but when you're this scared, everything becomes a sign. She tells me she's starving and all she had this morning was a bowl of Fruity Pebbles. Fruity Pebbles! Who eats that unless it's a pregnancy craving?

I bait her with questions like whether she has eaten any good sushi or ridden any exhilarating roller coasters as of late. She delivers monosyllabic answers—no and no—before shooting me a curious look and asking me if everything is okay. I say of course, just making conversation, then ask her if she would be interested in joining me for a restorative water circuit therapy where the temperatures of the waters reach as high as 102°F. I wait for her to wince, to instinctually grip her belly with the realization that pregnant people cannot partake in hot baths.

"I would love that!" she cries, eyes wider than I've ever seen. "When? Can we do it soon? I desperately need a spa day."

I relax a bit. This is a good sign. If she were pregnant, she would've turned me down and made up some excuse.

Still, I need to be sure. I need more proof.

Short of following her into the bathroom and testing her urine, the only way to know for sure is to see if she would actually go through with this plan. I book us a one-hour time slot at the spa for that afternoon. When we arrive, we are asked to fill out a consent and intake form. There's a question near the bottom asking if there's any chance you are, or could be, pregnant. I peek over at Paloma's form. She has ticked off the box that says no.

I feel as if I might cry from sheer relief. Those little pangs of abandonment start to dissipate.

It's not like I expect Paloma to never bear children ever again. I just think it's only fair she abstain for the next little while. After all, is it not one of the cardinal, unspoken pacts of friendship, to not date your friend's exes, to not befriend their enemies, to not get pregnant after their baby has died?

We strip down to our bathing suits and step into the saltwater pool. Paloma dips her head in the water, surfacing with a thick veil of hair that shrouds her face. She pulls all that hair away from her face and throws it up into a lush, wet bun. If I were to gather all my hair, it would not be so much a bun as it would be a sad little mound. For the past few weeks, my hair has been falling out in clumps. It is everywhere and sticks to everything like dog hair. It clogs the drains and catches on the rotating brush of the vacuum. I thought it was due to my lack of eating, but the internet tells me it's due to a precipitous decline of estrogen and progesterone levels that naturally occurs after childbirth.

"How much hair do you think you've lost?" I ask Paloma, hoping to give vent to at least one shared postpartum experience.

"I haven't actually," she replies. "I think it's actually gotten thicker."

"Oh."

I'm not sure what else to say and neither does she. I catch her gaze deviate towards my receding hairline and because things aren't uncomfortable enough, a clump of black hair floats between us. *My* black hair. We fall silent, feeling the enormity of the divide between us.

A pair of giddy women enter the pool and remark at how incredible this place smells, to which Paloma immediately perks up and responds as if she's known them forever. "I know, right? I could practically live here!"

I get the sense she'd rather be with those two women. They're bursting with happiness and hair, not a single woe or bald patch in sight. When the two women waddle to the other end of the pool for privacy, I could have sworn Paloma looked disappointed.

"How is Freddie doing?" I ask, because that's what best friends do, inquire into the other significant person in their life.

"Good, he's really been stepping up to the plate lately." She tells me he's always putting his clothes *in* the hamper and not *around* the hamper. That he folds the baby's clothes in neat little stacks. Empties the diaper pail before it gets unpleasantly full. Even anticipates when the diapers need to be restocked and the wipes refilled.

"There was this brown stain on the carpet in the nursery that had been driving me nuts. Every time I nursed, it was all I could see. Then one day it was just gone."

Her eyes stay on me a little longer than they should.

Does she know? Is she testing me?

I tense up and provide a routine, unsuspicious comment. "What a good husband."

"I know! And I didn't even have to ask. And you know the best part? He never even mentioned doing it. He used to have this terrible habit of pointing out every single task he does around the house. 'Babe, I reorganized the Tupperware drawer. Babe, I cleaned the toilet.' It's like he wants formal acknowledgment of every single domestic contribution." She rolls her eyes. "Now? Not a peep!"

I analyze her expression and body language for any signs of deception, but she looks genuinely delighted. She really believes in her husband's sudden and unadulterated helpfulness, so I don't pursue this conversation any further. Paloma will go on believing Freddie has been the one tidying up the nursery while Freddie will go on believing it's Paloma. No one will suspect it's me, walking around their house like a ghost who can't let go.

21

Is crying good for you? I type those words into my phone and click on the top result.

> Crying is a normal, natural response when emotions become overwhelming. It can accompany feelings of sadness but also elation, anger, excitability, fear, and exhaustion. Crying has been shown to have a calming effect as it releases feel-good chemicals such as oxytocin and endorphins.

I type in another question. *Why do we cry?*

> Humans are the only animals to produce tears as an expression of emotions. All other animals produce tears solely for the lubrication of their eyes. It is believed humans produce tears as a way to flush out chemicals associated with strong emotions. Scientists have discovered that emotional tears—versus tears created from physical irritation—contain high concentrations of manganese, a mineral associated with irritability and anxiety.

I type in another question. *Is it possible to cry too much?*

> Excessive crying can deplete the body of water and lead to severe dehydration. If you find yourself crying frequently or for no apparent reason, it may be a sign of depression and you should consider talking to a doctor.

I haven't spoken to Dr. Posey since she bungled my prescription. Her decorum and compassionate care model leave much to be desired, but I can't get the crying to stop. The sleeping pills are all gone, the cough syrups have not been cutting it, and vodka makes me cry even more.

"What brings you in today?" Dr. Posey asks.

Of course the moment she asks this, I burst into tears. It's embarrassing. I proceed to tell her about the excessive crying as mucus dribbles down my nostrils.

"And on top of that I haven't been sleeping very well," I add, stifling the tears.

"Well that does not surprise me given all your problems." She scribbles on her prescription pad and rips off the sheet for me. "Here, try this. Should knock you right out."

I take the piece of paper, incredulous at the ease of all this. I look down to make sure she spelled my name correctly. "I don't know what's wrong with me. D-do you think I should talk to someone?"

"You mean like a friend?"

"No, a psychiatrist."

"A psychiatrist? Oh heavens no! Why would you do that? All they're going to do is insult you and drain you of your hard-earned money. Rotten scumbags! Besides, there's nothing they can do that I can't do better. If you want to talk, talk to me. Here, let's start: How sad would you say you are?"

I was not prepared for that question. Was it possible to quantify sadness? Was there an equivalent 0 to 10 scale like there is for physical pain, where 0 to 4 meant you were mildly sad but can still carry out usual activities, 5 to 7 meant you were moderately sad and have a bit of difficulty concentrating, and 8 to 10 meant you were so unbearably sad you can't even talk or think straight?

Even so, sad doesn't feel right. It doesn't feel big enough a word to capture how much I miss you.

"I don't know," I tell her.

She furrows her brows. "Well then tell me, what makes you sad? Other than, you know."

I brush off her flippancy and think about her question. I could list off so many things. Old people sitting by themselves. Terminally ill children. Abandoned dogs. A lone adult swinging on a swing. I once cried after quickly glimpsing a news ticker about an orca in the Pacific Ocean who had been carrying her dead calf for several days. There was no image, no video. Just a crawling sentence that came and went in less than three seconds.

"Hmm . . . this is an unusual amount of sadness for one person to present."

"Do you think something is wrong with me? Is it normal, all this crying?"

I wait for her to provide answers but all I see her type on the screen is a successive stream of question marks.

"Hard to say. How many milliliters of tears would you say you produce a day?"

"Milliliters?"

"Yes, ballpark will do."

How am I supposed to answer that? I want to say an ocean's worth because that's how it feels. That's how much your absence has extracted from me. But I fear the pragmatic response would be something far, far less. Not even enough to fill a two-liter bottle of Pepsi.

Dr. Posey types up <2L *tears* in her notes directly underneath my blood pressure levels, as if it's a universally recognized measurement of sorrow. Her computer pings with a notification. She toggles to another window where a game of Texas Hold 'Em is underway. It's her turn to place a bet. While she ponders her move, I look up on my phone how many tears a person can produce.

The average volume of a human tear is roughly 6.2 microliters. If every single individual on the planet were to shed exactly 55 tears, this would be enough to fill an Olympic-size swimming pool.

Dr. Posey toggles her screen back to my medical notes. "Where were we? Right. And what do you think would be the cause of your current bout of sadness?"

I pause, scratching my head. "Isn't it obvious?"

"I would prefer if you spell it out, my dear. For my records."

"I guess I've realized how fragile and fleeting life is and I'm angry that I had to learn this the hard way."

"How so?"

"I beg your pardon?"

"How did you learn this the hard way?"

"My baby died," I remind her.

Dr. Posey's listening face goes blank. She reaches for a tissue, and I expect her to hand it to me but instead she uses it to squash a spider crawling across her desk. "Gotcha! You leggy bastard!" She squishes the spider between the two pieces of ply and unfolds it, examining the blackened bits with violent glee before crumpling it up and tossing it into the bin.

I hold my tongue and wait for her to apologize for her inappropriateness, but she does not. "I'm so forgetful, can you remind me again when that happened?"

"Seven months ago." As I hear the number fall out of my tongue, I wonder how can that be. Didn't I hold you yesterday? Didn't I say goodbye a lifetime ago? This yawning expanse of time is so incomprehensible it triggers another bout of tears.

"Oh my, seven months and you're still this emotional? This is not normal. Not normal at all. According to DSM-5, you should have been over this by the six-month mark."

"I should have?"

"Do you still experience an intense yearning for your baby?"

"Of course."

"Is it constant?"

"Yes."

"Do you think about her when you wake up?"

"Every day."

She lets out an exhausted groan. "Answer these questions for me please. You feel as if a part of you has died, true or false?"

"True."

"You feel bitterness, sorrow, and anger about the death, true or false?"

"True."

"Life has lost all meaning for you, true or false?"

"True."

"You feel detached from other people, true or false?"

"True."

"Oh dear, oh dear, oh dear." Her face turns serious as she types something into the computer. "I'm afraid I'll have to diagnose you with PGD. Prolonged grief disorder."

"Is something wrong with me?"

"Yes, this is a very serious condition. People with PGD are at a higher risk for medical issues such as cancer and high blood pressure, mental health disorders, not to mention you're more likely to be hospitalized or commit suicide. Is that what you want?"

"Of course not."

"Then you should put more effort into reducing the severity of your grief."

"But, but . . ." I'm at a loss for words.

"You had your time to be sad. Now the real work must be done to get you reintegrated into society. Have you been taking the propranolol like I said?"

I explain to her the mix-up at the pharmacy.

"Oh gosh, I'm terribly sorry about that. That might explain these unusually long spells of crying. How about I write you up for the maximum dosage to make up for it?"

She hands the sheet to me and places the tip of her pen back on the pad. "Is there anything else you want to try? There are some very effective mood stabilizers that would help with your issue. Just say the word."

I think of all the pills that could quell my sorrows. Lexapro. Effexor. Zoloft. Bupropion. Anything I want, I could get. But I find myself too flustered by this diagnosis that I tell her, "Just the propranolol."

"You sure? How about some minoxidil?"

"Is that an antidepressant?"

"It's for hair loss, which I see you're exhibiting. Must be distressing looking at yourself like that. No wonder you're crying so frequently."

I balk at her disparaging comment and get up to leave. "No thanks."

"Suit yourself."

After I leave the doctor's office, I order an obscene amount of Rogaine on my phone and select the fastest delivery option. A gust of wind blows in my direction and as I turn back, I see strands of black hair floating in the air. I instinctively reach my arms out to save as many as I can, but they belong to the earth now.

As I walk home, I think about all the hair that has fallen off every exhausted mother's head. I think about the mountains we could make out of them, the soil we could nourish, the clothing we could weave. We could form a new society where we celebrate each surrendered strand. Choppy hairlines would be praised. Naked temples would be lauded. The baldest of us all would be the most revered.

I walk into a hair salon and ask for a blunt bob to create the illusion of thickness. When the hairdresser is finished, she gives me a mirror to hold. I check my reflection to find there is no illusion. Not even a little bit. And now all my hair is on the floor, being sucked up by a Roomba.

22

I turn on my computer. I pop some propranolol and extra-strength Tylenol before drowning myself in work. I tackle my inbox. Then I tackle Kenneth's. I put in orders for caskets and urns and flowers and boxes of tissues. I answer phone calls from nurses whose patients have just died. I take down all the information they give me and double-check the spelling of the names. I print materials for upcoming services. I send out holiday cards letting families know we're thinking of them. Finally, I am left with the task I least want to do: telling next of kin their loved one's ashes are ready to be picked up.

Once the calls have been made, I can't help but google *What do people do with ashes?* The search generates a list:

- Crystallize into diamonds
- Turn into jewelry
- Paint onto a canvas
- Compress into a vinyl record
- Tattoo into your body
- Conceal inside a stuffed toy
- Fill an hourglass
- Set off fireworks
- Load into a caliber of ammunition

Scattering appears to be the most common practice. Particularly over famous bridges and oceans. Some divide up the ashes and scatter them in different parts of the world, or different parts of their favorite city.

Disney attractions are popular, too. Despite the fact that it's illegal, people secretly scatter ashes in Cinderella's garden and the moat underneath the Dumbo ride. A Disneyland custodian is quoted in one article: "A warning to you all: Don't even think about dumping Grandma's ashes here. We'll just vacuum her all up."

If you want to be really unique, you can put the ashes inside a weather balloon and have it sent into outer space where it gets released into the atmosphere. Slowly over time, the ashes will come back down to Earth, become incorporated with the clouds, and eventually turn into precipitation. Every time it rains or snows, you can say your loved one is literally washing over you. It costs $20,000.

I peruse the other search results and happen upon a news article about a police investigation into an Oregon funeral home after multiple families reported their loved ones' ashes had gone missing. It turns out the funeral home director had been secretly stashing the ashes underneath the floorboards, right under everyone's noses. Why? Nobody knew.

I think about Kenneth, how strange he was acting when he handed over your ashes, all fidgety and awkward and sweaty, like he was hiding a secret, like he had guilt lodged inside his throat. The way he snuck up on me like he didn't want me snooping in the wrong area. Something was off. My eyes dart towards the hutch. Could that explain why there was so little of your ashes? Could the rest be hidden in there?

No, no. It couldn't be. I'm clearly losing my mind.

I go back to researching creative ways to scatter ashes. I'm so lost in this topic that I forget to take a break or drink water and just like that, it's time to go home. What a blur of a day.

The clock reads 4:29. April 29. Your birthday. These numbers follow me everywhere. It's always 4:29 and the bill is always $4.29 or $42.90 and the spam calls I keep getting always come from some number ending in 429. When I told Paloma this, she squealed and insisted this was not a coincidence, that these sightings hold spiritual significance and represent messages from the beyond. I really wanted to believe her, really wanted to know nothing of the Baader-Meinhof phenomenon, so I kept my mouth shut and allowed myself to believe, just this one time, in something that escapes scientific explanation.

I go to the bathroom. It must have been sanitized because it reeks of bleach. Even the toilet seat is still damp. The solution tingles against the underside of my thighs and as I get up to flush, one whiff of the noxious fumes sends me into a hysterical frenzy.

All of a sudden I'm in the NICU, cradling you against my chest and rocking you back and forth. A janitor kindly asks me to lift my feet so that he can mop the area underneath me. I oblige and the room fills with an overwhelming scent of disinfectant. The janitor tells me he's sorry. I don't know what he's sorry for, but I thank him and he's gone. I rest my bare feet on the floor. I look down at your sweet face, your plush cheeks pressed against my chest like clouds. I give them a kiss but they're not like clouds at all. They're cold and hard like they've never been touched by the sun.

One blink and I'm back in the bathroom, staring at myself in the mirror and dabbing tears that have accumulated under my jaw. I splash my face with water in hopes of flushing out the bleach from my nostrils. These flashbacks have been occurring more and more lately. They pop in whenever they want, even if I'm busy doing things, even if I don't want the memories. All it takes is a smell or a glimpse or a jingle and there I am, free-falling to a past that can't be undone.

On my way out the door, I run into Kenneth and he asks if everything is okay.

"Yes, I'm fine," I respond, not looking at him, afraid his expression might unleash another tsunami of tears. He just looks at me, perhaps intuiting that I'm not being truthful and that I might need a little more goading to say what's really on my mind.

"Are you sure? You know you can talk to me about anything, right?"

I instantly feel buoyed by his kindness and ponder what he says. He's a good listener. I've witnessed him hold long conversations with bereaved customers without once appearing annoyed or inconvenienced. Maybe I should tell him about my flashbacks. What is it people are always saying? How it's good to talk about things? Gives the problem less power, reduces your stress, yada yada yada.

I try to put myself in Kenneth's shoes. If someone I knew looked as distressed as I did, I would want to know what was wrong so I could help them. I would hope they trusted me enough to share their deepest secrets.

I take a deep breath and let it all out.

"Do you think we could instate a no-bleach policy around here?"

23

According to the internet, taking walks in nature can significantly reduce flashbacks. Here we go again with the walking. The supposed cure-all for everything.

Fine. I'll give it another try.

I put on my winter boots and parka and walk to Kew-Balmy Beach, then from Kew-Balmy Beach to the water treatment plant. I rest here for a moment, watching one man chuck balls across the snow-covered sand as his dog feverishly runs for it over and over, mesmerized by the exacting repetitiveness of it all.

I walk back towards Queen Street. I pass by restaurants full of people seeking refuge from the cold. My gaze stops at a bubbly group of mothers. They've all got forks in one hand, stroller in the other. One of the babies is crying. Its mother puts the pacifier back in the baby's mouth, but it does not appear to be working so the mother picks up the baby and offers up one of her breasts. The baby is now content.

The mother looks up and stares at me. The other mothers do the same, followed by the rest of the diners. Why is everyone looking at me? Can they tell something is wrong with me? Is it my horrible haircut? Something on my face? Do I emit some type of unignorable aura?

I run away from the leering eyes and turn onto a residential street, stopping to catch my breath. There's music blasting from somewhere. I walk towards the source. It's coming from Sonia and Dave's house. They're a retired couple who hand paints birdhouses and hangs them off the maple tree in their front yard. Sonia spots me from across the street. We don't know each other well, but it appears we've exchanged enough hellos that she invites me in to the party.

"You have to come in, there's lots of food inside!" she exclaims.

I should've kept walking, told her I had somewhere to be, but she keeps insisting and now I'm inside the house, removing my boots, and it's suddenly clear I've made a mistake.

Because this isn't just any party.

It's a birthday party. For a two-year-old.

His name is Wilfred but everybody calls him Willy. He's Sonia's grandson. He likes planets, astronauts, and the solar system based on the space-themed decorations and the big banner on the wall: "TWO THE MOON."

I can't be here. Not after what happened at the baby shower.

Before I can slip out, other guests—neighbors I barely know—come up to me one by one to express their condolences. One neighbor tells me about a stillbirth from decades ago, how she went in for an ultrasound and all she saw on the black-and-white screen was a static baby. No squirming. No heartbeat. She tells me she still thinks about that baby to this day. She says it still hurts. I tell her I'm so sorry and she gives me the longest hug I think I've ever had in my life.

The attention comes off me (thankfully) and everybody starts regaling stories of their Nordic cruises and vegetable gardens and luxuriously long bike rides. I suppose this party isn't so bad. Most of the guests are in their fifties and sixties, so there's no talk of sleep regressions or long daycare waitlists or the merits of baby-led weaning. Sonia and her friends also have healthy attitudes about death. I overhear Sonia talking about a recent health scare that sent her to the hospital overnight. It turned out to be nothing, but Sonia says if it was her time to go, she would go in peace. Death is a normal part of life, nothing to fear. It's the price we pay to live, she tells the whole room, to which everyone nods in agreement.

"Cleo, don't you work at a funeral home? Monarch, right?"

Suddenly everyone's eyes are back on me, wide with intrigue. Now my heart is pumping, the pressure to say something interesting reaching a boil.

"Y-yes, I do."

"I've been there once," says Sonia. "A service for an old acquaintance of mine. Kidney failure, sadly. From what I recall, it was quite a lovely establishment. What an interesting career choice. You must have seen all kinds of things."

I nod, unsure what would be an appropriate thing to share. People must think I'm brimming with gruesome stories about dead bodies, entertaining anecdotes about erratic customers, or eerie tales about ghost encounters. The truth? The stories I've collected are much more ordinary in nature. Elderly couples who die within months of each other. Parents who die before they could walk their child down the aisle. Graduates who die just when their life was about to start. And yet despite its ordinariness, death still never fails to bewilder us.

A galactic-themed cake emerges from the kitchen, and they all start singing happy birthday for Willy. I mouth the words but make no audible contributions to the chorus. I wonder if it's palpably obvious how uncomfortable I am singing happy birthday for one child while housing the ashes of another at home. People rush to the front to take pictures. The child is giddy with both nerves and delight.

I imagine you in Willy's place, standing in front of the crowd, showing off your four tiny teeth, fidgeting with the stupid birthday hat that keeps falling off your sweet little head, your cheeks flushed from all the attention you're getting. You don't know which camera to look at because there are so many pointed at you, so you look straight at me. You give me the biggest smile you've ever given, then you cover your face because all the flashing lights are too bright. You run up to me and whisper in my ear, *Can I have cake now?* And I say, *Of course, it's your birthday! You can have all the cake you want!* I ask you to hold the paper plate while I cut you a slice and you do so willingly, with both hands for extra security, because you are such a good helper. You let me put a spoonful of cake in your mouth and when that frosting hits your tongue, your eyes sparkle like confetti and you ball up your fists to contain all the excitement inside your little body. I tell you, *It's okay, let it all out,* and you do. You let out the purest, most perfect shriek of joy.

"Would you like a piece of cake?"

Sonia presents me with a plate. I take the plate and stab my fork in it. I refuse to eat it. It feels wrong, like I'm cheating on my child. I watch the birthday boy eat his cake with glee, the chocolate buttercream smeared all over his lips and fingers. The sight of a happy child eating birthday cake fills me with an inexplicable grief made worse by the fact that if I tell this to anybody, I will sound like a horrible person.

Despite the cake being cut and the birthday song being sung, Sonia won't let anybody leave until the presents have been opened. "Please, just another half hour! Willy wants everyone here," she pleads when she sees me reach for my coat. "Fine," I say for lack of an excuse.

I pull out my phone as the birthday boy opens his gifts. I look up Paloma's Instagram. There's a new post—a picture of her child on a fluffy white bed next to an even fluffier blue bear. The caption is brief. My little angel followed by an emoji of a baby with wings and a halo. I'm seething with rage at her selection of emoji. I know I'm no child of God but this emoji is not hers to use. I scroll through the comments to see if anyone else has taken umbrage with this, but there's just a stream of positivity:

This is the cutest thing I've ever seen!
Wow so big now!
Stop it my ovaries!!!

I decide to flag her post. The app asks why. *Spam. Nudity. Sexual activity. Hate speech. False information. Bullying.* I can't seem to find what I'm looking for until I scroll to the bottom. *I just don't like it.* I select that one. The app tells me that unless the post violates specific community guidelines, it cannot do anything to help me. It suggests I unfollow any accounts that don't align with my values or speak with the account holder privately.

I hide myself in the bathroom and call Paloma three times but there's no answer, so I sit on the toilet and wait for her to call me back. Why is she not picking up? Why is she not tending to my grief like she always does? Why do I want her here and also the hell away from me?

Every time the bathroom doorknob jiggles I yell out *Just a sec!* and sit tight for what feels like a year until I hear them give up and pitter-patter to the upstairs bathroom.

Paloma finally calls back and I answer before the first ring completes.

"What's wrong?" Paloma asks.

The plan was to berate Paloma for her improper use of emoji, but the sound of her voice throws me into an involuntary fit of sobbing.

"Tell me where you are and I'll come get you," she says.

———————————

Twenty minutes later, Paloma is knocking on the bathroom door and picking me up off the floor. Everybody has retreated to the basement where it sounds like they're whacking a piñata. We slip out the front door. There are rows and rows of loot bags by the entrance. I take one.

Paloma gasps. "What are you doing?"

"It's for guests, isn't it?"

"It's for the kids!"

I grumble and set the bag down, sour that my presence at this party is not worthy of at least a stupid favor. We're in her car when I realize I forgot my fanny pack inside. Paloma says she'll go in. "It's in the bathroom, on top of the tank I think," I tell her.

She runs inside and returns with my fanny pack. Before I know it, she's pouring out all the contents of my bag on my lap and shouting, "What the hell are these?"

I look down, my sight blurring before coming into focus. I assume she's not inquiring about the wallet or lipstick or house keys but instead the Benadryls and NyQuils and sleeping pills and propranolol and half a dozen mini bottles of vodka.

"What on earth are you doing with all of this?"

"I've been having a hard time sleeping."

"A hard time *sleeping*? Then make a tea, meditate, put on soothing ocean sounds! You don't go mixing pills and vodka! Are you an idiot?"

This is the side of Paloma I haven't seen in a while—the brash, no-nonsense, get-it-together Paloma. While I give credit to my mother for giving me life, Paloma was the one who taught me how to survive. She warned which intersections to avoid at night, how to aim for the eyes and throat if I'm ever attacked, and when to tell if I'm being scammed. I don't know where I'd be without her. Likely bankrupt and rotting in a ditch somewhere.

I ignore her and start putting all my things back in the fanny pack until she grabs my arm. "Nuh uh, not so fast. Give me those!"

She takes the pills and bottles and shoves them in her own purse. I want to punch her in the throat—just the way she taught me—but she might end me with a sucker punch of her own. "Don't you know you could seriously get hurt taking these?" she yells. "You could *die*! How could you be so stupid?"

I want to throw the exact same question back at her. How could *she* be so stupid? Can't she see how unbothered I am by that scenario? Haven't I made it blatantly obvious?

"Can we talk about this later?" I say instead.

Paloma relents, calms her breathing, and drives us home in silence. She parks in front of my house and turns to face me, her expression turning serious.

"You have to stop," she says.

"I will," I tell her, though I had no intention of doing so.

"Don't lie to me!" Paloma suddenly shouts. "You know what? I'm fucking sick of this self-sabotaging shit. I know life dealt you the shittiest hand in the world but it doesn't give you the right to blow up your life. Do you know how many people care about you? Do you know how much patience you've been given? It's like you *love* being defeated. Well, guess what? You're not! You can get pregnant again. You can have another baby. Hell, you can have all the babies you want. But you'll never get there if you don't get a fucking grip and stop playing the victim!"

Paloma lets out the longest exhale, like a thick, heavy shroud has just peeled off her. I'm glued to my seat, shocked. She really just said that. Wow, good for her. I wonder how long she's been holding that in. This is the angriest I've ever seen her. She won't even look at me.

I've finally done it. I've pushed her to her edge.

Good. Now I'm free to hate her and be liberated from the bitterness and jealousy that poisons me.

I get out of the car and before slamming the door, I give her my coldest look. "Babies don't replace babies."

24

Dear diary,
We had a successful day in the pool today. What a water baby
I have! We kicked and splashed and blew bubbles and pretended
to be speckled frogs. I think she could very well be an Olympian.
I will make a mental note to sign her up for lessons in the future.

Dear diary,
That's it, I'm never flying with a baby again! She had an explosive
blowout as we were landing. The flight attendants would not let me
get up. No matter how much I begged. I had no choice but to just
sit there, murky brown sludge smeared all over us and offending
all my senses. I can't believe I survived that. I think I could survive
anything.

25

🌼

Birthdays. I can't seem to escape them because the moment I walk into work Rachel informs me it's Maggie's birthday and she's recruited me to blow air into a pair of deflated sixes. I can't believe Maggie is still working here at her age. I wonder when she'll retire. I wonder if the company will reward her long tenure with a fifty percent discount on her funeral.

One thing I've observed from working here is how much this team loves to celebrate birthdays. No matter how old you are or how much you insist it's not that big a deal, you can bet there will be balloons and cake and silly party hats in your honor.

"That's not even the best part," Rachel tells me after we finish decorating the break room.

"There are parts to this?"

"Just wait."

As the other staff members file in, they instinctually form two rows facing each other and Rachel motions for me to get in line. The room is quiet. I ask her what's going on, where's Maggie, why it feels like we're about to perform some type of sacrificial ritual, but she shushes me and the room goes dark. Disco lights beam onto the ceiling and the Bee Gees blare from a pair of Bluetooth speakers. Maggie enters the room with a silly party hat and star-shaped sunglasses and struts down the aisle we have created. Everyone claps and cheers and shouts in unison, "Ah, ha, ha, ha, stayin' alive!" She gives us a little twirl, slaps a few high fives, and throws her fists in the air as if she has just won the country an Olympic gold medal.

When it's all over, Maggie blows out her candles and looks as giddy as a child on Christmas morning.

The lights have turned on again and the music is set to a more pleasing volume. Kenneth comes over to me with two plates of red velvet cake.

"Well, what'd you think?" he asks me.

I accept a plate. "I have to admit that was kind of cute."

"Maggie's a pro. She's probably done this more than thirty times."

"She must really love the Bee Gees."

"She doesn't have a choice. We play that song for everyone."

"Everyone? Every time?" I balk.

"Yup."

"Doesn't that get old?"

"You would think, but I haven't received any complaints yet."

"Was this all your idea?"

Kenneth nods like a proud father. "I just think it's important to celebrate being alive while we're still alive, given the type of work we do. Sometimes we wait until it's too late to appreciate what a remarkable thing it is to be born. I think most people get caught up in the stress of life that they forget what an improbability it is to just exist. That of all the possible people that could be here on this earth, we are the lucky ones."

What Kenneth says stuns me into silence. I watch as he shoves a whopping spoonful of cake into his mouth, and I am finding it difficult to reconcile the fact that a person with such philosophical inclinations can be the same person with frosting on his mustache. I'm scared to point it out, afraid he'll put his facial hair in one of the drinking cups.

"You really think we're that special?" I reply. "You and me? Just because we're alive?"

"Why yes. So many unlikely chains of events had to occur for me to be here. For you to be here. Our parents would have to have met, obviously, but our grandparents would have had to meet, too, and their parents, and their parents, and so on and so on. Not to mention they'd all have to live to reach reproductive age and successfully conceive a child with a very specific DNA combination." He swallows another bite. "Do you know about the turtle and the yoke?"

I shake my head.

"It's a Buddhist parable about a golden ring that floats on the surface of the ocean and a blind turtle who lives at the bottom of the ocean that comes up only once every thousand years. The odds of being born today is about the same as that little blind turtle sticking its head out of the water, right in the middle of that ring, on the very first try." Kenneth raises both eyebrows. "Basically what I'm saying is the odds of us being here are practically nil!"

It's startling to be around someone who loves life this much—especially with all the people dying, the forests burning, the starving children, the constant exhaustion, the endless dishes, the unexplainable kink in your neck, the never-ending question of what to eat all the time, the bills and the taxes and the *don't forget to call your mom and keep up with the news and respond to the group chat* and *oh, remember to wash your face.*

"If I can play devil's advocate," I say, "has it ever occurred to you that maybe it is luckier to have not been born at all? What if the unborn are having a grand old time, laughing at our misfortune for existing like this?"

Kenneth swallows his last bite of cake and sets his plate down, frosting still perilously dangling from the tip of his mustache. "Who says we're not having a grand old time ourselves?" He points to my untouched plate. "Look at this cake. We're the privileged few who get to know the taste of this sweet, delectable treat. Are you telling me you'd rather choose nonexistence over *this*?" He licks his lips as he eyes my plate. I hand it over, telling him I'm not all that hungry, and he happily takes the spoon and shoves more red velvet into his mouth.

"But if I were never born, then I wouldn't know what cake is, let alone what it tastes like, therefore I wouldn't know that there was anything to be missing out on," I respond.

"Please, you're telling me you wouldn't be missing out on *this*?" He hovers a spoon of cream cheese frosting in the air before devouring it. I watch as he empties the plate, scraping the last smears of icing with the edge of his plastic spoon, and just like that the cake is gone. Everything good has to end.

"I just think there's so much suffering in this world, so much despair," I say. "It's hard to see how being alive is all it's cracked up to be."

"Ahh, I see," he says, softening his eyes and putting down his plate. "You know, I've seen firsthand how extremely difficult it is to be a human." He places a hand on my shoulder and gives it a light squeeze, as if he's acknowledging everything that's too unbearable to say. "Life is an endless seesaw of things being terrible and things being wonderful. That pain you talk of, I like to believe it's a by-product of love. And look at all the things we also gain from love. Laughter, security, comfort, joy." He pauses to pick up the plate again. "And cake."

I dab at my eye. His words bring out something in me that's only been reserved for the end of the day—when I'm shrouded in duvets and darkness.

"I know death is a painful part of life," he continues, "but to die means having gotten to be loved and, in my opinion, that is what makes being alive worth it."

"You really think the pain is worth it?" My voice cracks when I say this.

"I really do, dear."

How would you know? I want to ask him. Have you ever lost any-one? Do you even know the specific agony of waking up every day to the realization that the person you loved with your whole entire being is dead?

I already know what he's going to say: One does not need to have lived an experience to understand, that all one needs is an open heart and an open mind.

Kenneth wipes his mouth with a napkin and the frosting has finally vanished. "I've been meaning to tell you this, Cleo. I think you're doing great, coming here every day and helping others say goodbye to their loved ones despite the grief you're experiencing. That makes you a re-markable person. And an even more remarkable mother."

Warmth spreads throughout my body as if I've been draped in a heated blanket. It's the first time somebody has called me a mother despite having no baby to hold, no baby waiting for me at home. I want to hug Kenneth but worry it might be too weird, so I raise my glass and say a cheer he would be proud of. "To life."

I must have been in the bathroom too long because I miss Maggie's whole speech. There's a loud applause when I return to the room. I ask the person nearest me what I missed.

"She just announced she's bestowing her inheritance to all of us!"

"Oh my god, really?"

"I'm kidding. She just thanked us all for being here."

"Oh."

"Sorry, I'm a bit of a jokester. Dylan, by the way."

It's only after turning to fully face him that I realize I don't know him. "I'm Cleo. Sorry, I'm sort of new here. Have we met before?"

"I work at the crematorium in Milton. I've known Maggie for years, so I thought I'd drive over and join in on the fun. Our office is kind of dead right now." He belts out a laugh and I laugh, too, to demonstrate my tolerance for hearing the same joke over and over.

I think about your ashes, how there was so little of it, how I came across a news article about a funeral director who was secretly hiding people's ashes. A long list of questions form in my mind. I want to ask him every single one of them without appearing suspicious, so I pretend to be a studious intern wanting to glean as much information as I can about the industry in preparation for an upcoming exam. How long does the average cremation take? How many cremations do you do a day? What are the profit margins on cremations versus burials? Finally, I ask Dylan the question I really want to ask: "How much should ashes weigh after the cremation process?"

"Well, it depends. Are we talking about a six-foot, three-hundred pound man or a petite lady under a hundred pounds?"

"Um, what about an infant?"

"An infant?"

"Yes," I say, "for the purposes of my education."

He looks at me quizzically but answers my question anyway. "It's very little, I can tell you that. Sometimes not even half a cup. We do everything we can to try to maximize the recovery of ashes—"

"How?" I blurt out. "Sorry to interrupt, but how do you do that?"

"Well, there are a number of ways. We use a specialized tray that helps us collect as much of the ash as possible. We turn off the main chamber burner to decrease the turbulence—" He pauses for a beat. "Do you want to write this down or . . ."

I momentarily forget that I'm an intern and should be taking notes, so I pull out my phone and pretend to get this all down. "You were saying?"

"It's very important to keep the airflow to a minimum so that the ashes aren't blown out of the tray. Either we will turn down the jets or place the casket close to the door where it's less turbulent. Like I said, we do the best we can to recover as much tangible ashes as possible but we have had some upset families for sure. It's not uncommon to have folks call and ask where the rest of the ashes are. Sadly we've had to explain to them that this is the process and . . . I'm sorry, should I stop? Is this too much to share?"

He passes me a tissue as I realize tears have been falling down my face. Ugh, what is wrong with me? I excuse myself, not wanting to make a scene, and walk out of the building and into my car.

I replay what Dylan said—how common it is to receive only half a cup of ashes. This whole time I wanted to believe there was another explanation—some kind of human error or gross negligence that would account for why there was so little of you in that box. But Dylan shattered my delusions. The hutch, the fixation, the relentless scrutiny of Kenneth—who, despite all his mysteriousness and idiosyncrasies, has turned out to be the sweetest, most thoughtful human being I've ever met—were just distractions. Ways to avoid facing the one truth I couldn't bear to believe.

There is no more of you out there. No more of you ever.

———————

I text Kenneth that I'm not feeling well and because he's Kenneth, he doesn't probe or lay on the guilt, just tells me to take as much time as I need.

I check my other messages. There are dozens I haven't responded to. A lot of *how are yous* and *thinking of yous*. I keep meaning to reply but then feel overwhelmed by the task of forming a cohesive response, so I ignore it, forgetting about it for months until it becomes this big monster I'm too afraid to confront.

I tend to the most recent messages. There's one from Paloma—I'm really sorry about what I said, can we please talk?—followed by three flashlight emojis, our way of saying *I love you.*

Fuck your apology. Delete.

The next text is from Fatima, informing me they had their baby last night. A healthy beautiful girl, seven pounds, two ounces, Sadie is doing well. Attached is an image of all three of them.

Fuck your beautiful family. Delete.

The next message is from my mother, a quote from Jalaluddin Rumi:

What hurts you blesses you.
Darkness is your candle.
Your boundaries are your quest.

Fuck your basic quotes. Delete.

The last message is from Ethan. Sorry babe I won't be home until nine, somebody called in sick.

Fuck. I don't want to go home to an empty house, so I drive aimlessly around the city in hopes of killing time. Ethan hates that expression. Killing time. He's a time evangelist who counts every single minute we get on this earth as a gift. Time is not something to be hurried along. Most certainly it is not something to murder. "We don't *kill* time, we *fill* time," he would always say. I'm convinced he and Kenneth would get along swimmingly.

Regardless, I need to make it to the end of the day somehow. That niggling loneliness creeps its way up again. I need a distraction, something to push it down. I connect my phone to the Bluetooth speaker and do something preposterous. I call people. I pick numbers at random because it doesn't matter who is on the other end, I just need to hear any voice other than the ones in my head telling me to step on the gas and cross the median.

Everybody is shocked when I call out of the blue. My old college roommate. My accountant. A dude I went on one date with many, many years ago. They wonder if something is wrong, if I need a favor of some sort, if there's some special announcement I'm making. I tell them no, that I'm just calling to say hi, and they all accept that as a perfectly viable reason because who doesn't miss the good ol' days when people called people unannounced and without agenda.

The conversations are surface-level and superficial because I brush off every personal question that is asked of me. Instead, I turn it around on them, ask them question after question and every single one of them laps it up. They love talking about themselves. And I'm more than happy to listen. It's comforting hearing other people's problems, even if they feel trivial by comparison, because it reminds me we're all a shade of miserable.

I find myself parked at a grocery store. I don't know why. I don't need anything. I just want to feel normal. I want to be like all these people pushing their squeaky carts up and down the aisle and pressing their grubby fingers into the avocados until they find the right one. I start loading up the cart. Puffed rice cakes. Crunchy peanut butter. Frozen bag of pierogi. When my cart is full, I abandon it and walk out of the store.

My stomach lurches and my legs feel weak, and I quickly grab on to a lamppost to steady myself. Not again. My body is crying for food but my brain won't let me eat. The hunger feels like it's gnawing at me from the inside.

I force myself to stop inside a restaurant and order a platter of sourdough toast and chicken liver pâté from the bar. I get a drink, too, a dark and stormy, because the waitress insists it goes well with what I'm ordering. When the plate arrives, I'm immediately repulsed. My lips tighten and my body involuntarily leans back, like a child refusing to eat what's in front of him. I push myself to have one bite, then another.

I can't do it.

I scrape the pâté off and eat just the bread. This makes it more tolerable, but only by a negligible amount. The bartender sees my rejected mound of thirty-dollar pâté and shoots me a disparaging look. The old me would've been so embarrassed at appearing wasteful, or worse, culinarily unadventurous, and would've atoned for the misstep with profuse apologies. But I am no longer the old me. I am the new me and the new me does not give a shit. This is perhaps the one and only gift of grief: Welcome to zero-fucks land! I drop the bread, down my drink, and leave a fifty-dollar bill on the bar.

As I walk back to the car, a craving travels its way up my throat, telling me it desires something sweet, something cold. All the want in my body points towards the unbelievable: a Brownie Batter Blizzard. The thing I craved the most when I was pregnant with you. The thing that always made you kick your hardest kicks.

Are you kidding me right now?

It feels unfair that my body betrays me with this reminder. I focus on driving in hopes of quieting the craving, but it persists like a dog that hasn't been fed in days. I drive to the nearest Dairy Queen. I order the usual. The cashier flips it upside down. And I pay, hating myself as I tap the credit card. I eat the Blizzard in the car. My hand instinctively rests on my belly, knowing there will be no kick but waiting for one anyway. Sometimes we break our own hearts more fiercely than anybody else.

My phone pings with a text from Ethan, telling me he's home and where am I? I drive towards the house, passing a car accident. It looks bad. Three vehicles involved, one turned over, multiple fire trucks and ambulances on scene. I see two people crying and hugging each other and think they must be having the worst day ever.

Then I realize I am, too. It's just not as flashy as theirs.

Ethan hugs me when I come in. He asks how my day is. I shrug. Then he asks what's wrong, which is a strange question because he knows better than anyone what's wrong.

"Nothing," I tell him.

"Are you sure? You've been acting a little . . . different."

I want to ask him different how? Different since when? Aren't we all changing and expanding from one day to the next?

I go to the bathroom and remove my makeup. He follows me in and monitors me like I'm one of his sedated patients. My lipstick is not budging no matter how much I rub and I remember it's because earlier, I swatched one of the homemade formulas Ana uses on her decedents.

It's part dried-up lipstick, part grease paint, which she sets with a translucent powder. "The key is to put a layer of Elmer's glue down first and let that dry. That way the color stays put much better," Ana explained.

I look at myself in the mirror, fruit punch lips and all. My lips, the shape and curves, look so much like yours. I weep, parting my lips to taste the salt, and Ethan envelops me in his arms. He says *it's okay* over and over and I don't know if he means it's okay to cry or that everything is going to be okay. I look up at him and find not a single drop of wetness around his eyes and suddenly I'm enraged. It's as if I'm shouldering the grief for the both of us. Like a household chore I bear the sole responsibility for. He does the laundry and lawn maintenance. I do all the feeling.

"It's the funeral home, isn't it?" Ethan says. "I don't think it's good for you to be there. Look what it's doing."

I shoot him an infuriated look and say, "I'm going to bed."

I slip under the covers, relieved another day is over and all that's left to do is sleep. I find a lone sleeping pill in my purse that Paloma failed to confiscate and swallow it. I wait for my eyelids to get heavy, for grogginess to kick in, for that split-second state of not remembering anything at all.

26

My parents get word that I've taken up a job at the funeral home, despite my best efforts at keeping this fact hidden. They insist I've gone mad due to a lack of nutrition, so they come over and cook some steamed rice, fried lemongrass fish, and bitter melon soup. The look and smell of all that food makes me nauseous, but I know they will not leave until I eat something. I dig through my dresser and find an old edible in hopes it will stimulate my appetite.

"Ethan tells us this job is quite stressful, is that right?" my father asks.

Everybody glares at me with the sharpness of a razor.

"Not really," I say defensively. "I like the work I do. The people are nice. And it gives me purpose."

My father shoots me an exasperated look. "I just don't get it. What's someone like you doing working at a funeral home? It's the last place you should be. I'd understand if you were desperate for a job but you had one. A very good job. Probably due for a promotion soon. I don't understand why anybody would give that all up for . . . for whatever this is."

Ethan and my mother both lower their heads in unison as if to avoid my gaze. What did they want me to say? How do you tell the people you love that you dream about cranes crashing down on you and loose wheels barreling towards you on the highway, and that the only way you're able to shut down these terrible thoughts, if only temporarily, is to work work work until there is no space to think or feel? What is the correct way to break it to your family that you'd rather be surrounded by the dead than the living, that to get through an evening with them you have to wear a mask so you can present as a remotely normal person? Surely there's a template for telling your loved ones you prefer the funeral home over your actual home because it's the one place that makes you feel safe and seen—the one place where there's no such thing as grieving too much or too wrong or too long or too little. How do you look them in the eyes and tell them they are the sources of the very pain they desperately wish to extinguish from you?

In the absence of a blueprint, I tell them, "I like helping people, it's like a calling," and hope that is enough to get them off my back.

"But you shouldn't even be working," Ethan chimes in. "That's the reason Shane put you on leave, right? So you can take some time to heal? It's not healthy, working that much, especially in that environment. You should be taking things slow, being gentle on yourself."

Hearing this come from Ethan, someone who has been working himself like a dog, feels like total hypocrisy. Has he always felt this way? Why has he waited until now to say all these things?

"We worry about you, that's all," my mother joins in.

It's never a good feeling, being told by the people closest to you that they worry about you. It makes you feel like a helpless injured bird whose wings are clipped. Worse, it makes you feel like a burden.

"You haven't been yourself lately," my mother continues. "You don't leave the house unless it's to go to work. And when you're home, you're holed up in your room all day. You don't hang out with your friends. You don't respond to your text messages. People keep reaching out to *me* asking if *you're* okay. What am I supposed to tell them?"

"Tell them I'm fine."

"But are you? From what I can tell, you're not. If you keep wallowing like this, you'll turn your sadness into a sickness that you'll never recover from."

I sit there, fuming in silence. I look at Ethan, waiting for him to defend me. We make eye contact, briefly. Something in his expression feels weighted. I know something is on his mind, so I dig it out of him. "If you have something to say, say it."

He swallows hard and stares directly at me.

"They're right. It's not healthy, all this crying. And now this—this career change, if you can even call it that, it's concerning."

I don't know where this is coming from.

I'm tired of being seen as the troubled one, the weak one, the why-can't-you-get-your-shit-together one. I don't need to justify myself. Anger bubbles inside my throat. I'm unraveling as my wounds give birth to the most vicious words I can think of. I look Ethan dead in the eyes and tell him: "You just don't love her as much as I do."

The shock on his face is unlike anything I've ever seen. I wish I could take it back but it's too late.

"I can't fucking believe you just said that." He forces his chair back and storms off.

I look down at my food. I can feel my parents' eyes burrow into me as if I'm an unsolvable problem. They are probably wending through history wondering where they went wrong with me. Maybe they should have placed me in daycare to help tame my emotions. Or maybe they should have tried for another child so I had a sibling to decenter my outbursts. Or maybe they shouldn't have stuck me in front of the television so much given the growing evidence that it increases aggravation. Everything can be traced back to upbringing, and I can tell my parents are beating themselves up right now.

"That was not a very nice thing to say," my mother scolds. "He's been through a lot."

My irritation rises. "And *I* haven't?"

Her reaction confirms an incredibly infuriating thing I've noticed. Ethan is praised for looking on the bright side and maintaining a positive attitude while I'm shamed for doing none of those things. When Ethan runs his knees into oblivion or works illegally long hours at the hospital, people remark at how great it is he's getting back in shape and moving on with life, whereas if I so much as lie in bed one minute longer than the allotted eight hours, I'm met with the suggestion that perhaps I should talk to somebody.

My mother exhales. Her patience is running thin, I can tell. "At least he *wants* to get better. You? It's like you enjoy being miserable!"

That's what Paloma said. I look at my father for help but he crosses his arms and grunts in agreement.

I can't believe this. They all promised to be there for me, to help me get through this. How quickly their sympathy has run its course.

Oh no.

I can feel it come up.

More ugliness.

"Well, it's a good thing the other one died so you only have to deal with one child's emotions."

My mother gasps. My father exhales with such ferocity it creates tiny ripples on the surface of his tea. I'm being cruel, I know, but I can't stop. It's like an addiction.

You'd think my parents would have stormed off the way Ethan did, but they remain seated. That's the thing about Vietnamese parents. They're as steeped in familial duty as their children. No matter how many awful things I say, they'll never leave me. It was something I gleaned through various observations as a child. When I called my father an idiot for getting a parking ticket, he still packed my school lunch the next day. When I told my mother she wasn't very pretty, she still kissed me multiple times before bed. It was like I had unlocked a superpower. I could be as cruel as I wanted and still keep all the love that had been granted to me.

Just as I expect, my mother stays put, simply scooping another handful of rice into her bowl and pinching flecks of fried fish off the plate with her chopsticks. We eat in silence for what feels like the length of winter.

My mother finally speaks after a while.

"Do you know what chia buồn means?"

I shake my head.

"It means to divide the sadness. It's what we Vietnamese do. We all take a piece of the pain so that one person is not bearing the entire burden of grieving. I have a piece. Your father has a piece. Do you understand?"

I don't know what to say.

"No, of course you don't. I bet you don't even realize why I cooked this meal for us tonight."

I look down at the rice and fish and bitter melon soup. Nothing inherently special. She scoffs and points to the bitter melon. "Do you know what this is called?"

"Bitter melon."

"In Vietnamese."

"Khổ qua."

"And what does that mean?"

I shrug.

"It means the suffering will pass. Do you remember when we first fed you this soup? You hated it. Said it was too bitter, that it burned your throat, and you cried and cried until we removed it from the table. We told you it would get easier the more you eat it and now here you are, on your third helping. You see, my child, things may be difficult now, but it won't always feel this way."

I look down at my bowl of soup, not remembering a time when I ever despised this dish.

"It is not exceptional, losing a child," she says. "Mothers have been losing their children for centuries. You are not the first and you will not be the last person to know of this anguish."

Her words feel like a punch in the gut, a kick to the face. Like tough love without the love. It had never occurred to me to think of myself as part of a long and ongoing tradition of loss—to break from the illusion that my experience was singular.

"It is a rather Western practice," she goes on, "to devote so much time dwelling on one's suffering. Lying in bed all day. Replaying events over and over. Meditating at length about how you've been wronged. What a privilege it is to have all that time tending to one's ego."

I grip my bowl of rice. Where does she get off? When did her edges get so sharp, her eyes so steely?

"What's the alternative then?" I push back. "Pretending it never happened?"

"No, of course not. But the more you drag the past into the present, the less at peace you will be."

Was she right? Was I doing this all wrong? Had I been feeding my grief too much, stuffing it and stuffing it until it had swelled into an unconquerable monster that terrorizes everyone I love, including myself?

"Try to be happy, please," my mother pleads.

It's getting late, and I'm out of energy and comebacks. We eat all that's left on the table until there remains one lone bitter melon in the soup, floating on the surface.

———————

With my parents gone, I take a shower. I undress myself and wait for the water to get as hot as I can bear. Before the mirror turns foggy, I check my reflection and am immediately startled. Have you ever looked at yourself and wondered how you got to be so extraordinarily dull and decrepit looking? When did this happen? How did I not see these lines cracking open, these veins trickling along my cheek?

I know I shouldn't be surprised given how poorly I've been treating my body, like some kind of unwanted stray. No matter how fast I run from it or shoo it away or throw scraps in the other direction, it's always there. I wake up and it's there. I go to sleep and it's there.

I can't keep doing this forever. If I want to get better, I need to take care of myself.

I wash my hair and gather it into a luscious lather. I take a loofah and run it over the dry patches on my body. I shave my legs, grate the calluses off my heels, push back my cuticles. I open a new bottle of tuberose-scented oil and slather it all over my body until I'm as friction-less as a dolphin. When my hands reach my stomach, I pause. I pull on the fat so it stretches and spans like raw pizza dough. Why are mothers in such a rush to flatten their bellies? Maybe it's because they don't need proof they birthed a baby. Their baby *is* the proof. I rest my hands on my belly, feeling it rise as I take a breath, and for once I'm proud of it because it made you.

When I get out, I wrap myself in a towel and check on Ethan. He's in the guest bedroom, and I know he's not sleeping because the door is left ajar. He has a thing about sleeping with the door open, a latent fear about waking up engulfed in flames. Besides, he doesn't believe in going to bed angry. In fact, he proclaimed in front of our wedding guests, all 170 of them, that he promised to always resolve all disputes before resting his head on the pillow.

I tremble with nervousness as I walk up to him. He's under the covers, his breath slow and deliberate. He's pretending to sleep so he won't have to talk to me. I decide to accept my wrongdoing. There will be no shouting match, no defending my actions. I will let him say his piece and listen quietly, without pushing back. That way, this can all blow over quickly.

"I'm so sorry," I start. "I know what I said was unforgivable, but can you ever forgive me?"

I steel myself for his wrath, but he opts for the silent treatment.

"I don't know why I said that awful thing. I didn't mean it. Of course you love her with all your heart. That's not even a question. Anybody with their head on right can see how much it pains you that she's not here. Can we just move along to the part where you tell me *It's okay, baby, I know you didn't mean it?* You know I'm an idiot. Can we just move past this, please?"

Still, he doesn't budge. I tap him harder, but he pretends to not feel it. "Are you kidding me right now? Look, I know what I did was un-called for but what you're doing to me now is far worse. I get it. You're mad. But I don't understand why you can't just put it aside for one minute and be like, *Okay fine, let me have an adult conversation with my grieving wife, hash out my feelings with her, and give her a kiss good night instead of sulking in bed like an avoidant man-child?* Now can you please sit up so we can talk about this?"

His entire body jerks, then becomes suddenly still. I turn on all the lights and discover his eyes shut, mouth wide open, ear plugs in. He's been dead asleep the entire time.

27

Weeks go by without a single dialogue between me and Ethan. I fear if this goes on any longer, the space we have occupied in each other's lives will become obsolete.

I decide to apologize, just get it over with, and wait for him to return from his second run of the day. When hours pass and he still isn't home, I assume the worst. He's been hit by a car. He's been struck by a stray bullet during a brazen daylight shooting. He's tripped and smashed his head on a rock and is out there hemorrhaging somewhere. I call my parents to see if they've heard from him but they don't pick up and now I fear they're dead, too. Everyone I love is dead or about to die.

Ethan marches through the door, sweat beads dotting his forehead. There seems to be no signs of hemorrhaging or gunshot wound. He's peering down at his smartwatch as it beeps excessively. There's a coffee and croissant in his hand. He chows down and does not ask me if I want a bite. I can't believe he has the audacity to go about his morning routine while I've been worried sick over here.

Breathe.

I force myself to calm down. I know if I meet his quiet fury with my own, we will reach a stalemate. I think about what Dr. Posey said—how most marriages don't survive the death of a child. I can't let her be right.

I walk over to the table and pull out a chair, the same chair I sat in when those ugly words spewed out of me. He does not look up, his eyes fixed to something on that tiny watch of his.

"Can we talk?"

He sips his coffee and says, "Depends."

It's the first word he's said to me since the fight. I inhale, mulling over everything I've been too terrified to say, and just say it.

I begin by telling him why the funeral home is important to me. I tell him about the intrusive thoughts, the flashbacks, the wanting to die. How I just needed to drown out the noise. And though I went into the job for all the wrong reasons, I want to stay because it's the only place where I feel like myself.

I tell him the people there treated you with so much love, more love than we could have ever hoped for. A care so deep and unexpected and rare it gave me my first taste of peace in a long time.

"It's nice being around people who see me as a person and not a tragedy. They just get it, you know? They accept me for all my messiness and brokenness."

Ethan doesn't respond, only sets his drink down. Maybe it's hopeful thinking, but I notice the bands in his neck softening and the scrunch in his forehead flattening, like all the anger he harbors for me is slowly washing away. He runs his hand over his entire face and lets out a laborious exhale. "I had no idea you felt this way. Why didn't you say something? Did you think I wouldn't understand?"

I shrug, staring at a water stain on the table. "Sometimes it's the people closest to us who understand the least."

He drops his head as if he knows I'm right.

"And I'm sorry about—" I choke. "About that thing I said." Someone once told me the art of a good apology is to state the harm that was done. But I can't do it. I can't repeat those ugly words. It wasn't me. It's not who I am. "I hope you know that's not how I feel. Of course I know you love her. And I know everyone grieves differently. It was wrong of me to even say such an awful thing."

He waits a moment before speaking up, palming his chest. "For a second, I wondered if it was true."

"If what was true?"

"Whether I loved her enough." I reach for his hand and realize it's shaking. His watch suddenly beeps to inform him his heart rate is elevated. He taps ignore and when it beeps again, he swiftly removes the watch in frustration.

"Oh my god, please don't ever think that. I was completely out of my mind when I said that. Of course you do. There's no question."

He pulls his hand away from me, as if embarrassed by his trembling. "So why does it feel like I've moved on too quickly?" He looks at a point behind me, beyond me. "I barely took any time off work. I have never missed a run. I'm in the best shape of my life right now. Someone at work even said they'd never seen anybody bounce back so quickly from a big loss. And she said it in such a way that I don't think was supposed to be a compliment." He pauses. "Do you know the last time I cried?"

I try to recall but our grief has been so private, so individual, that I honestly can't remember.

"Three months ago, on her six-month anniversary. Three months."

"It doesn't mean you're not grieving. There's no right or wrong way to do it."

"The other day, I had to pull up a sad movie just to make sure I could still cry."

"And did you?"

"Yes. But I shouldn't have to pull up a sad movie. I should be able to think of her and that should be enough. But when I think of her." He sighs. "I don't feel anything. It's like I've reached the end, you know? I've cried out all the tears I'll ever cry."

I go quiet for a minute, trying to imagine what it would feel like to get through an entire day without bursting into tears. I picture a life without constant makeup touch-ups, without pulling over on the side of the road, without carrying around a wad of tissue paper wherever I go. It sounds liberating—to live without sorrow's grip constantly around your throat. But then I remember your funeral, my complete inability to shed a single tear, and I get Ethan's point. Not being able to release the screams inside your body is a hell of its own.

"Grief is weird," I say, trying to make him feel better. "Just because you can't cry doesn't mean you don't care."

"What if—" He stops, holding back. I give him a moment. "What if I'm forgetting her?" he says. "What if I forget how she looks, the way she sounds when she breathes, the way her hair feels between my fingers? I feel like it's already begun."

My eyes well up with tears. I quickly dab them away for fear I'm rubbing my emotional whims in his face. "You will never, ever forget her."

"How do you know? I've caught myself going an entire day without thinking about her."

"Because I won't let you. I will make sure of it."

I pull him into my arms and run my hands through his hair. He sinks into my chest and we stay there for a long while.

"Did you watch *Grave of the Fireflies*?" I ask, remembering Melody and Dolores's conversation.

"No."

"What movie did you watch to make you cry, then?"

"You won't judge?"

"Promise."

He hesitates for a moment, then spits it out. "*Mamma Mia 2*."

I pause, waiting for him to say he's kidding but he's serious. The corners of his lips turn up and we both burst into laughter, our bellies clutched in a familiar but pleasurable kind of pain. It feels good to give humor another try.

"Ethan?" I say.

"Yeah."

"You're crying right now."

He lifts his hands to his face as if to make sure the tears are real. He licks the tears off his fingers. He licks and licks and licks, as if these are the first drops of rain after a horrendously long drought. That night, we make love for the first time since you died, in the pitch-black, where he can't see the tears pour down my face, a secret just for me and the pillowcase. It feels good to be in each other's arms again. It feels like a defiant act, a desperate attempt at resuming cheer and taking back the pleasure that was ripped from us.

So why does it feel wrong? Why does it feel like we're dancing in the streets as atomic bombs fall from the sky?

28

Dear diary,
I think I want another. I know, I know, adding another child into the fray would be disastrous, but I miss the newborn days. The scrunching of the legs, the intoxicating snuggles, the blurring of time and space. I want it all back.

Dear diary,
The baby's birthday is coming up! We're going with a book theme. I'm thinking we could do a cute banner that says "Chapter One" and hand out bookmarks as party favors and get a cake shaped like a stack of books. It's going to be perfect. I'll invite everyone. It'll be the biggest party the neighborhood has ever seen because she deserves it. She deserves the world.

29

Monday morning starts with a pickup. By now, I've done at least five—white-knuckling my way through each one until the process became muscle memory. Park at shipping and receiving dock. Follow attendant to deceased patient. Zip up body in plastic bag. Tag bag with identifying information. Obtain signature on consent form. Transfer body to cot. Bam, bam, done.

There's profound relief knowing there's a meticulous, time-tested system to get people's loved ones where they need to go. No body gets lost. No body goes unaccounted for.

As I hop into Kenneth's car, a flashback appears. No, no, not again! We're in the hospital, packing our things. Gathering everything we want to take home. Except for you. You're in the hospital bassinet, surrounded by a ring of stuffed animals. We've said every variation of goodbye. Kissed every inch of your face. As the nurse walks us out the door, I stop and ask, "Will she be all alone?" The nurse assures me you won't, that she'll stay in the room until the funeral home staff arrives. "What if you have to use the bathroom?" I ask, and the nurse promises me that somebody will always be in the room. We take her word for it—what else could we do?—and walk away from your body.

Kenneth's phone rings, breaking me out of the memory. I hear a female voice on the other end asking where something is. Kenneth tells her they're probably inside a drawer, next to the utensils, shoved in the back probably, but make sure to check the expiry date as it's been a while since Napoleon has had a dental chew. Before hanging up, he says to my utter bewilderment, "Okay, bye bye, honey bun."

I bite the inside of my cheek. Kenneth has a dog? Kenneth named his dog Napoleon? Kenneth has a person he calls *honey bun*? I want to know more. I want to ask who *honey bun* is, what kind of breed Napoleon is, what brand of dental chews he buys.

"Bad breath isn't normal," I say unexpectedly.

"Excuse me?"

"People assume dogs are supposed to have bad breath, but it could be a sign of a serious health issue. Possibly bacterial growth or tartar buildup. Or worse, it could be a symptom of kidney disease. Kidneys filter and process toxins and if they're not working properly, one of the first signs is bad breath."

There's a palpable silence afterwards. Kenneth fiddles with the controls on the multimedia dashboard and I fear I've accidentally insulted his dog.

Finally, he speaks. "You're right, we should really take him in for a proper cleaning but we've been so busy with the upcoming move. My wife's siblings offered to help us pack but they mostly piled on the guilt. They're so upset at us for moving farther away from them but we're literally only an extra fifteen-minute drive away. They're disturbingly codependent."

In the span of twenty-two seconds, Kenneth has divulged more information about his private life than he has in the past nine months. It's like a field of freshly ripened strawberries, so much to pick at. Should I ask where he's moving to, inquire about his wife, or encourage more bitching about the in-laws? Kenneth chimes in before I can ask any follow-up questions.

"How do you know so much about dental care for dogs anyway? Do you have one yourself?"

I look out at the snow-topped trees that straddle the Don Valley Parkway. "My best friend had one growing up. A labradoodle. His name was Stephen. With a 'ph.' He was such a good dog. Horrible breath though. They spent a fortune keeping the plaque off his teeth. Her parents still have the receipts stored in a Tupperware container to this day. About once a month, they like to whip it out to show people how exorbitant the vet bills were."

"Did they ever get another dog?"

"No. After Stephen died, Paloma's dad couldn't get out of bed for months. Said he would never put himself through that heartbreak again."

From the corner of my eye, I see Kenneth nodding his head in agreement. "I hear that quite a bit in this line of work. Many people are scared to love something so much afterwards. Widows have told me they'll never remarry." He pauses, clearing his throat. "Parents have told me they'll never have another child."

I stir in my seat. "And what do you tell those people?"

"Oh, it's not my place to be imparting advice on families in their time of mourning. It's such an emotionally taxing time for them. They're not in the right headspace to think about tomorrow, let alone the future."

I nod. "But if you could, what would you say?"

He pauses, thinking about his response. "Truthfully, I'd say go ahead. If you want to ensure a life of little pain, then it might be wise to keep to yourself, not attach yourself to anything too much, keep the people in your life at a distance. To love anything is to jump on a speeding train to heartbreak."

"You'd really say that? Is that how you really feel? You don't think a life without love is heartbreaking, too?"

"Yes, one could see it that way. It depends on how much suffering you can tolerate. For some people, their hearts can tolerate very little."

Kenneth merges lanes and takes the next exit. I think about what he said. I think he meant it to be comforting but that kind of life feels hollow, lonely, just all around sad. As awful as everything is, I could never give up the time I had with you. I'd rather have these wounds than none of it at all because they're a reminder of the mark you've left on this world. Your time here may have been brief, but my god—what a glorious gift it was.

My phone vibrates with a message from my mother. It's a quote from the Lebanese American poet Kahlil Gibran:

When you are sorrowful look again in your heart, and you shall see that in truth you are weeping for that which has been your delight.

I look out at the road, wondering if she's following me. It concerns me how increasingly well-timed her messages have become.

"Can I ask you a question?" I say.

"Mm-hmm."

"Do you think some people are more resilient than others?"

"To be honest, I think resiliency is a bunch of bullshit."

I choke back some saliva. Did Kenneth just *swear*?

"I think somebody's ability to withstand a tragic loss has nothing to do with resilience," he goes on. "Everybody, no matter how strong-willed you think you are, will experience a permanent rupture of catastrophic proportion. They will be forever changed. They will weep. They will scream. They will plead for all of it to be over. And then the day will come when they go to bed and realize they got through the whole day. They'll notice a loosening of that constant wrenching in their gut. They'll be able to pull up memories of their loved one without breaking down. And let me tell you, that has nothing to do with resilience."

"Then what is it?" I ask, intrigued. "What gives somebody the ability to overcome such tragedies?"

He pauses to think about his answer. "It's simple really. People. Community. Connections. Nobody can get out of a pit by themselves, particularly if it's a deep, cavernous one. We depend on one another, like it or not. Why do you think we have funerals? People need to be reminded they have a community of support around them. *That* is how they will get through it. Not grit. Not positivity." He pauses. "Certainly not inspirational quotes." He lets out a throaty laugh and I realize he has been glancing down at my phone. I quickly turn my screen off. He snickers. "I'm only joking. I love a good quote as much as the next guy, but that's probably no surprise to you."

I cringe as I think about all the framed quotes peppered around the funeral home. The cheesiness and genericism of them all. And yet for some reason, I always see people standing in front of them, taking a picture with their phones, as if they plan to pull it up later or send it to a friend, with the belief this quote will impart a renewed sense of hope.

"Okay, we're here."

I look up from my phone and a chill runs down my neck. My chest swells with fear as I realize where we are. The hospital where it all happened.

Another flashback. My hands are suddenly cold, clasped around something stiff and hard and I realize it is you. No more tubes and wires and beeping. Your chest has stopped moving up and down and your hands are balled into tight fists. I try to uncurl them so I can wrap your hands around my fingers, but there is no give. It's like your hands are glued shut. Ethan asks me to pass you to him, but I'm afraid if I don't keep you pressed against my warm body that you will turn into stone. The nurse tells us to take our time, there is no rush at all, but just so we know her shift will be ending in an hour and somebody else will be taking over. This makes us feel like we need to hurry our hugs and goodbyes, but how can we when we just said hello?

"Are you coming?"

The flashback is over and I'm back inside the car, parked in the loading dock of the hospital, as Kenneth knocks on the glass of the passenger door. My heart is racing, pumping blood to all my extremities and yet my limbs feel numb. I can't get myself to open the door. My body is frozen. My senses sharpened.

Breathe.

Breathe.

Breathe.

I look around. Big, burly, uniformed men unload boxes out of trucks. Medical equipment. Fresh linens. Soft drinks for the vending machines. Is this where they wheeled you out? Covered in an opaque sheet of plastic so that anybody walking by would not know what was underneath? Nothing to see here. Just another FedEx package going out for delivery.

"Is everything okay?" Kenneth knocks on my window again.

Thump.

Thump.

Thump.

Each knock is loud and thunderous, causing me to jolt from my seat. My heart is pounding. My breathing quickens. Why can't I get out of this car?

Kenneth opens the door and I feel naked. I am exposed to things that will hurt me. My mind races through all the possible ways I could die. Someone slashing my throat. Coyotes gnawing at my ribs. Airborne toxins entering my lungs and polluting my bloodstream. I have welcomed the idea of death, flirted with it, beckoned it. So why am I suddenly terrified?

"Close the door," I say to him.

"What's going on? Are you feeling all right?"

"Please close the door."

"Did something happen? Should I call someone?"

"CLOSE THE FUCKING DOOR!"

Kenneth's eyes go wide with shock. He gently closes the door, takes the cot out of the back, and disappears inside the hospital. I need to get out of here. I think about pulling on the door handle, but my arms won't leave my lap. Why can't I move my arms? I think about lifting my feet off the floor but they remain planted. Why can't I move my feet? I can't move. I can't do anything. I'm going to be stuck here forever. Is this it? Is this how it ends for me? Inside a parked mortuary van at the shipping and receiving dock of the hospital where my baby died?

"Cleo?"

Ethan is standing outside the car. I don't know how much time has passed. He opens the door and takes my hand. I will my body to move and it listens to me. It's slow, like it has just come out of major surgery, but it's doing what I want it to.

"How did you know I was here?"

"Kenneth called me. I came as fast as I could."

"He had your number?"

"You put me as your emergency contact."

I had forgotten I'd done that. What had I been thinking? Filling out forms and accepting a job I had no business having? I'm too messed up and broken for this. Why did Kenneth even hire me? Surely he's going to fire me now. He will finally see me for who I am. Pathetic. Weak. Good for nothing.

30

Ethan is convinced I need a break from the funeral home. He demands I eat a hearty meal, drink a big glass of water, and get a solid night's sleep. But I know what I need. I need to be with Dumpling.

In the middle of the night, despite Ethan's watchful eyes and worried protests, I push my luck and slip out while he's sleeping. Earlier I saw Paloma and Freddie pack up their car and drive off for the night, probably staying at his parents' house again. I couldn't pass up the opportunity to step into a version of my life where I am normal and happy and nothing bad ever happens. Every time I step inside that house, I feel safe, swaddled, surrounded by everything I want: love, warmth, laughter, markers on the wall, drool stains on the couch, rubber duckies in the bathtub, itty-bitty shoes by the door, cuddles until sundown. There's no darkness, no place for it to settle.

I set Dumpling on the changing table and put on a fresh diaper. I pick a onesie out of the drawer, a plain white one with three buttons on the crotch, and snap those on. I put my finger on Dumpling's nonexistent hands, wishing it would do that thing baby hands instinctively do where it squeezes anything that touches it. Nothing happens.

I pick her up and bob around the house, narrating everything I see. *Talking to your baby regularly will encourage them to speak while strengthening their communication skills.* "Let's go see what there is to eat in the kitchen. Oooh, grapes! We love grapes. What color are they? Why yes, they are green! So juicy and delicious and *green*! Let's see, what else is in the fridge? We've got yogurt and cheese and zucchini and milk. So much miiiiilk. Do *you* love milk? Yes you do!"

There are multiple bottles of breast milk in the fridge. They have started to separate, thick fat floats at the top. They all have today's date on it. Paloma must be an oversupplier. I wonder if I am still producing. I go back upstairs and lie Dumpling down in the crib. I turn on the sound machine and draw the blackout curtains. I pull out Paloma's breast pump and secure the plastic shields to my breasts. The machine whirs awake and the suction begins, first short and quick, then shifts to a slower, deeper rhythm. The flanges are too wide for my nipples, so each pull stretches and pinches my areolas. I grip the armrests and breathe through it because that is what mothers do. Endure the pain for our babies. I wait for white drops of milk to flow down the plastic tubes, but nothing is coming out. I increase the suction strength, wincing through the pain, praying the bottles will fill up with something, anything, but the only droplets that emerge come from the condensation of my body heat. I turn it off. There is now an angry ring of red around my breasts.

Pathetic.

Weak.

Good for nothing.

I make myself useful in other ways. I tidy up the nursery. I do a deeper clean this time, wiping the baseboards, sanitizing the light switches and doorknobs, de-pilling the rocking chair, but by the end of it I still cannot rid myself of this restlessness. I walk around the house. I enter the primary bedroom and sift through the contents of Paloma's vanity. I dab on a brightening serum. Spray on a musky perfume. Hold up a yellow-gold diamond crawler to my ear to see if it looks good on me. It does not.

I look around the room. The bedsheets are different, cotton percale this time. Books are stacked on each side table, not for reading but for the propping of lamps. I pull out Freddie's drawer. Glasses. Spare change. Lubricant. I peek inside Paloma's table. Hand lotion. Eye mask. A crinkled packet of birth control pills. Tucked in the back of the drawer is an unopened box. A pregnancy test. The tiny inscription on the bottom says it's been expired for months. I wonder if it still works. I pull out the stick, take it with me to the bathroom, and pee on the absorbent strip. The pink control line appears. The second line does not. My heart sinks, then quickly buoys back up with relief. You can't lose another child if you don't have them in the first place.

I remember when I found out I was pregnant with you. It was the middle of the night. I had rolled onto my stomach to get in a more comfortable sleeping position, suddenly yelping in pain. My breasts were tender beyond belief, unable to bear the weight of my body despite all that thick memory foam underneath. That's when I knew. I didn't need a pregnancy test to confirm the existence of you.

"What the hell are you doing here?"

Paloma.

She's at the bathroom door, eyes wide, brows crinkled, mouth agape. I quickly get off the toilet and pull my pants up. I didn't hear her come in. No car pulling up. No thermostat chime. No steps up the stairs. Had I heard anything like that, I would have dashed inside a closet. Crawled under the bed. It's my fault for not paying attention. Why hadn't I paid attention?

Pathetic.

Weak.

Good for nothing.

I open my mouth to say something but what could I say? There's no justifiable reason why I'm in *her* house, using *her* bathroom, peeing on *her* pregnancy test. We may be best friends, but there are boundaries you just don't cross. Why had I done this? Why am I such a terrible friend? I close my eyes and hope when I open them, she'll be gone. But she's still standing there, the creases in her forehead more pronounced as she awaits an explanation.

"Well, are you going to say something?" she shouts.

"I—"

I'm so bad at defending myself. How am I supposed to justify this? The longer I'm mute, the more Paloma figures it out on her own. Her eyebrows twist as she pieces it all together: the stains that magically disappeared; the diaper pail that was always conveniently emptied; the onesies with the inexplicably crisp folds. I see questions all over her face. *How long has this been going on? Why did you do this?*

"Oh my god," Paloma cries. She puts her hands over her mouth, having finally put together the full picture.

This is it. She's through with me. She's going to tell me to get out, to never come back here again, to stay away from her and her family. All of our friends and neighbors will side with her after she tells them what I did. *How horrible! How inexcusable! I don't care if she's lost a baby, she has no right to do what she did!* People will stop by her house with food and flowers. They will peer over their shoulders, take one look at my house, and mutter under their breath, *What a sad, sad woman.*

The more I lay out this imagined future, the more its edges become defined like a Polaroid coming into sharper focus, and a realization comes to me: I'm about to lose her, too.

"I'm really, really sorry, I shouldn't have done what I did—" My voice is cracking, each word breaking up like a bad connection. I wish there was a flashlight I could flicker three times, to remind her of our decades-long friendship, to declare a truce. As I look at Paloma, I think about the kids we were, shy yet precocious, cautious in life but daring in our dreams. I think about our fake daycare and all the plushies we wrangled together. That could've been us for real. We could've been raising our children together. But I ruined it. I ruined everything. "I—I don't know why I did this. At first I was getting your package out of the rain, but then I just kept coming back for some reason and—"

"You're pregnant," Paloma says, pointing to the stick on the counter.

Confused, I look down and wave my hands. "No, no, no. I was just testing it out. The box said it had expired and I wanted to know if it would still work."

She steps into the bathroom, picks up the stick. "There are two lines."

"No, just one."

"No, Cleo. There are *two* lines."

I take the test from her. I squeeze my eyes shut, then open them. The other line. It is faint but it is there.

31

There's nothing left to do but tell Paloma everything. The break-ins. The cleaning. The pretend games with Dumpling. And I don't stop there. Because I have nothing left to lose, I tell her all the things I've wanted to scream in her face since we left the hospital. How seeing her with a living baby feels like a knife to my throat. How unfair it is that she got what she barely wanted. How infuriating it was the way she doted on me when all I wanted was one valid reason to cut her out of my life and when she finally gave me that reason by saying what she said in the car, it shattered me beyond words.

"I'm sorry," I repeat like a broken faucet that won't turn off. "I should have never come into your house like this. It was wrong of me. I'm such a mess. It's hard for me to look out my window and see your perfect house and perfect family, living out the life I should have had. I just wanted to know what it was like. To have everything go according to plan. I wanted to know what it would have been like if she had . . . if she had . . ."

Why is it so hard to say the thing I want the most?

"Lived. I know it doesn't make any sense. Do you know I haven't stepped inside her nursery in months? I can't stand it. It's so cold and quiet. The opposite of this room." I look around the nursery, where we're sitting cross-legged. "I like it here. It's warm and calming. You've done such a good job of this space. When I'm here, I feel like I'm with her, you know? Nobody ever brings her up and I just wanted to pretend she was here. I'm sorry, I know this sounds bizarre. I won't blame you if you never want to see me again. Please, just kick me out. I won't be mad. I promise. You deserve a friend who doesn't have a hard time being around you. A friend who can be happy for you."

When I finish, my whole body immediately loosens. I can breathe easier, deeper, without all that guilt clogging my airways. Paloma is taking it quite well. She does not shout or scream or slap me. I think being pregnant helps. Most people look down on berating or hitting a pregnant person.

She grabs my hand with both of hers and squeezes it tight, not letting me go.

"It's okay," she says. "I get why you did what you did. I had no idea how painful it was for you to be around me. And I'm sorry I don't talk about Daisy. It's just that . . . I didn't think you wanted to." My heart flutters. It feels wonderful to hear your name come out of another person's mouth.

"It's just not easy to talk about," I say. "To be honest, it's not easy talking about it with you because—"

Just blurt it out.

"—your baby lived and mine didn't."

Paloma's face scrunches in horror as tears stream down her face. She lets me keep talking.

"To be honest, I resented you for a while. I hate that I feel that way. I know what happened is not your fault, but I can't stop wondering why me? Why did this have to happen to me? Not that I would want anything to happen to your child. No, no, please don't get me wrong. That's the last thing I'd want. I just . . . I just wish things were different."

I look down at both of our hands, so tightly intertwined I don't know whose is whose, just like the day we went into labor. I'm surprised she hasn't pulled away.

"It never occurred to me you felt this way. I'm so sorry. If I can confess, I've felt so much guilt about what happened."

"You have?"

She swallows hard before speaking. "Because I'm the happiest I've ever been. My baby has brought so much wonder to my life and every time I catch myself bursting with joy, I feel guilty that that was taken away from you. When I think about losing my own baby, my world goes dark. I can't move. It feels like somebody has ripped my heart out. And then I snap out of it and realize it's just a fleeting thought. For you, though, it's your reality. If I could take away just an ounce of your pain, I would do it in a heartbeat."

Hearing these words feels like the first sip of water after a long entrapment. An intense relief washes over me. I appreciate her saying all of this because it means she has imagined the unimaginable. Until now, I didn't realize that's all I wanted this entire time. For the pain to be acknowledged. For others to know how much this hurts.

"And I'm so, so, so sorry about what I said in the car," Paloma continues. "Of course no baby could ever replace Daisy. She could never be erased, not by anyone or any amount of time in the world. You'll always be her mother and she'll always be your girl."

I could feel the tears coming so I shut my eyes. Paloma leans in for a hug and I sob into her chest, letting my body sink into her. She doesn't flinch or buckle under the pressure. She just holds me tight on the floor of the dark nursery, keeping me from collapsing to the ground. It's the type of embrace that tells me *I've got you, I won't let you fall*. And I will never forget it. The sensation of being held when it feels like the weight of the world is on me.

Once it feels like I've expelled all the tears from my body, I pull back and dry my face. I remark at the large wet spot on Paloma's shirt and feel terrible for soiling her clothes.

"Oh god, your shirt! I'm so sorry!"

She looks down and laughs. "Please, this is nothing. I've gotten far worse excretions on this thing—"

Paloma stops talking and her eyes go wide with panic.

"I'm sorry, I didn't mean—"

"It's okay. Really."

Silence fills the air, floating in and around our tense bodies, until Paloma speaks up. "I'm a little mad, to be honest."

I lower my head in shame. "I know you are. I shouldn't have broken in like this."

"It's not that. I'm mad that Freddie wasn't the one that's been doing all this cleaning! I should've known. The onesies. Of course he doesn't have a clue about the KonMari Fold!"

Despite my deception, we both laugh out loud like old times.

I change the subject, my heart pounding as I say this next part. "I'd love to meet Jude one day, if that's okay?"

Paloma's eyes turn dewy. It's the first time either of us has mentioned her son's name. I'm ashamed to admit I didn't know his name until I saw her Instagram post. I didn't want to know anything about him but now I'm ready. "That would make me so happy." Paloma beams.

I rest my hand on my belly and think about the cluster of cells rapidly multiplying in my uterus. I think about how strange it is our bodies know what to do without any instruction from us, how it carries out functions we can't even fathom. I worry something will go wrong. What if I'm missing a crucial genetic material required to keep a baby alive? What if my grief rubs off on the baby and they become destined to live a life of misery? I have become too privy to all the ways babies can die that I wonder how any of them make it home alive. I can't bear to lose another child. It will be the end of me.

Paloma senses my dread, grabs my hand again.

"What if it doesn't work out?" I ask her.

"What if it does?"

I think about how much I want this baby and how scary it is to want something so badly. It would be so easy to never want for anything. I think about Kenneth's words. *To love anything is to jump on a speeding train to heartbreak.*

But it's unshakable. The want. The hunger. The desperation to be slathered in joy again.

I picture a baby in my arms. Not a plush toy. A real baby. One that cries and coos and clasps my finger when I stroke its palm. One that outgrows its clothes and shoes and toys. One whose eyes light up when I enter the room.

A sweet tickle spreads inside me. It's so foreign; I have to remind myself what that feeling is.

Suddenly a wave of nausea hits me. At first I mistake it for morning sickness, the kind that creeps up your throat and wets your mouth, but this is different. This is burrowed deep in my gut, wedged in there like the head of a tick. I recognize the guilt immediately. It is punishing and relentless and mean, screaming all kinds of things at me: How dare you make plans for the future? How dare you want to be happy? How dare you abandon her?

I collapse into my own body. It's exhausting, all this feeling. My instinct is to numb myself with pills and vodka and screens and work.

I think about the clump of cells again, how it's expanding and growing and multiplying into something that will one day walk and talk and breathe and dream. I remember the trivia I learned at Sadie and Fatima's baby shower. How a baby's fetal cells stay in the mother's body for years. How the cells transfer to future brothers and sisters. How we all live on in some form or another as long as we have people here who love us. I rub circles on my belly, hoping all of it is true.

32

Before I leave Paloma, she makes one request of me. To tell Ethan everything. The pills. The intrusions. Everything. I promise her I will and actually mean it this time.

When morning comes, I think of ways to break it to him. He'll be disappointed, that I know for sure, but what he'll do with the information I don't know. Will he ransack every inch of this house and remove every possible medical substance that could be abused? Will he track my whereabouts to ensure I have not trespassed onto anybody's property? Will he send me away to a facility that can knock me to my senses? So many scenarios run through my mind, but the one I'm most afraid of filters its way to the top: Will he leave me?

I find him in the living room, sitting on the sofa's edge reading a book. Probably another one of his grief books. I get closer, trying to make out the title on the yellow spine when—

Shit. That's the diary. *My* diary.

"What are you doing with that?" I shout.

"What the hell is this?" He shakes the diary in the air, exposing all the pages I'd written in.

"Give it to me!"

"What the hell is this?" he repeats, eyes wide with rage.

"Nothing."

"Cleo!" He barks my name so loud it scares me.

"It's not mine. It's Paloma's."

"Jesus Christ, you don't think I can tell that this is clearly your handwriting?"

My jaw is clenched so tight I can feel my teeth shifting. "Fine, it's mine."

"What is this?"

"It's nothing. I'm just . . . experimenting."

"With what exactly?"

"I'm trying my hand at fiction writing, that's all."

"Oh it's fiction all right! And not a very good one!"

"Fuck off!"

"Get serious, Cleo. You told me from now on we were going to be honest with each other. About everything. No holding back. So maybe start by telling me what the fuck this is!"

I reach for the diary, but he holds it up high where I can't reach and reads aloud a passage.

"The baby is here. She has a bit of jaundice but otherwise is feeding well and pooping lots."

"Stop it!" I jump up to grab the diary, but his wingspan is preposterously long.

"I'm writing this as she sleeps in my arm. I can't stop staring at her. She's so peaceful, so serene."

"I'm serious, give that to me!" I grab his crewneck and twist the fabric with both my hands.

"The baby's birthday is coming up. We're going with a book theme."

I try to scratch his face but my arms can't reach so I deliver one strong punch to his gut, causing him to clutch his stomach in agony. The diary drops from his hand. "You're a fucking asshole," I say.

He coughs a couple times before straightening himself. "You're living in a goddamn fantasyland!"

"No, I'm not!"

"Does this make you feel better? Pretending she had lived?"

"I'm not pretending anything. It's . . . it's just for fun."

"For fun? There's pages and pages and pages of this. That's seriously messed up!"

I fold my arms and look away. It is easier not to look at the bewilderment on his face. I wait for him to shout some more, to call me out, to diagnose me with a disorder that will prove I am and have always been unfit to be a mother. But all he says is, his voice now weak: "Why didn't you tell me?"

"Because if I told you, you would've packed your bags and left. I know it's all too much for you. Me and my impossible emotions."

"That's not how I feel."

"Well, it certainly comes across that way."

He groans, his eyes darting to the diary in my hands. "Why did you write all this?"

I can feel myself tearing up just thinking of a response.

"Do I really have to spell it out?"

"Yes, please. I want to understand."

"Because! Because I want to be that mother. I want to live that life. I want the sleepless nights and the mysterious rashes and the fucked-up plane rides where I'm covered in shit! It's not fair! It's not fair that we did everything right and she still died anyway. We picked the best doctor. We went to the best hospital. We did all the tests. I even prayed. *Prayed!* You know me. When have I ever prayed? What an idiot I must have looked begging to a god I don't even believe in."

A violent rage comes over me and I whack a cup off the table so hard it goes flying towards the media unit. Coffee and ceramic pieces go everywhere. Sofa, rug, feet.

God, that felt so *good*.

I look for more things I can destroy. I flip over a chair. I knock over a lamp. I kick the stupid ottoman that is always getting in my fucking way. There's a vase of dead funeral flowers on the table. There's not a single drop of water in it—that's how much it's been neglected.

"And I'm sick of all these fucking flowers!"

I lift up the vase—Ethan's eyes scream *don't you dare*—and I throw it against the wall. Broken glass scatters like glitter, crispy flowers lifeless on the floor. When the last shard stops spinning, Ethan looks at me in horror before grabbing my arm and saying, "You're coming with me."

———

We've been driving for over an hour and Ethan has still not told me where we're going. I have a few guesses in my head. He is taking me to (A) a psychiatric hospital, (B) a rehab center, or (C) the middle of the woods where he plans to abandon me and let me slowly rot into wolf dinner.

The emptier the highway gets and the more rural the surroundings, the more C starts to sound like the most plausible answer. I'm tempted to break the silence. To tell him I'm pregnant so that he'll have to spare my life. He'll have to turn this car around and come back to me. I cannot bear the feeling that I've taken a sledgehammer to the most vulnerable cracks in our marriage, leaving deep fissures beyond repair. We've lost so much, and I've bludgeoned what little we have left.

We arrive at a parking lot where there's nothing but trees surrounding us. He gets out and I follow suit. He heads towards an unmarked trail and I do the same. Each time we hit a bend, I expect him to finally tell me what we're doing here, but he keeps marching forwards. We go on like this for a while. He maintains a lead of about twenty to thirty feet, his pace never slowing, and I wonder if he is purposely trying to lose me. I am getting tired. My breath clouds are getting bigger, more frequent. I wish he would stop. I wish he would just tell me what's going on inside his head. Just tell me it's over. That it's one thing to be with a woman who can't keep her baby alive, but it's another to put up with her infuriatingly destructive behavior.

We stop at a cliff overlooking a sparkling blue lake. He brushes the snow off a rock and takes a seat. I notice he has left a little bit of room, so I wedge myself in and sit there as he throws small rocks over the cliff. His pitch is strong, forceful, as if he's picturing me on the other end of those stones. I hold my breath, waiting for a tirade of fury, a final warning, a declaration of divorce. I brace myself for what he might say and remember what my father said to my mother all those years ago. *I can't do this anymore! You need to get over it! You suck the life out of everything!*

"I've been coming here a lot to clear my head," he finally says. "This is Daisy Lake."

My mouth falls open. I was not expecting that. My heart flickers at the sound of your name and I rest my hand on my chest, trying to still it. Ethan tells me he came across it when he was aimlessly driving around, looking for somewhere to go, and when he plugged in your name into the GPS, it took him straight here.

"I've been thinking this would be a good place to spread her ashes."

I'm silent. He's not mad? He doesn't want a divorce? He doesn't want to throw me into an institution and leave me there for good? Ethan pulls down his toque and slides a finger underneath his eye. I feel my chest lurch, as if his aches and pains are mine to bear, too. I lean my body into his, not sure what to say. He stares intently at the blank space beside him, like he's attempting to conjure you to life.

When you lose a child, you're forced to live two lives: the one in your imagination and the one rooted in reality. You skip back and forth, sometimes inhabiting one more frequently than the other. One moment the high chair is covered in Cheerios and yogurt and the next it is spotless, empty.

"What do you think?" Ethan asks and it dawns on me that I have to make a decision about your ashes. It never once occurred to me to scatter them, despite helping countless families decide if they should do exactly that. We've already let you go once. How much more of you must we relinquish?

The angle of the sun shifts, casting a spotlight on the area we are sitting. I close my eyes and face the warm rays. The idea of saying goodbye all over again crushes my heart. And yet every inch of my body wants to free you from the confines of a ceramic container and introduce you to the majesty of this lake because that's what you deserve—the world.

The lake is beautiful, wild with serenity. Birds fly overhead while white wildflowers bloom from the cracks in the rock we are seated on, somehow defying winter's wrath. I rest my head on Ethan's shoulder and give him my answer.

"Let's show her the world."

33

Somebody is at the door for you," Ethan tells me as I lay motionless under the duvet after a terrible bout of vomiting. I can't believe I'm going through first trimester hell again, then remind myself the nausea is good; it means the baby growing inside me is alive, and quickly I'm overcome with gratitude.

"Tell Paloma I'll call her later."

"It's Kenneth, actually."

Kenneth?

I hadn't been at the funeral home in a week. I didn't want to face Kenneth after what happened in that van. I lied and told him I have early-onset arthritis, hence why my body seized up in the van and why I can't come back to work for a while, and to my relief he didn't request a doctor's note. I'm not sure who I was trying to fool because it was clear he didn't buy it. I wonder if he's come here to gently terminate me.

I pull the duvet off and go downstairs. Kenneth sits on the couch. He's not wearing his usual attire. He's disturbingly casual with a brown wool sweater and khaki pants. The sight of him without a collar or lapel or waistcoat makes me uncomfortable, like seeing your teacher in a robe.

He points to the basket of Bartlett pears on the coffee table. Tells me they're Ontario-grown and have reached perfect ripeness. Then he looks at me with those concerned eyes of his and asks, "How are you feeling?"

I worry my breath smells putrid, so I speak with my head lowered. "Listen, about what happened at the hospital. I just—"

"You don't have to explain it. I should have known that location would have been a triggering place for you. I'm sorry I put you through that."

"It's not your fault. I—I didn't know I'd react that way."

"We can't always control what happens in these types of situations. You did the best you could."

We are silent for a moment, and I wonder how much longer this will go on for before he inevitably fires me. I hope he does it quickly. I can't shake the feeling that I've disappointed yet another person with my inability to meet the demands of being alive. Bad wife, bad daughter, bad friend. And now a bad assistant.

Kenneth pulls out something from his pocket. A wallet, then a small picture. He shows it to me. It's a picture of a baby boy swaddled in a hospital blanket. A deluge of envy runs through my veins, ready to gush out, as I wonder why he's showing me a picture of a baby.

"This is Teddy."

I hand the picture back.

"He would've been forty-one this month."

I'm unsure if I heard him correctly. Did he use past tense? "I'm sorry, what?"

"He died when he was three and a half months old. We found him in his bassinet. He just stopped breathing in the middle of the night."

I clutch my chest. My vision goes blurry with tears. "Oh my god, oh my god, oh my god," is all that comes out of my mouth until, thankfully, my brain kicks into gear and forms a few more words. "I had no idea. I'm so sorry."

"I don't talk about Teddy very much, though I think of him every single day." His voice cracks when he says his son's name, as if it's been teetering on the tip of his tongue for years. His face goes solemn, like a shadow has been cast over his head. "It's a pain like no other. Something only people like us can understand."

Like us. Several feelings rise one after the other. Sorrow that this happened to him. Betrayal that he didn't tell me sooner. Solace to have found someone who knows this singular pain as viscerally as I do. In that moment, I wish I could see the picture again. I feel terrible for pushing it away so quickly. It's probably one of the only pictures he has of Teddy. I wish I'd studied the shape of his nose, the curvatures in his face, the texture of his skin. That's all there is left to do with our babies: lose ourselves in the few images we have of them.

Kenneth goes on to tell me what happened. How it was an ordinary day, as ordinary as it can be, with a colicky new infant. They'd finally got Teddy to fall asleep in his cot, so he and his wife drifted off to sleep, knowing they'd be woken up in a matter of minutes, an hour if they're lucky, by Teddy's cries for milk. But hours passed and the cries never came. Kenneth recoils as he recalls the first thought that came to his head—how wonderful it was to enjoy a luxuriously long stretch of sleep. He went to check on Teddy and that's when his world went black.

He called 911 and answered all their questions. He hated the answers coming out of his mouth. *No, he's not breathing. No, I can't feel a pulse. Yes, I know CPR.* By this point his wife had woken up, screaming hysterically on her knees. As they waited for the ambulance to arrive, Kenneth put his two fingers between Teddy's breastbone and pressed, pressed, pressed. The operator told him he needed to press hard, about one and a half inches down, so he pressed harder, afraid he was hurting the baby.

When the first responders arrived, they wheeled in a stretcher that seemed awfully large. They took over chest compressions right there on their bedroom floor, the tummy time mat kicked out of the way so the paramedics wouldn't accidentally slip. Kenneth swears he held his breath the entire time, waiting to hear the sweet sound of Teddy's cry.

Just like I did.

After thirty minutes of resuscitation, they transferred the baby to the stretcher. Teddy looked tiny on that thing. They had to adjust the harness to the tightest setting, the surplus straps practically dangled on the floor. As they were getting in the ambulance, he spotted his neighbor standing on their porch, cloaked in a loose bathrobe. This neighbor had a child of his own, ten months older than Teddy, and in that split second, a horrible thought flashed before Kenneth. "I remember wishing I could trade places with him. I wanted it to be *me* standing on the porch watching *him* step inside the ambulance instead while Teddy slept safe and sound upstairs."

To this day, he doesn't know why Teddy died. SIDS was the diagnosis, but the doctor may as well have written IDK in his chart. There was no explanation for his death. That was the hardest thing to get over,

Kenneth said. Not knowing why it happened. If he and his wife were to have a fighting chance of getting through this, they needed a reason, something worth pouring all their rage into, something they could dedicate their life's mission to eradicating. A charity, a good cause. But there was nothing. A bad thing happened for absolutely no reason.

Kenneth goes on to tell me about Teddy's funeral. How the first place they called turned him away because he'd requested an open casket service and the director said nobody wants to see that. He couldn't believe what he was hearing. It made him so angry, so hurt. He channeled all his rage into opening his own establishment so that nobody would ever have to go through what he went through.

"When they told me it had to be closed, I lost it. How could they tell me my boy was not the most beautiful thing in the world?"

A sob escapes me. I've never met Teddy but my heart longs for him the same way it longs for you. I hope Teddy was there to greet you wherever you are, to tell you everything is okay. I can see it now. The two of you stacking wooden blocks on a lush green meadow under the shade of an apple tree. A generic utopia, I know, but who can prove me wrong?

"I can't believe you had to go through that," I say to him, blinking through tears. Kenneth continues talking and I let the words roll out of his tongue without interruption. Even when he stops speaking, I don't rush to fill the silence, instead letting it swell with everything he has been holding in over the decades. I nod ferociously at everything he says, as if he's telling me my own story. I had no idea this part of me was conceivable to other people. I had believed nobody except Ethan could come close to understanding this experience, much less articulating it the way Kenneth is.

We talk about our babies, how peaceful they looked in their casket, how remarkably good the makeup artist was at bringing the pink back to their faces. I have never talked about this with anybody else. Not many people are comfortable getting into it, but for us, we happily clutch at any chance we get to talk about our babies. We swap stories of our children like any other parent. We share our dreams for them, what values we wished to have passed down, and laugh as we come to the agreement that Teddy and Daisy would've grown to be incredibly attractive and talented individuals.

"Is that her?"

He points to a photo of you on the wall of the staircase. Ethan and I had it blown up and framed so that we could see your perfect little face every time we walked by.

"That's our Daisy."

"Breathtaking," he whispers.

He pauses to gather his thoughts and suddenly the mood turns serious. "I know we've gone through similar losses," he says, "but it would be foolish of me to say I know exactly what you're going through. Everyone's grief is as unique as their love for their child. I loved that boy more than anything in the world." He shuts his eyes, as if to stop the flood that threatens to spill out. "What I've been wanting to tell you is that you will survive this. The road to healing is anything but linear. One day you'll think you've made progress and the next day, you're right back at the bottom of the pit. But it's all part of the process. Grief is a beast, but I promise you: You can handle it.

"I'm not going to lie and say it goes away. It never goes away, but it won't always hurt this much. You'll feel like yourself again. Maybe not who you used to be. But something close to it. Something you can look at in the mirror and recognize beyond a shadow of a doubt."

I want to believe him. If he can emerge from the quicksand of grief and still love life as much as he does, maybe I can, too?

"Do you remember what you asked me all those months ago?" he asks.

I shake my head, unable to recall.

"You asked me what happens after we die."

"Right, I remember." How had I forgotten to follow up on this? I lean in, eager to hear his response.

"I think what you were really asking, what anybody who asks that question actually wants to know, is whether they'll see their loved ones again. I know many of our families believe in reunification, that their loved ones are waiting for them on the other side. I don't doubt that's the case, but I like to believe we don't have to wait until our passing to be with them again. The reunion is already happening. It's taking place right now. Our relationship with the dead carries on so long as we lean into the most tender parts of ourselves and carry them wherever we go. We're so much more than these physical bodies." Kenneth lets out a soft sigh. "It's taken me a while to come to this conclusion but I truly believe love transcends flesh. I may not be able to see Teddy or touch him or hold him, but I can feel him. Every single day."

I look over at Kenneth as he clutches his chest. How is he not bawling right now? I wipe tears from my cheeks and take in his words. The more morsels of grief he shares with me, the more I feel connected to him. Our ten months of acquaintanceship now feel like sixty. The gaps in my understanding of him as a person have diminished to a speck. I no longer feel like I am a problem to be fixed. I am part of something bigger. A community of parents who have lost children. Who light candles for them on anniversaries. Who press their lips to the cold glass of framed photographs. Who search for their children in a mighty maple tree or a sparkling rainbow or a flicker of a passing butterfly. We may not know each other. We may walk among each other, unaware. But we are tethered—by our grief. And by the desperate, aching need to keep our babies' memories alive.

"I'm sorry, I know you didn't ask about me, about any of this, and I apologize if this is bringing back painful memories," he says, curling deeper into his lap as if embarrassed to be sharing so much of himself.

"No, please, I don't mind, really. It means a lot that you shared this with me. And I don't want to sound disrespectful at all, but it feels good to know I'm not alone. These past few months have just been so fucked up. It feels like I'm living on another planet."

Kenneth relaxes his jaw as tears finally stream down his cheeks and all I can think is, *Holy shit, he can cry! I have to tell Rachel!*

"Every time we get a funeral for a baby, it all comes rushing back," he says. "It's like I'm back there all over again, hunched over his body, pressing his mouth against my ear and begging to feel his warm breath against my skin again."

He plants his eyes on me and what he says next makes me think he can read my mind. "I saw what you were going through and I wanted to help you, to keep you close. That's why I offered you the job."

It all makes sense now, how this job practically fell into my lap. "You mean it wasn't because of my sheer charm?"

We allow ourselves a little laugh.

After a beat, I ask the question that's been niggling at me. "If I may ask, did you ever have any more children after Teddy?"

Kenneth's face crumples and his frown lines etch deeper into his skin. He shakes his head. "We tried for years afterwards. Went through all the fertility treatments, emptied our bank accounts, even considered surrogacy and adoption. It took a long time, but my wife and I eventually found peace accepting a life without living children. We've had a good life, despite everything. Teddy will always be our child and we'll always be Teddy's parents." Kenneth sniffles into the back of his hand. "I had to work through a lot of things back then. A lot of self-blame. I should've set an alarm. If I had set an alarm and woken up when I was supposed to, he might still be alive. I should've known something was wrong when he slept through his feeding. He always needed milk. Every two hours on the dot. But I let four hours go by. Four damn hours."

Kenneth's eyes go to a place I'm familiar with. The deepest, loneliest pit that can only be dug out by guilt. I want to tell him I have those thoughts, too. What if I'd gone to the hospital sooner? What if I didn't push hard enough or fast enough? What if there was something in my genes that caused this? These recurring what-ifs keep playing over and over again in my mind. I cannot shut them down. They are incessant, dangling the possibility of a world where you had lived.

My knee has been shaking this entire time and I place my palm down to stop it.

"Why did you decide to live?"

I didn't mean for my question to come out so bluntly, but even if I tried, I couldn't imagine a gentler way to ask it.

"I can't say I haven't thought about ending everything. If you ask any parent that has lost a child, I can assure you they've thought about it at some point or another. But there was one thing that always stopped me."

"What was it?"

He pauses to clear his throat. "I couldn't stop picturing my funeral. The things they would say at the service. They would say I died because of Teddy. Because I couldn't live in a world without him. I hated the thought that Teddy would forever be associated with my death. That his life brought nothing but pain and heartache. Because it's not true. He showed me a kind of love beyond my wildest dreams. He injected so much joy and color into my life. He made me laugh like I'd never laughed before. That's how I want people to remember Teddy. So for that reason, as much as I wanted to end my misery, I couldn't do it. I couldn't let Teddy be the reason for my demise. I wanted him to be the reason I lived."

I sit up straight and cling on to his words, repeating them back in my head. I wonder how many years it took for Kenneth to get to this level of peace.

"I know you've heard me say this countless times in the office," he goes on, "but everyone dies eventually, why be in such a hurry to get there early? Why not stay a little longer? Yes, there is disappointment and death and so much horror, but there's also beauty. So much beauty. Why not stick around to bear witness to all the beauty that's created before you die?"

Kenneth switches the subject and asks when I might feel well enough to come back to the funeral home. "There's no rush. Take all the time you need. We all miss you."

I know better than to answer on the spot. I need time to think about what I'm doing, whether it's good for me to be working or if I've been using it to salve my grief. Shane is expecting me back in a few months, but I don't think I'm ready to go back to a place that reminds me so much of the old me. I don't know her anymore.

I tell Kenneth I'll let him know. He nods and we hug, the compression stilling the pace of my heartbeat.

After he leaves, I grab one of the pears and take a bite. The juice falls down my fingers and seeps into my sleeve. I swish the pulp between my teeth and savor the sweetness. Have these always been so delicious?

34

I return to the web forum where I asked the question *Does it ever get better?* and am stunned to find the conversation is still going. There are hundreds of new responses. A resounding majority share how counseling helped them tremendously. They say the more they talked about the pain the more demystified it became. They all speak of this practice like it's eating broccoli or lifting dumbbells, an inarguably healthy habit one is supposed to do as regularly as possible.

"I think you should give it a try," Ethan says when I show him the forum.

I'm reluctant at first. Therapy sounds like a predatory scam akin to juice cleanses. Sure, it *seems* like you're doing something good, but afterwards all you feel is nauseous and like you might poop your pants.

"Then how about a group?"

"A group?"

"One for mothers who've recently lost children," he says. "You won't have to talk the whole time. Frankly, you don't have to say anything at all. And you can meet people who've gone through a similar thing. It can be really validating."

I crinkle my brows and look at him. "How do you know so much about this?"

Ethan looks at his feet. "I've been to a few."

"Y-you have?"

He tells me about a support group held at the hospital every Thursday evening. It's for fathers, but lately it has expanded to include non-birthing parents of all genders. He tells me about how the facilitator takes them through breathing exercises and neck stretches. Everybody is encouraged to talk but there's no pressure if you're not feeling up to it. There's one man who hasn't said a word other than his name and *excuse me* the one time he sneezed. Ethan is the newest person in the group. The others have been there longer. One person has been going for two years. They not only talk about the babies they've lost but also how the grief shows up differently for them.

"What do you mean differently?" I never thought to see our grief as two disparate entities. I always imagined us dragging the same load, the equivalent of a sixteen-foot semitruck hauling the entirety of Mount Everest, the only difference being that Ethan was able to cover more distance than me.

Ethan clears his throat. "I always assumed there was only space for one person to grieve at a time, that we weren't allowed to both feel the loss at the same time. So I pushed it down, thinking there would be time for me to feel the feelings later. After you got better."

I stretch out my arm, clutching his knee. "I'm so sorry if I made you feel like you couldn't grieve."

"It's not your fault. I just wanted to be strong for both of us. It's what people kept telling me to do. *Be strong for Cleo.* It took me a few sessions, but I know now that this loss is as much mine as it is yours."

I can hear the shakiness in his voice as if tears are about to erupt, but he blinks them back and stretches his neck from side to side, a succession of pops blasting from his joints. There he goes again, doing that thing men do when they want to appear tough. I've seen it before in my father and uncles and cousins. The puffing of the chest, the flexing of the muscles, the quick brushing off of the subject—all to keep the sadness from spilling out. It's heartbreaking, seeing Asian men pursue a version of masculinity that doesn't benefit them in any way.

"It's a stupid thing people say, to be strong," I reaffirm.

"I know that. I can't help it though. I can't help but feel it's my responsibility to keep it together. For you. For us. I mean, that's my literal job! I relieve people's pain for a living and it killed me that I couldn't do anything to relieve yours." He stops to swallow whatever has been building up in his mouth.

I can see he's hurting, but I can't help what I say next. "Well, I did ask you to put me under and you said no."

Ethan chuckles, thankfully in the mood for joking. He loosens his whole body, grabs my hand, and brings it to his lips. "Just think about the sessions, will you?"

The thought makes me bristle again. I didn't grow up in a household that believed in talking it out. My parents certainly believed in demons that muddled the mind, but their solution was to absorb the demons, not expel them. "Say their name and they will come," was how they put it. Because of this logic, they seldom brought up difficult subject matters and no sin was worse than talking about the dead. When my grandmother passed away, all the photos of her disappeared from the house. There were exposed nails in the wall and blank pages in the album where her pictures once lived. Then one day, a framed photo of her appeared on the altar, tucked behind a ceramic bowl of joss sticks and a towering glass Bodhisattva. I asked my father why we couldn't keep Bà Nội's photo in the living room where we can see it all the time. He kneeled down to eight-year-old me and said, "The living room is for the living."

He explained that portraits of the dead are placed on the altar to help usher them towards a fortunate rebirth so they don't stay trapped in a bardo state. He forbade me from saying her name for forty-nine days lest her spirit overheard and strayed from making the proper transition. I didn't believe any of it. It seemed all too much, these rites and rituals. I think he just couldn't bear all the reminders of what he'd lost.

Ethan looks at me with a desperation I can't ignore.

"Please, just try it," he begs.

"Fine." I dig out the card Paloma gave me months ago and call the number.

When I think of group therapy, I think of cold plastic chairs assembled in a circle. This is the arrangement I'm expecting when I arrive at the twelfth floor of a tall building wrapped in glass panels. Before I even knock, Bonnie Spoon, Grief Counselor Since 2005, is already at the door as if she could sense the melancholia from a mile away. She's a white woman in her fifties, short hair, piercing hazel eyes. She wears an improbably chunky necklace that looks to weigh about a hundred pounds. She flashes me a bright smile and I catch a glimpse of her permanent retainer.

"Hi, I'm Bonnie Spoon. You must be Cleo?" she asks.

I nod, wondering how she knew it was me, whether she looked me up beforehand or whether I simply look like a Cleo the same way Bobs look like Bobs. Bonnie, on the other hand, looks nothing like a Bonnie. Her head appears to be shaped like a spoon, though.

There are already five other women here. I take my seat and study the brokenness scribbled all over their faces. Their slumped shoulders and reddened eyes reveal a desperation for healing. I'm not convinced there is any healing to be had, but I promised Ethan I would try at least once. That way I could go back and say to him with complete plausibility, *It's just not for me,* and we could leave this whole silly counseling business behind us.

As we wait for the last person to arrive, I scan the offerings on the small table in front of us. Hand sanitizer, tissues, and—bizarrely— a handheld scalp massager. Through the glass panels, I see office workers in the building across. They're clad in blazers and shiny shoes, and they have passcards clipped to their waists. Running from meeting to meeting, keeping up with the flurry of emails, rushing to file deliverables before day's end. Everyone is busy. Too busy to feel anything. Numbed by the pressures of work, like lidocaine had been injected into their veins. Oh, how I miss it.

I wonder if they can see us. I wonder what they are thinking, a group of forlorn women seated around a scalp massager and dabbing their eyes. I want to wave my arms and signal to them I am not like these sad women. *I am one of you!*

The last chair is finally filled and Spoon closes the door.

"It's nice to see some familiar faces," she says, smiling. She takes a seat on her chair, which looks more comfortable than the plastic ones we're sitting in. I take a closer look. It's an authentic Hans Wegner upholstered in soft wool, marked by its curved silhouette and deep-pitched seat. My back stiffens at the sight of it, how perceptibly expensive her chair is. I wonder how many patients she had to see to afford that chair. How many tears had to be shed, how much pain had to be extracted.

"Why don't we all go around the room, say our names, and tell everyone a bit about why you're here?" Spoon says.

I look down, appearing engrossed by a speck of dirt on the surface of my boot. I wait for someone to start. Anybody. Perhaps one of the familiar faces. It would seem incumbent on those with the most therapy to say something first. Finally, a woman in a red-knit sweater speaks. Her name is Amina, her baby Lucas was stillborn over a year ago, this is her fifth time here, she is happy but sorry to meet all of us. Next is Patricia. Her baby Kelis was born premature with a heart defect and passed away in the NICU after forty-five days. It's only her second time here; she feels like she's drowning. There is Marta, whose baby Julia was terminated after amnio tests discovered trisomy 13; it has been four months and her three-year-old keeps asking when the baby is coming home.

Every single person chokes back tears as they whittle their stories down to a brief paragraph. It's not enough time to encapsulate such life-altering events. But we're on the clock. Forty-five minutes remain. And there are still four more people to go.

I realize all eyes are on me. I am next. I tell my story as quickly and efficiently as possible. I can't believe these words are coming out of me so nonchalantly, like I'm recapping a movie I've seen a dozen times. The women all shake their heads and clutch their chest, as if they're hearing the story of their own child dying. How is it possible, after what they've gone through, that they still have space to be awed by tragedy?

When the circle is completed, we all let out a collective sigh. It's hard enough carrying our own stories of loss. It's even harder carrying those of others. Observing this, Spoon leads us through a diaphragmatic breathing exercise. She instructs us to fully engage our diaphragm to create more space in our chest cavity.

"Let's all do it together now," says Spoon, placing one hand on her chest, one on her belly.

I have no clue what she's talking about. Isn't a diaphragm a kind of condom? I stick out my belly like everyone else seems to be doing and suck it back in.

"Good, good, you're all doing very good," Spoon says. Patricia nudges me with her elbow and gives me a look that says, *I don't know what I'm doing, either.* We both chuckle. What a whiplash to sob your eyes out one minute and giggle like little girls the next.

Spoon has us going around in a circle saying how we're feeling in this moment. Nobody says *good* or *fine* as we're probably wont to do outside of this room when we're just trying to make it through the day. Instead we say words like *tired* and *angry* and *like I've been run over by a truck.* We are asked to elaborate. After one person volunteers, the others join in like a symphony reaching its crescendo. There is so much that comes with loss. A marriage on the precipice, a friend disappearing off the face of the earth, a questioning of faith, a career trajectory that has completely stalled. It's a pattern I'm noticing. Death begetting death of a different stripe.

When it's my turn to speak, I spit out the truth, as brutal and blunt as it may sound. What do I have to lose? I will never see these people again. "Frankly, I'm not all that interested in being alive right now. I always joke that if a crane were to fall from the sky, I wouldn't be in a hurry to get out of the way."

Silence befalls the room. I shift in my seat and keep my head down a beat, afraid to see what looks of horror are planted on the faces around me. I look up after a few beats. There are no grimaces, no quizzicality. My confession is met with several approving head nods, even a triumphant "I hear that."

"Thank you everyone for sharing," Spoon says. "I know that was not easy." She looks down at her notepad, which contains scribbles too indecipherable to make out. "When someone in your life dies, it's quite normal to experience a secondary loss. As you've all exemplified, it can come in the form of our relationships, our jobs, our beliefs, our outlook on life." She looks intently at me as she says this last bit. "Not only are you grieving your child, you're now grieving something that was once a staple in your life. It can be very overwhelming. It can make you feel more lost and alone than ever before, which is not what we need in such a vulnerable time." Spoon crosses her legs and leans forward in her expensive chair. "Death is very cruel. It doesn't care how kind you are or how often you go to church or how very much you wanted this baby. The thing about death is it takes and takes and takes with complete randomness. And I can sense in some of your voices that there is a lot of anger because of this. I'm curious, how does everyone cope with these struggles you mentioned? What do you do to release some of that negative energy?"

One by one, the women all speak up.

"Yoga."

"Walking in the park."

"Shopping. Lots of shopping."

"Screaming in the shower."

"Playing with my dog."

"Going to therapy."

I'm the last person to say something. Nothing comes to mind. I can't think of a single thing I do to release the negative energy, at least nothing that doesn't involve pills and vodka and chugging back a bottle of cough syrup. I think about the other answers, how entirely appropriate they all sound. Have I been doing this healing thing all wrong?

Spoon presses me for an answer, and I shrug, stewing in shame that I have failed to do the most basic human instinct of coping. "There must be something you do to let out the pain," she implores.

I shake my head.

"Do you exercise? Meditate?"

"No."

"Take long baths, call your friends, write in a journal?"

"No. Wait, yes."

"Which one?"

"I have a journal."

"That's great!" she says with glee. "Writing about our stresses and struggles has been shown to have significant benefits to our physical and emotional health."

I'm confused. I'm not sure what she's talking about. "That's not what I write," I clarify.

"Oh? What do you write about then?"

"About what should have been."

Spoon sets her notepad down. "Would you like to tell us more about what you mean by that?"

"Not really."

"This is a judgment-free space."

I shuffle in my seat, wishing I hadn't invited everyone's attention on me with this admission. "It's not very interesting. They're just snippets of what my life would've been like if my baby had lived."

Nobody says a word. The drawn-out silence makes me uncomfortable, so I keep talking in spite of myself. "For example, there's an entry where I talk about the first time we flew with her on a plane. She had quite the blowout. Shot up her back and neck, even got all over me. But the seat belt sign was on and the flight attendant wouldn't let me get up. I begged and begged her to please make an exception. I showed her the mess. She even wrinkled her nose at the stench. But still she said no. And the entire time Daisy is just bouncing and laughing without a care that she's got poo smeared all over her."

A chuckle comes out of me as I picture the scene again. It feels more vivid than the first time I imagined it, almost as if it really happened. If you think about something enough, could you trick your brain into believing it's a real memory?

There's no reaction from the group. Perhaps it was not my most compelling journal entry. "Like I said, it's not very interesting."

"And how does it feel to write out these scenarios?" Spoon finally says. "Do you feel a sense of catharsis when you do it?"

"I don't think so," I reply, though truthfully it's hard to say. I don't think or feel much of anything when I write. It's almost as if I black out, emerging without a clue as to where I am and how I got there.

"I'm curious," says Spoon, "how many entries would you say you've written so far?"

"I don't know. A hundred?"

"Wow, that's . . . a lot."

"Well yeah, there are many experiences and milestones to document within a child's first year of life. I want to capture it all."

Spoon clears her throat. Her brain seems to whir with many more follow-up questions until she finally lands on one. "So, these entries, are you still writing them?"

I nod.

"And what are you thinking for the ending? I mean, all fantasy stories must come to an end, right?"

I chuff at her statement. "Um, I suppose. But I wouldn't call it a fantasy. It's my life."

"I'm sorry, Cleo, I didn't mean to overstep. But I must be rather blunt with you. As painful as it may sound, these stories, these diary entries, are in fact a fantasy. You are fantasizing about reuniting with your baby. You make up events that have never happened. They are not rooted in reality."

I sink back into my chair and cross my arms. There she goes again with that word. *Fantasy.* It sounds like something a child does—make up silly little imaginary tales about dragons and elves to rid themselves of their boredom. This is not what this is. "Like I said before, this is *not* a fantasy." My voice comes out sharp, raised. I don't mean to yell, but I am feeling rather defensive in this moment.

"I understand this is a difficult time for you. Everyone has a right to cope in their own ways." Spoon leans back and scans the group. "How many of you here have thought about reuniting with your child?"

All arms shoot up.

"Of course you all do. It's a very natural response in grief to yearn for the person we lost. We want our child in our arms again. We will do anything to have them back with us. We want things to go back to the way they were when they were alive. And from time to time, it's okay to think about what could have been. But what we want to watch out for is when that sort of thinking becomes a constant. While it may seem harmless to fantasize, it can become unhealthy when we play out impossible scenarios over and over again. Our brain starts to spend all its energy on reestablishing an unrealistic bond and this can push us further and further away from reality. Does that make sense to everyone?"

All heads bob up and down. Except for mine.

I feel hot. The fabric on my clothes sticks to me. The socks on my feet feel damp with sweat. The back of my neck is like a radiator. Is she saying I'm delusional? I thought the point of coming to this thing was to feel better, not worse. She's just like Dr. Posey. Cold and uncaring. I bet once this is over, she'll pat herself for a job well done and treat herself to another Hans Wegner.

"Now, I'd like to go back to what you said earlier," Spoon continues, making clear she is not going to change the subject anytime soon. "You said you were not all that interested in being alive, that you wouldn't be mad if you got hit by a bus."

"Crane," I correct for some reason.

"Well, whatever it is, what you're describing is something called passive suicidal ideation. You think about death but have no plan or means of ending your life. This condition is more common than you think. Especially among people who engage in reunion fantasies. They think dying is the only way to reunite with their loved ones. Is this what you believe?"

"I—I don't know. I haven't decided what I think of the afterlife. There are lots of theories to parse through. I just need to spend a bit more time researching."

"I see. Well, whatever conclusion you come to, would you like to . . . you know . . ."

"Die?"

She nods.

"I mean, I don't actually want to die. I just want to close my eyes forever."

"That sounds like you want to die."

"Well no, not really, I merely wish the logistics of living were slightly altered so that I don't—" Everybody is staring at me like I've got chickens laying eggs on my head. I'm suddenly hyperaware of the sound of my voice and can hear myself bumbling, tripping over my words.

"Go on," says Spoon.

"So that I don't have to feel the pain all the time."

"I see. Let me ask you another question. Would you say you're at risk of harming yourself?"

"No, no! I could never do that. My husband, my parents—they'd be heartbroken!"

"It seems you have several solid relationships in your life, which is promising. Relationships are important for keeping us tethered to reality. If healing is the goal, it is essential to turn our attention away from these fantasies and direct them towards our real attachments."

Why does it feel like I'm on trial? I look at the door. All it takes is one tug of that handle and I'm out of here.

"I'm sorry," I blurt out, "but I don't see the harm in engaging in a little imagination. You make it sound like I'm on hallucinogens. I know the difference between what's real and what's not."

Spoon recrosses her legs, elbows on her lap. "That's all fine and well. As long as you know it has to end at some point."

"What are you implying? That I need to stop writing altogether?"

"You don't have to if it's helping. Writing can be a very effective and transformative exercise. But my dear, I'm afraid what you're doing is quite destructive to your well-being and I would not be doing my job if I did not interrogate this."

My heart is pounding fast and I feel a tugging in my chest. This is an ambush. I have stupidly walked right into it. I don't want to stop writing. These stories are all I have. Where does she get off telling me what I can do? I don't need this. I don't have to be here. I'm going to get up and walk out that—

"Well, it looks like our time is up," Spoon interjects. "Gosh! An hour is just never enough, is it?"

The other mothers all start gathering their things. I feel awful. I have taken up their time. They probably think I'm inconsiderate for making it all about myself. I want to tell them it was not my doing; it was fucking Spoon with all of her invasive questions. Surely somebody had something else they wanted to talk about, something more urgent than some silly little diary entries. I want to tell them all I'm sorry, but I fear saying one more word will only add to the evidence that I'm an attention-seeking mess.

We all say goodbye and cautiously tell each other we hope to see each other next week, though we know grief has a way of changing our plans on a dime. Plan-making is a fool's game.

A few of the mothers stay back to chitchat with Spoon. I get out of there as soon as possible and jump into an elevator. Before the doors slide closed, one of the participants rushes in. I think her name was Amina. We acknowledge each other with a nod. I ask her if she's going to the ground floor. She says yes.

We stand in silence until my guilt gets the better of me. "I'm really sorry for taking up so much time back there. It wasn't my intention at all."

"It's fine, really," she says, smiling. "Better you than me in the hot seat." A giggle comes out of her. The sound helps melt away my guilt.

"She really did grill me hard, didn't she?" I say. "Spoon? More like Spear!"

We're both cackling now. I wonder if she knows this is rare for me, to be laughing this abundantly. I wonder if it's the same for her.

"I'm really glad you came," she says. "I know Bonnie can be tough but these sessions have been very beneficial for me. Honestly, I wish I found this group earlier. I kept to myself a lot and it wasn't doing me any good. I was in a dark place for a while. But now I get it. Healing is only achievable through our connections with others."

"Geez, you sound just like Spoon," I inform her.

"Oh no, don't say that! It's *not* a compliment!" she replies, laughing in return. "By the way, I loved your story, the one about the plane. I can picture it so clearly." She pauses, her eyes glistening. "I wish you got to have that experience, even if it does seem a little disgusting."

We laugh some more, the lump in my throat melting with each chortle. "Thank you."

"Can I see a picture of her?"

I'm suddenly taken aback. It's been a long time since somebody has asked to see a picture of you. I think they think it rude or intrusive, or maybe they fear what they'll see: a baby wrapped in wires and tubes, a baby on the brink of death. We all know everyone dies, but we hate being confronted with visual reminders of life's fragility.

I pull up a photo on my phone. You're wearing a white eyelet bonnet.

The bow is neatly tied under your chin and the way you're sleeping with your head slightly tilted to the side makes it seem like you're smiling. It's one of my favorite photos of you.

"She is beautiful," says Amina.

I ask if I can see hers, too. She pulls out her phone and shows me a photo of Lucas. She tells me this was taken moments after he was born still.

I gasp. "He has so much hair!"

She beams with pride. "I know. People always ask if we put a wig on him. Of course we didn't!"

"He's all you," I tell her. She wipes away a tear and says something so faint it is practically inaudible, but because I recognize the rhythm, I instantly make it out. *I miss him.*

The elevator doors open, and she tells me she's going right. I tell her I'm going left. We hug each other goodbye. One would expect a hug between strangers to be curt, a blink of an eye, but this was not one of those. It's the kind of hug that slows a quickening heart and eases an erratic mind. The kind that can only be shared between grieving mothers.

As I walk to the car, my path illuminated by a single streetlamp and the moon, an unusual sense of calm courses through me, a feeling I haven't felt in a long time. It felt good to be in the company of people like me, people who are decidedly not okay. Maybe that's what my mother meant by chia buồn. The more you share your grief with others, the lighter it feels.

Don't get me wrong; Spoon was an absolute pest to the tenth degree and I wish her a lifetime of stepping on LEGOs, but I have to admit this session left me with something that made my attendance worthwhile— the possibility that I could begin to hope again.

I pull out my phone and thumb to my calendar app. I set up a recurring event on my calendar. Every Thursday at 7 p.m. Group therapy w/ Spear.

35

Now that there's a tiny beating heart in my body—and a whisper of hope—I commit to behaving like a normal person. I wake up with the sun and retreat with the moon. I listen to guided meditations before bed in hopes of getting my circadian rhythm back on track. I drink multiple cups of water a day. I am now the kind of person who always keeps a water bottle within arm's reach.

I throw out all the intoxicants. The alcohol, sleeping pills, cough syrups. Even the dimenhydrinate pills I take for nausea, just to be safe, since the label warns too much can lead to severe neurologic deficit. The only pills I take now are vitamin D and prenatals, and even those I make sure to buy organic, free from unnecessary additives.

I reply to my unread text messages and fill my calendar with plans that involve getting out of the house. So far this month, I have plans to attend a highly anticipated movie premiere and join a spin class at a brand-new gym. I told my parents I'd take them out for dinner, where I plan to apologize profusely for the horrible things I said. I even reserved an afternoon to visit Sadie and Fatima and their new baby. They told me not to bring anything, but I insisted on bringing a stir-fry because I know they would appreciate eating something other than Pop-Tarts and beef jerky. After making these plans, I noticed a tingle of excitement coursing through my body and smiled at how pleasant it feels to reconnect with the people most important to me.

I pay off the credit card bills I'd been neglecting. I get my teeth cleaned. I buy a cute dress in hopes there will be a future occasion to wear it, then conjure that occasion by making dinner reservations for me and Ethan at an Italian restaurant. Instead of dreading it all, I find myself getting excited at the prospect of dressing up and eating delicious carbs.

Speaking of food, I start eating fruits and vegetables and protein on a daily basis. I snack on raw almonds because they're rich in vitamin E, magnesium, and phosphorus. Eating still does not come easy, I admit, but at least I'm putting on weight and my skin is looking bright.

I take photos again. I snap the sunrise peeking above the clouds and the light bouncing off the ripples of Lake Ontario. Sometimes I'll flip the camera and take a picture of myself. I flatten my postpartum baby hairs and present a little smile. When I review the photo, I'm taken aback by how alive I look. How these lifestyle changes are already making a big difference.

I scour the internet for a new family doctor and put myself on the wait list. It takes an hour to get to this new doctor, but she has stellar reviews and has never gone before a disciplinary committee. I remove myself from Dr. Posey's patient list and delete her number from my phone. This is something I should have done a long time ago. It took me far too long to realize how terribly wrong she was about everything. I understand now that my grief, as messy and stubborn and unruly as it is, is not a disorder but a natural human response to losing someone I love so deeply.

I send Shane my resignation letter. I thank him for the many years at the company, for his unwavering faith in my skills and talent. I assure him this decision has nothing to do with him and everything to do with me. How the person he hired ten years ago and the person I am today are too incongruous to piece back together. How this is a good time for a fresh start. I wish him and the team my best and PS please remember to water the fern behind my desk.

I go for long, unironic walks and treat my body to deep, purposeful stretches in the park. I wait for traffic lights to turn green before crossing. I don't stand too close to the road. I occasionally look up at the sky for falling cranes that may kill me in an effort to avoid dying. This is perhaps my biggest improvement yet.

When I come across people, I try to acknowledge their existence. I make small talk in stores. I say good morning to the crosswalk guard. I even muster up the courage to say hello to a gaggle of preschoolers but they are too focused on a tree or a squirrel or the mittens on their hands to notice me. I wonder if everyone can sense the exertion of my performance. I hope it doesn't come off as disingenuous, or worse, creepy.

Another piece of good news is I'm no longer barging into people's homes without permission. I knock, or ring the doorbell, and wait to be let in like a normal person. Paloma is especially happy about that. She and I agreed to go to the Royal Ontario Museum with Jude. He's almost turning one, which means you would've been turning one, too. As the anniversary nears, all I want to do is hide under the covers, emerging only when that date has come and gone. Maybe I will. But today, I will gather all the courage I have to spend a quaint little afternoon with my best friend and her child.

We agree to meet at the Queen's Park entrance. I bring a gift for Jude because that's what normal people do—they shower children with little delights. It's nothing big, just a rubber teething toy in the shape of a seahorse. *Baby teeth start coming in between six and twelve months and teethers are an excellent way to soothe some of that discomfort.* The teether I purchased has multiple ridges and textures to massage the gums, plus it can be put in the fridge for added cooling relief.

When Paloma sees me with a gift bag in my hand, she tells me I shouldn't have. But I can see the twinkle in her eye, and I know she's secretly thrilled. This is a big step for me, being here, a toy in hand, mere steps from her child. Paloma pulls back the hood of the stroller and there he is.

My first reaction: He's huge! My second: He's so stinking cute! My third: I wish you were here.

The first two I verbalize. The last one I keep to myself.

I tickle the tip of Jude's chin and he giggles uncontrollably until I stop. I count four teeth, lower and upper central incisors, possibly a lateral incisor erupting from the top. I pull out the seahorse and he immediately starts gnawing on it. An unholy amount of drool starts running down his chin and I instinctively take a napkin from my bag and dab him gently. Paloma taps me on the shoulder and I realize I have overstepped. Right. This is her baby. Not mine. I take a few steps back but Paloma stops me and hands me a bib. "Here, this absorbs better." I bend down and secure it around Jude's neck. Paloma mouths the words *thank you* and we head inside to get our tickets.

As we walk through the various exhibitions, I'm surprised at my ability to hold it together. There are children everywhere. They squeal at the giant albatross hanging from the ceiling and say *cheese* in front of the southern white rhinoceros. But I'm not stirred. Even when it's glaringly evident how I'm the only adult whose hands are completely empty. No stroller to grip, no snacks to carry, no little hand to hold.

That's okay.

I am okay.

I can do this.

I grab a map and take over navigations, keeping note of the nearest elevators and bathrooms with change tables. I fill up Paloma's water bottle while she nurses and hold the diaper bag when she changes him. I am useful. I am productive. I am normal.

I'm doing rather well until we run into some old friends from high school. One is now a mother of three under five. The other has two under two. I do not announce my pregnancy because I know the question that will inevitably come up—Is it your first?—to which I will have to decide whether to tell them about what happened or act like it never happened, both of which don't feel particularly good. So I say nothing and allow the conversation to veer towards talks about our jobs, where we're living, whether we still keep in touch with so-and-so. The topic segues into parenthood and suddenly my contributions to the conversation stop. I'm no longer an active participant, merely an eavesdropper, as they talk about their kids' various activities and interests. Surely they don't mean to exclude me or make me feel like an outsider, but it starts to feel that way when ten minutes pass and nobody has observed the fact that I haven't said a word. I excuse myself to the bathroom.

My exit doesn't disrupt the flow. I can hear their voices getting more animated as I walk away, as if my removal has permitted them to speak more freely.

I don't need to pee but I sit on the toilet anyway. The sadness greets me without fail. It sits in the background, huddled against the darkest corners of me. It is calm. Not seeking attention. Just there. Part of me wants to extinguish it, cut it out of me. The other part wants to nurture it like a seedling tucked underneath soil. I think about what Kenneth said. How he didn't want Teddy to be his demise. How he decided to live for Teddy. I think I'm starting to get it. It's going to take a long time to learn how to live without you. It won't happen today. Or tomorrow. Or ever. All I know is I want to live. For you.

When I return, the high school friends are gone. Paloma is bouncing Jude on her hip, attempting to put a pacifier in his mouth but it keeps coming out. She apologizes if that interaction was weird. I tell her it was weird but it's fine. It's always fine.

"Should we check out the gemstone gallery?" Paloma asks.

"Actually, if it's okay, I think I'd like to go home."

She doesn't ask what's wrong or pressure me to stay. Instead, she says, "I'm really proud of you for coming out. I know how hard this must've been."

My fake self sneaks in for a second wanting to say, "Oh it's nothing," but I turn it off because I realize it's not nothing. I made a lot of progress today. It might not seem like much to others, but to me, it's everything.

The pacifier falls to the ground again and Paloma hands Jude to me so she can clean it. I take him without thinking. I haven't held a baby since I held you. He's heavier than I imagined. I try to guess his weight. Fourteen, maybe sixteen pounds? I wonder if this is how heavy you would've been. Is this how many thigh rolls and knuckle dimples you would've had? I sniff Jude's powdery head and try to remember your smell. You smelled like warm cotton, fresh out of the dryer. I'll never forget it.

Jude squeezes my cheeks with his tiny hands, wet with some questionable substance, but I don't mind. I make fart noises with my mouth every time he presses my face and he giggles uncontrollably. I keep doing it again and again, his laughter more manic each time. Paloma returns with the pacifier but he's over it now, obsessed with my mouth farts. Paloma steps back and takes a picture of us, a sparkle in her eyes. "Let's do this more often," I say to her, to which she promptly agrees.

36

Despite how much I imbue my life with normalcy, the grief still follows me like a needy toddler. It screams at me all day no matter what I'm doing. Truly. It could be anything. I could be unloading the dishwasher or shaving my legs or lying in savasana and suddenly I hear, *She's dead, she's dead, she's dead.*

Still I trudge on. I keep on with my attempts to be normal again, which entails attending routine prenatal checkups.

I'm stripped from the waist down, my ass smashed against the crinkly paper, my belly smeared with globs of jelly. The sonographer apologizes for how cold everything is, the jelly, the probe, her hands. I tell her it's okay because I want her to like me. If she likes me, then that will earn me several karmic points, which will go towards ensuring the appointment going well and the baby being fine.

On second glance, the sonographer looks familiar. I look down at her name tag. Stephanie. Stephanie with the stars tattooed behind her ear. I can't believe it, it's her! I met her when I was pregnant with you. It was my twenty-week anatomy scan. She turned the screen towards me and pointed out your fingers and toes. Told me your organs were healthy. That you were growing right on track. That your amniotic fluid levels were fantastic. She told me everything looked great. *Unremarkable* was the medical term she used, and I remember being offended by that word because everything about you was remarkable. Ethan and I left that appointment feeling so elated that we got two medium Blizzards despite it being below freezing that day.

I wonder if Stephanie remembers us. Most likely not. I imagine she sees dozens of expecting couples a week. One ultrasound after another, all the grainy images of bloated blobs blurring into one. They could all be stock photos for all she cares. A part of me wants to tell her what happened to you as if she has been itching to hear an update about that Asian baby with the fantastic levels of amniotic fluids that she scanned more than a year ago.

But I don't say anything. I fear she'll say something that will shake my cool, something along the lines of *That's too bad but at least you're pregnant again*. People tend to disregard your past when the future is right in front of you.

Ethan points out that I've been crumpling the crinkly paper between my fists. Oh, I say, unaware of my own body's movements. He takes my hand and squeezes it. I squeeze back. It's something we've been doing at every doctor's appointment. We like to think it is out of love, or at the very least, habit. Truthfully, it's more out of terror. It feels like bad news is always around the corner, waiting to swallow us whole.

Ethan has been holding it together rather well since I told him I was pregnant. When the words came out of my mouth, he simply sat with that information as if I'd just told him today's forecast calls for a thirty percent chance of drizzle. I could tell he was excited, but then fear took over and he froze. It was as if he was too afraid to celebrate, too afraid to want it. I didn't feel slighted by his reaction. It seemed to be the only correct way to respond.

The sonographer tilts the screen to show us the baby, but I can't look. I shut my eyes. I'm afraid of what I'll see. I'm convinced the thing growing inside me is not a fetus but impermeable dread that's draining my energy and pushing my organs aside so it can take up residence inside my body.

Then an audible *oh wow* slips out of Ethan's mouth.

I open my eyes.

A glorious blob pulses on the screen, and Ethan and I exchange a look of visible relief.

The sonographer tells us there's not much to see as it's still early days. Not much? I want to tell her it's the equivalent of an entire planet to us. She zooms in on the flickering heartbeat. It looks like it's dancing the cha-cha. I could watch it for hours.

The technician asks if we would like a picture. I hesitate. I know if we say yes, that picture will hang on the fridge where it will stare back at us every day, filling us with the kind of hope that could later betray us. The technician senses my discomfort and tells us there's no need to decide now, that those pictures will be saved in my file if we ever change our mind. I sigh with relief. I wonder if I'm the first person to say no to a picture. I wonder if she thinks I'm a bad mother.

"Do you have any questions?" Stephanie asks.

I have many—forty-two to be exact. I had frantically created a list of questions the night before to manufacture some semblance of control over this pregnancy, convinced that if I leave one stone unturned something will go wrong. How many heartbeats per minute? How is the brain developing? Are there any congenital conditions? Where is the placenta positioned? Is the fetal-to-placental weight ratio healthy? How is the blood flow to the placenta? Are there additional screenings I can do? How often can I come in for a scan? Does she see any concerning precursors?

"Hold on, hold on." The sonographer puts her hand up to stop me and points to a sign on the wall. *Ultrasound technicians are not permitted to communicate results to patients.*

"These are great questions but it's something you should address with your doctor."

"But if you could just tell me—"

"Sorry, it's our policy."

I exhale, feeling defeated. Ethan tells me it'll be fine; we'll get all the answers we need from the OBGYN. Stephanie tells me I can get changed and leaves the room. I lean back on the bed. There's a brown stain on the fissured ceiling panels. I stare at it for some time until an image comes forth, a woman caressing her ample belly.

"Does that look like a pregnant woman to you?" I point to the ceiling.

Ethan looks up. It takes him a moment to locate the stain. "Whoa, it actually does."

I've been wary of signs given the lack of scientific explanation surrounding the phenomenon. Nothing more than wishful thinking. Still, I keep staring at the pregnant woman in the ceiling, clinging to the belief it's a message from you that everything will be okay.

37

Four weeks come and go, and I am due back at the funeral home. Kenneth had encouraged me to take time off. He said it wasn't healthy to bury myself in work, no pun intended. I pushed back because I didn't think it was such a bad thing to work. It was what everyone had encouraged. Go back to the swing of things! Build a routine! Get on with it! After much persuasion, Kenneth helped me see that grief is inescapable no matter how much I distracted myself, that leaving it unaddressed for too long could manifest in very unhealthy ways. I didn't want to find out how much uglier this grief could get so I obeyed.

On the day of my return, I'm shocked by how much I look forward to it. During my time off, I realized that this work had become central to my happiness. When I arrive, I am met with an overwhelming tide of open arms and delightful greetings. Rachel, Maggie, Ana, even Stuart—they're all here.

"We missed you!"

"So happy you're back!"

"We were dying without you!"

That last one is an inside joke that's articulated whenever an employee returns after taking some time off. The joke lands better when the person has only been away for one day, or even better, an afternoon. I belt out a genuine laugh and return big smiles to all of them. I'm not sure if they knew why I was gone. In any other workplace, such as my former, nonsensical speculation would have run rampant. But here, I don't suspect that to be the case. Everyone is genuinely concerned for my well-being. If they weren't, I don't think they'd be working at a place like this. Every day they're faced with a revolving door of people on their worst days. They cast aside all judgments and treat these broken strangers with nothing but reverence. Because of that I know my grief is safe here. My body knows it, too. I can tell by the way my lungs expand with ease each time I take a breath.

After catching up with everyone, I become overwhelmed by all the attention and revert to my default state of seldom saying a word. I excuse myself and head to my desk where there's a trio of purple helium balloons tied to my chair and a silver foil banner that says, "WELCOME BACK!" My cheeks go warm. Tears form in my eyes, and I quickly dab them away with my sleeve. I turn on the computer and momentarily forget my password until the muscles in my fingers plug it in for me. The screen buzzes to life and I'm thrust into an endless list of things that need to get done. This is how I could exist all day. Alone in a room illuminated by a bright blue light and never interacting with a single soul.

Raucous laughter erupts outside and suddenly a pang of longing thrums in my chest. I wonder what they're laughing about. A struggle between solitude and companionship play out in my head. My instinct is to stay put—to be alone where it's safe and easy and predictable. People hurt you. People leave you. And yet, I can't deny the part of me that longs for connection.

For once I let myself move towards that desire. I turn off my screen and rejoin the others.

That afternoon, a man named Harold is getting laid to rest. He's in his eighties. He's dressed in a crisp black power suit, a navy-blue tie, and solid brass cuff links. He's the head of an important company that distributes refined granulated sugar across North America. He has a Wikipedia page with links to a handful of news articles written about him. In one interview with the *Toronto Star*, he said his favorite candy is SweeTARTS. "I pick out the cherry flavor and give my wife the rest," he is quoted as saying.

That wife is seated in the front row beside his two sons, two daughters, three grandchildren, and English bulldog named Chester, who is ferociously licking a peanut butter–filled Kong.

The eulogies are full of emotion as they summarize his accomplishments and character and heart. He was a man devoted to success, not just in business but in his personal life. He strived to keep everyone around him happy, especially his wife and children. He knew how to live and was not afraid of adventure, evident by the slideshow featuring him in almost every continent. "He was the type of person who wanted to do everything, to collect as many experiences as humanly possible, making him a man of very little regrets," Harold's brother says, clearing his throat. "If my brother left this earth with any regret in his body, it would be that he couldn't physically be here with you all today."

Everyone in the room takes turn dabbing their eyes and putting their arms around each other. Smiles peek through pained expressions but soon the faces sink to a somber state again. Most people stare up at the pulpit. For many, the weight of grief keeps their head pointed down towards their shoes.

I feel a gentle tap on my shoulder. I turn around to find Kenneth, who bends down to reach my ear and whisper a request. "Can we chat for a second?" I hesitate, concerned about what my absence from the service might do. What if something happens? What if the A/V equipment decides to fritz out? What if there's a big kerfuffle and I need to jump in to placate the guests? Rachel sees my worry. "Go," she mouths to me, and I clasp my hands together in thanks.

I follow Kenneth to our office where he tells me to take a seat in front of his desk. Something is different. I've stared at this desk hundreds of times, imprinted it to memory, so I'm hyperaware when a piece of paper is astray or a pen goes missing or the keyboard is slightly tilted. What's changed? Ah! The framed photo beside his computer. It's new. The glare makes it hard to see the photo. I try to get a better look, but Kenneth blocks my view and loudly clears the phlegm from his throat.

"Am I in trouble?" I didn't mean to say that so bluntly, but when you're called into an impromptu private meeting with the boss in the middle of a service—especially after taking an unexpected leave of absence—my question is not terribly outside the realm of reason.

"What? No, no, of course not. That's not why I asked you here. I wanted to see how you were doing. Whether you feel ready to return to work? Because if you think you need more time, I'm more than happy to grant that to you."

I'm not sure what to say. I've only been back a few hours, so the question of whether I need more time off is something I can't answer at this moment. For now, all I can say is I feel fine. Truly, I do.

"It's good to be back and have things to do. Everybody has been so nice."

"That's good to hear. We can always take it on a day-by-day basis, too. If anything changes on your end, please tell me and I can make sure we're giving you the time and space you need. The last thing I'd want is for you to feel overwhelmed."

The gentleness, the thoughtfulness—it all feels unreal. Like seeing the shore after being lost at sea. I'm grateful for his kindness and do my best to not question his motives. "Don't worry, I'm not going anywhere."

"Good, you've been such a big help around here. I don't know what I'd do without you."

"Ah well, I guess you'd be doomed to an eternity of pop-up ads."

I instantly feel bad about the jab—he's been nothing but kind—but I remind myself that Kenneth has always been cool about these disparaging digs. He has admitted once or twice to being "a total dingus" when it comes to all this "*Star Trek* stuff."

He snorts. "Actually I wasn't referring to that, though you've proven to be quite valuable in that area." He picks up the photo on the desk. "After we spoke at your house, I decided to look through pictures of my son. I hadn't let myself look at the album since"—he looks to the ceiling as if the answer is up there—"well, since it all happened. I was too scared seeing him would keep me stuck in the past. That I would never move on. But then I saw that picture of Daisy in your home, how beautiful it was the way you honored her. And I decided to finally take this out."

He caresses the hard edges of the picture frame before taking the pad of his finger and playfully dotting Teddy's eyes and nose and mouth. He traces Teddy's head, the curves of his cheeks, the bulbous tip of his chin. To anybody else, it would appear to be any ordinary photo. But because it's us, we know the picture carries an incomprehensible heaviness that will never make any sense to anyone else.

I twist my neck to get a closer look. Kenneth hands me the photo and I hold it in my hands as gently as I would a day-old newborn. I think about Teddy and Lucas and Kelis and Julia and all the other babies who didn't get to stay. But most of all I think about you. All the firsts you didn't get to have, how your short time on earth was relegated to a series of lasts. Last kiss. Last photo. Last breath.

"Wow, he's perfect," I say, returning the photo to Kenneth. It's palpable how fiercely he misses Teddy, the amount to which has not abated even after forty years. I'm only in my first year of grief and it makes me shudder thinking I have to live with this deep pit in my soul for the rest of my life. They say time blurs the memories and dulls the pain, but what they don't tell you is that when it comes to the love, time doesn't lay a single hand on it.

He asks if I want to see more photos and I nod. He walks over to the hutch—the hutch!—and unlocks it with swiftness, pulling out a leather-bound photo album. "These are all the pictures we ever took of Teddy. All right here."

"*That* was what was in there this whole time?"

"Yes, I'm not proud of it but thanks to you, I'm reminded of how much joy his face brought me."

I let out a little chuckle, feeling silly for having thought Kenneth was hiding dead people in there. I guess, in a way, he kind of was.

I watch as he flips through the album, taking in each photo like it's a breath of fresh air. I give him a moment, but when he starts doing that thing with his mustache again, pulling out individual hairs and putting them in a jar, I can't help but blurt out, "Why do you do that?"

He looks up at me, eyebrows scrunched. "Sorry," I say, trying not to look disgusted. "I—I didn't mean to sound rude. It's just, that jar, um, I have so many questions."

He grins. "Oh, this? It's just something I've always done since Teddy died. I bring them to the cemetery and sprinkle it over his grave. He used to touch my mustache all the time, pulling at the strands with his tiny fingers and pulling back when it felt too prickly. I'll never forget the way he smiled every time he played with it." Kenneth strokes his mustache and his eyes start to go glassy.

I sit there frozen, feeling like an utter asshole. "That's really sweet."

"I know it's a little weird, but death is weird. Grief is weird."

Silence and sadness press down around us, coercing us into a complete stillness until Kenneth speaks up again. "Do you mind if I play a song?"

My eyes light up as I wait for him to pull up the song on his computer. He taps his mouse a couple of times before turning up the volume on the speakers. Nothing. He furiously presses some keys on the keyboard and jiggles the dial again. Still there's no music. He bangs his palm against the computer, as if all that violent rattling will jolt it into cooperation and when he realizes it does not, he lets out a number of expletives.

"Do you need some help?" I jump in.

"Please. I can't figure out this damn thing."

I lean over the desk to look at the pixelated screen. I problem-solve as best I can and quickly uncover the issue, rectifying it with a most simple solution—selecting the unmute icon—and the song finally plays. We sink into our chairs and surrender to the melody with childlike wonderment.

38

I haven't touched the diary since Ethan discovered it. I missed it. The writing. The imagining. It gave me permission to live outside reality, glossing over the harshest parts of being alive, molding life the way I wanted it to be. I knew these stories fringed on fiction, but I liked it. I liked knowing that this other world was taking place inside these pages, and I worry that if I stop now, all of it will cease to exist.

I pull it out from under the mattress. The yellow cover has curled at the corners, the pages bloated after having soaked up so many tears. There's one more blank page left. Several ideas come to mind with ease and pleasure. There are so many directions I could take this story. The baby could take her first steps. We could go to the zoo. Maybe catch the Wiggles live on tour.

I start to write but my hands are trembling. I shake them into submission, but they won't relax. I feel exposed, like all my clothes are off, like someone's watching me. I take a deep breath and remind myself these words are not meant to be read, only to be written. That this diary is simply a place where all my yearnings can live so they don't swallow me from the inside out.

I can't write, though. There's some kind of blockage. And when I hone in on it, all I can hear is Spoon's grating voice in my head telling me to stop. I think about what she said, how my writing is destructive. Could she be right? Could this writing not be healthy and restorative like I believe it to be? She doesn't know how good I've been to my body lately, all the nuts I've been eating and how little I think about death these days. If she did, surely she'll see that writing can be of little harm. I push aside her voice and start writing. I write as fast as I can before my heart catches up to me and floods my eyes with tears.

When I'm finished, I close the diary. I hold it to my chest and gently stroke its cover. It holds everything I ever wanted. Smooches and coos and the most devastating kind of love. Somewhere out in the universe, there's a version of me living out these pages. Wherever she is, I hope she's grateful for everything she has. I hope that when she cries at how fast her child is growing, she remembers how miraculous it is they get to grow at all. I hope that when she watches her child cross the convocation stage or come home for Christmas with the present she's been hinting at for months, she knows how close she was to never having any of it. I hope she notices those startling pangs of sorrow that occasionally reverberate through her body—and that, just for a split second, she thinks of me. Of what could have been. And in that moment, she's overwhelmed by the urge to rush to her child and never let them go.

39

Dear diary,

*Daisy would've been one today. Instead of putting up banners
that say "Chapter One" and singing happy birthday around a
book-shaped cake, Ethan and I got in the car and drove. The drive
was pleasant despite the heaviness of the day. It helped that all
the crab apple trees had bloomed to a stunning magenta color. We
drew the windows down and the scent of them soothed the cracks
in our souls.*

*The box was in the back. It didn't feel right that it was all alone
back there, so we stopped the car and moved the box to my lap,
wedging it against my growing belly.*

*The closer we got, the queasier I became. I couldn't blame it on
the bumps and curves because there were none. My eyes were glued
to the GPS, zeroing in on the minutes remaining. The less time
there was, the more it seemed the air got thicker with dread.*

*We parked and began the trek. We took turns holding the
box, careful not to trip on any large rocks or overgrown roots. We
reached a fork and took the one on the left. The trail and trees
eventually cleared away and revealed a secluded pebble beach.*

*The waves were calm. The water, clear. We kicked off our shoes
and rolled up our pants. We walked in until we were knee-deep.
I tensed up at the cold but quickly acclimated, thanks to the
intensity of my focus on not dropping the box.*

*Holding the box between us, we squeezed each other tight for
a long while. All the love we never got to express poured out and
filled the space around us, creating a force field that kept us safe.
When doubt creeped in, we reminded each other this was not a*

goodbye, not an abandonment. It was a surrendering to joy and hope and possibility. And as long as our hearts continued to beat for Daisy, she would always be coming with us into the future.

A row of birds cawed above as gentle waves lapped at our knees. We said a few words, words too hurtful to repeat here, before taking the ashes out of the box and scattering them into the lake.

EPILOGUE

Is this your first?" the nurse asks as she sticks fetal monitoring patches on my belly. For a question that often makes my entire body quake, I'm remarkably unflustered when I hear it this time.

"No, this is my second. My first child died last year." I have rehearsed this line so many times it feels no different than reciting my date of birth or my mother's maiden name. No more lying. No more pretending like it never happened. I'm learning to wear my scars instead of letting them wear me.

"Oh, I'm so sorry," the nurse says solemnly.

Another contraction comes and I clutch the sides of my belly, exhaling in rapid succession. Ethan kneads my lower back. The deep pressure of his fists provides absolutely zero relief, only distraction, which at this point I will take anything.

When it's over, the nurse turns her gaze to the fetal heart monitor that's beeping to life and says, "Beautiful." She places her hand on my shoulder. "Pretty soon you'll be meeting your rainbow baby, Mum," she says with a warm smile.

Rainbow. The gift that follows a storm. A sweet term I never much liked. Storms are loud and nasty and frightening. And you were none of those things.

Dr. Astrid pops in to check on my progress. "Seven centimeters dilated. You're doing great," she tells me. The sound of her voice calms my nerves. We've been seeing her once a week, sometimes twice on my more anxiety-ridden days. Excessive, some might say, but Dr. Astrid never showed any indication of being annoyed. She knew what we had gone through, what we had lost, and agreed there was no limit to how much caution we should exercise. It was a relief to have our fears acknowledged, though it didn't stop us from thinking the worst from time to time.

I continued attending group therapy. Though Spoon was still quite a pill, I had to admit she was very good at what she does. She had this preternatural ability to bring out the ugliest parts of me and somehow convince me of their beauty. I could talk about you, could see my pain reflected in the eyes of the other mothers, and walk out of these sessions with a tiny glimmer of hope. The moms were all in different tunnels of grief, but we were crawling through it together. We talked about everything. How it feels like the world has moved on and forgotten our babies. How exhausting it is to wear a mask around people but taking it off is just as hard. How bad days pull us underwater but good days wrap us in a life jacket.

No matter what the topic of conversation was, there's an unspoken understanding that this thing we were doing—healing, surviving, or just getting through the damn day—would span the entirety of our lives. There's no finish line. No end date. No embossed certificate waiting for us with the words "CONGRATULATIONS, YOU'VE GRADUATED GRIEF!" Once I accepted this, living became easier. I stopped resisting the loneliness and sadness and simply let them be, like thunderstorms rumbling in the night, scary and ominous for sure, but necessary for anything living to thrive.

"Sorry to interrupt but I think these are for you."

The receptionist walks in with a bouquet filled with gerbera daisies in the brightest pinks and oranges and yellows and other colors I didn't even know were fathomable. The nurses ooh and aah at the sight of it. Even Ethan looks gobsmacked. He reads aloud the card. "'From everybody at Monarch Funeral Homes, congratulations on baby no. 2!'" I can tell by the nearly illegible scrawl that it was written by Kenneth.

One nurse snickers. "I think that might be the first time we've gotten flowers from a funeral home. It's usually the other way around!" The other nurse chuckles as she presses some buttons on a machine.

Ethan lifts the bouquet and turns to me. "I'll get these out of your way."

"Wait, why would you do that?" I say.

He reminds me of what I said, how flowers are overrated and how I never want to see a single one of them again. How I trashed every single bouquet that came into our home. I stare blankly at him, recalling everything I said and did. This bouquet is different, though. It's the most dazzling thing I've ever seen.

"I suppose I can make an exception for these," I say, "seeing as how much trouble they went to get these delivered to the hospital."

Ethan smiles and sets them down. "Okay, just this once."

Two weeks earlier, I said my goodbyes to the staff before going on maternity leave. There was cake and candles and nonalcoholic champagne, which tasted so awful that I would have rather chugged gasoline. Missing from my party were baby gifts. I didn't want to tempt fate by having items in my home earmarked for a not-yet-guaranteed future. I had made it clear to everyone that there would be no presents under any circumstances. No toys, no onesies, not a single diaper.

Technically it wasn't a goodbye party since I would be returning in a year's time. Everyone kept telling me a year will fly by. There were lots of "the baby this" and "the baby that" as if the baby was a sure thing. The due date was weeks away and despite all my efforts at worrying less, I was still skeptical that we'd bring the baby home alive. I couldn't rid myself of it, the unwavering fear that history would repeat itself. Lightning found me once. Surely it knows where to find me again.

We kept the pregnancy a secret as long as we could. We thought if we could fool the people around us, we could fool the evil eye, too. Even when it became glaringly obvious my mid-region had ballooned, I still didn't speak of it. I could see eyes dart down towards my large belly, a *congratulations* sitting at the tip of their tongues, eyes widening at the anticipation of my announcement, and still I would stay mum.

"Nothing new going on with me," I would say.

Of course everyone knew. I wasn't delusional. There was a shift in the way people treated me. They opened doors and held things for me. Paloma offered to drive me everywhere. Kenneth kept telling me to take afternoons off. My parents dropped off pork bone soup weekly, a dish nobody eats unless you desire a strengthened uterine lining.

There was another reason I didn't want to share the news: I couldn't handle people's joy. I feared their joy would rub off on me, accidentally awaken a look of happiness, and they'd take that as proof that another baby had made up for what was lost—that I'd somehow been fixed. Then I'd have to tell them no, that's not true, I'm far from fixed. And I know this because the pain is still there, rooted in my body like an organ of its own, reminding me how easily I can splinter into a million little pieces again.

Fortunately, the pieces do come back together. Not perfectly but good enough. The tears and the pain recede like a memory from another life, and what remains is an indescribable love—a love so powerful it makes me go from wanting to die to breathlessly anticipating the future.

It wasn't long before I recognized a pattern. This fight between grief and joy was not a fight but, in fact, a dance. One didn't need to vanish for the other to exist. They were a pair, inextricably linked, twirling in the most dizzying, twisted, reckless fashion. You want to die and you want to live and you want to cry and you want to laugh and you want none of it and you want everything the world has to offer. That is the dance of life.

Ethan holds the phone in front of me, showing me a text that just came in from my parents. It's in Vietnamese. "What's it say?" he asks. Another contraction begins, saving me from having to translate the sweet yet mortifying message: We love you, Smelly Shit.

There's another knock on the door. The receptionist sticks her head in. "You've got a visitor here named Paloma. Can I bring her in?" I nod before gripping the sides of my belly, breathing through another contraction.

"I'm so sorry I'm late!" she cries. "I wanted to catch you before you went into labor. I won't stay long. I just wanted to drop off something."

"If it's flowers, I don't think you can beat the ones we just got," says Ethan.

"No, it's not flowers. Something else."

Paloma reaches into her bag and pulls out Dumpling. I can't believe it! My sweet little Dumpling! Tears start pooling in my eyes. "I know she meant a lot to you and I wanted you to have her."

I hadn't seen Dumpling since the day Paloma found me in her bathroom. I didn't dare step inside the nursery again after that, though I desperately wanted to. I thought about her a lot, wondered if she was getting picked up and played with, if she got kissed and squeezed on a routine basis. I missed rocking her in that chair, pressing her against my chest as I read her book after book. I was too embarrassed to ask about her. After all, she wasn't mine.

"Y-you want me to have her?" I say.

"Yes."

"But it's Jude's."

"We are literally drowning in toys. Please take her. You'd be doing me a favor."

Paloma tucks Dumpling into the nook of my arm and just like that, I'm reunited with her once again. Oh, the warm softness! I squeeze her tight as I breathe through the next contraction. Everything feels right now that Dumpling is here. Now that Paloma is here. I feel lucky to have a friendship like this. Some days I don't feel worthy of it, particularly when I think about how horrible I was. A tidal wave of shame has, at times, convinced me I don't deserve anyone's unconditional love. Yet somehow, here in this room, I'm surrounded by it.

This is another aspect of life I'll never quite figure out.

"It's time to push," the doctor tells me.

"Right now?"

"Yes, you're ready."

Paloma tucks a strand of hair behind my ear and kisses my sweaty forehead. She tells me I've got this and that she'll be waiting just outside the room. I grip her hand and tell her to stay. A smile slips across her lips and she stays put as Ethan squeezes my other hand.

The next moment is a blur of adrenaline and agony and *come on, come on, so close, push, push, you got this, one more push!* I keep glancing at the fetal heart monitor, watching the lines bounce across the screen. I remind myself I'm safe. The baby is safe. Everyone is here.

Including you, my darling Daisy. You are here. You have always been here, swimming in my bones.

I take a deep breath, shut my eyes, and release a most momentous wail. It echoes down the hall, bounces off the walls, and when it finally settles, I hear it. That pulsating, magnificent, merciful cry.

BEHIND THE BOOK

Dear reader,

I wish I could say this book was all made up. Some parts are. Some sadly aren't.

In 2022 while I was working on edits for my first book, *Sunshine Nails*, I went into labor with my firstborn, feverishly excited for her arrival, only to be later told by the doctor that she had suffered a severe brain injury during birth and wouldn't have long to live. We named her Gemma. She was with us for four breathtaking days. I never wanted to let her go.

The grief that followed was beyond anything I could put into words. For months I tried writing about this dark abyss, but all that came out was WTF, WTF, WTF.

Luckily words slowly came back to me, allowing me to write the story of Cleo Dang, a grieving mother who's trying to make sense of life after losing her baby. I poured all my pain into her, as well as the strength, hope, and humor I wished for myself. I tended to Cleo's grief like a garden, and remarkably it awakened within me a desire to live again.

If there's anything I've learned, it's that living is hard. Especially when the people we love die long before they're supposed to. There's no getting over it, no moving on. Just the lifelong job of carrying around the tenderized parts of ourselves where our loved ones now live. If this is something you know all too well, then I hope reading this book made your grief feel seen. Though grief has no end, this book does, and I'm beyond grateful that you've made it all the way through.

With love,
Mai

ACKNOWLEDGMENTS

Thank you first and foremost to you, the reader, for picking up this book. Despite what Cleo believes, life is short, very short, so the fact that you spent some of your precious hours reading this book means the world to me.

This is not a book I ever set out to write, but it's a book I'm glad I wrote. There are so many people who made it possible for this novel to come out from the depths of my drafts folder: my super-smart agent, Carly Watters; my brilliant editors, Loan Le and Brittany Lavery; the ever-reliable editorial assistant Natalie Argentina; marketing and publicity mavericks Cayley Brightside, Mackenzie Croft, Gena Lanzi, and Maudee Genao; eagle-eyed copy editor Lisa Nicholas; the very gifted cover designer Amanda Hudson and interior book designer Esther Paradelo, along with everybody else at Atria Books and Simon & Schuster Canada. Thank you for giving me the opportunity to share this book with the world and helping to demystify the stigma of grief and infant loss.

To the loss moms I've met online and in person—Shal, Lindsay, Tyla, Kristin, Diane, Daniela, Nina, Dora, Doreen, Heather, Nicole, Ceci, Laya, Jessalyn, Sara, Steph, Lili, Caroline, and everyone in the WhatsApp support group— I hope you know that all of the healing you see in me is only possible because of you. It's an honor to know your stories, to have seen inside your hearts, and to carry the hurt alongside you. Thank you for crawling through the tunnel with me.

To the real Maggie, Rachel, Ana, Dylan, and Rebecca, the NICU nurses at SickKids Hospital, as well as Hannah, our musical therapist, who looked after Gemma like she was your own. I'll never forget the delicacy of the care you provided during her last days of life. My world was pitch-black but you were all a flicker of light.

To the health care workers who helped me, Lindsay Witton, Sheila

Wijayasinghe, Melissa Goldband, and Kayli Balaban. The health care system can sometimes be cold, rushed, and unkind, but your warmth and humanity were great boons to my healing, and I wish your exceptional care could be felt by every patient. You are nothing like Dr. Posey, thank god!

To Cardinal Funeral Homes, for showing me what death positivity can look like. Thank you for normalizing death and grief in a way that made me, and countless others, feel seen.

To the Ontario Arts Council, the Canada Council for the Arts, and the Toronto Arts Council, for funding this book and granting writers and artists like myself the immeasurable gift of time and space to create art.

To Lucy Doan, for the sparkling new author photo, and to Julie Doan, for letting me wear your beautiful dress—I'm grateful to call you my sisters.

Thank you to all my family and friends, including my in-laws, for feeding me copious amounts of food, washing the dishes, folding my laundry, and getting me out of the house, but mostly for always speaking of Gemma. (And to everyone who ever sent flowers, please never stop sending them—I swear I love them!)

To Chris, who walked the path of grief with me with such steadiness and didn't even bat an eye when I said I wanted to write a book about our story. Thank you for always catching me.

And finally, to my daughters both living and dead. Together you cracked my heart wide open and poured joy into all its crevices. You are worth being alive for.

MAI NGUYEN is a Vietnamese Canadian author whose debut novel, *Sunshine Nails*, was longlisted for Canada Reads and named one of the best books of 2023 by NPR and CBC. Her journalism has appeared in *Wired*, *The Washington Post*, and the *Toronto Star*. Raised in Halifax, she now lives in Toronto with her husband, daughter, and French bulldog.